Say the Words

GENNY CARRICK

Cover Design & Illustration by Melody Jeffries

Edited by Zee Monodee

ISBN: 978-1-957745-03-9 (ebook)

ISBN: 978-1-957745-02-2 (paperback)

❀ Created with Vellum

content

Be advised this book deals with themes of grief.

For Mom & Dad
who loved my ridiculous stories from the beginning

june

IN THE GREAT hierarchy of wedding responsibilities, the Maid of Honor falls slightly beneath the bride. The groom is third, the Mother of the Bride fourth, and as far as I could tell, the Best Man rattled around somewhere at the bottom of the barrel.

I was currently second in command for my favorite cousin's wedding, in addition to designing and decorating it, and I took all these jobs seriously. I'd spent months putting together a suitably bookish aesthetic for librarian Eden and her high school teacher fiancé, complete with custom color palette, props, and detailed floor plans. I'd helped her choose the bridesmaids' dresses, the catering menu, and the reception playlist. I might have had a tiny hand in encouraging her toward their honeymoon bungalow in the Florida Keys. In short, I was *invested* in this wedding.

The Best Man, though? Debatable. Ty Hardy hadn't responded to my texts with anything more than *"I'm on it"*, so here I was, slogging out to his ranch to verify that he was indeed "on it." Most likely, he'd stopped reading my texts weeks ago and just pasted *"It's covered"* or *"Don't worry so much"* in response to anything I messaged him.

Not that I expected a warm reception to my messages. As his younger brother's ex-girlfriend, I probably didn't rank as one of his favorite people in the world. We'd been friends once, or so I thought, before his cheating brother went and cheated on me like a cheater. Everybody took sides in break-ups, and I couldn't very well expect Ty to side with me over his brother. Still, we needed to work together on this, and I was done being blown off by *Mr. I'm Too Busy to Get Back to You Rancher Man.*

I turned my little hatchback onto the dirt road that wound to Ty's house, running through his checklist in my head. At T-minus seventeen days to the ceremony, he hadn't confirmed with me the groomsmen's suit rentals, the groom's gift, or what he'd planned for the bachelor party. I hadn't asked for details on the last one, assuming the worst when it came to a group of mostly single men in their early thirties. For all I knew, Ty would have the groomsmen show up to the wedding in jeans and button-downs, and toss Booker a wad of cash at the reception. He'd hire Dave's Discount Dancers for the bachelor party, obviously.

Me? I'd sent him briefings on the successful bridal shower, not-so-subtle hints about my plans for the bachelorette party, and polls on his reception playlist opinions—all of which he'd ignored. The man could have faked a little polite interest, at least.

But this trip out here wasn't just about me going all maid-zilla. Each day closer to the wedding date, Eden's panic level went up another notch, and no amount of reassurance could stop her endless texts and emails. Were the decorations too subtle, were they too much, did we order enough flowers, was the cake over the top, was the book theme too obvious? She hovered one canapé decision away from a breakdown, and the lack of communication from Ty didn't help. I'd do anything to make sure my cousin's wedding went perfectly to plan, and that included pinning down the Best Man.

Metaphorically speaking.

Plus, we had the whole *brother's ex* thing to deal with. The relationship hadn't lasted long, and I'd never known Ty to be the vindictive sort, but we were supposed to spend a whole weekend together smiling, laughing, and making nice for the guests. I needed to be sure that what happened between me and his brother last year wouldn't throw a wrench in that.

The GPS told me I'd reached my destination as soon as I'd pulled off the main road a mile back, but I hadn't reached Ty's farmhouse yet. A lot farther from the turnoff than I remembered, it lay hidden somewhere down a long drive through green pastures and shade trees. I'd been out here a few times growing up, back when it still belonged to his grandmother, but I didn't recognize anything. For all I knew, I could have been inching closer to a serial killer's cabin and not the horse ranch of my childhood dreams.

Oh, the horses. Ty's grandmother had helped my Girl Scouts troop get our horse-riding merit badges when I was twelve. Over five or six Saturdays, Abigail Hardy had taught us the basics of how to mount, dismount, how to hold the reins, the different parts of a saddle, and a hundred other things that made being around horses seem like glitter and fairy dust. As far as I could tell, horses only had one real drawback. I'd long forgotten the details of saddles and halters, but I still remembered every pungent minute of mucking out the stalls. You couldn't pay me enough to do that again.

The farmhouse finally came into view, and my stomach twisted so hard, it might as well have been the murder cabin. Ty's beat up old truck sat out front like it had gone there to die. The kind of heavy-duty truck popular on farms, it stopped just short of being a classic, but was still well past its prime. Surprisingly clean, though. I parked next to it and got out to survey the area. Not much had changed in almost twenty years. An old red garage sat across from the house with its doors wide open to reveal the all-terrain vehicle inside, but no sign of the man.

A bead of sweat inched down the middle of my back as I climbed onto the wide porch. Punching down a shiver of nerves, I smoothed my skirt, threw my shoulders back, and rang the bell. Somewhere inside, an old-fashioned chime echoed like nobody was home, and nobody would ever be home again.

I really needed to stop watching true crime documentaries.

I knocked on the door, but the house stayed silent. Cupping my hands around my eyes, I tried to peer in the front window, but the sun punished me with temporary blindness. I moved to push the bell again, but before I reached it, a man's voice drifted to me from the yard.

Following the sounds, I marched toward the barn behind the house. Probably should have tried there first. Ty wasn't a man to sit around with his feet propped up in the middle of the day. I didn't love the idea of creeping around on his property, but if I wanted to find him, I'd need to creep.

His central Texas property stretched for I didn't know how many acres, with giant elms and ashes dotting the green pastures beyond the farmhouse. Here in the yard, though, tire tracks cut through the grass, and dust blew up in little eddies every time I took a step. I regretted my bold choice to boost my confidence by wearing heels and my favorite skirt more by the minute.

The property's smell took me back to my time here as a girl. Not manure exactly, but the strong aroma of large animals mixed with the sharp scent of hay. And okay, plenty of manure.

Yet, it also proved oddly comforting, like the fruity whiff of my dad's orchards mid-summer.

I rounded the corner of the barn and stopped cold. In the center of a large, circular paddock, Ty faced off with a horse in a battle of wills. Hard to say who was winning. He held a coiled rope in one hand as he encouraged the horse to move its feet, his broad back to me, his attention fixed on the horse's motions. Something skittered around in my chest at the sight of him, but I ignored it. It would go away.

It always did.

Standing in Ty's back yard watching him work, I had second thoughts about my great plan to confront him here. Even in my cute outfit, I had the weaker footing. Here, he was in his element, full of power and confidence. I should have texted a request to meet at a coffee shop or a diner. Some nice, neutral spot where we wouldn't be under the blazing sun, and nobody looked like they'd been sculpted out of muscle and denim.

Not that he would have responded to that text.

Unaware of my presence, Ty's silent instructions to the horse led them in a strange sort of dance. If the horse moved away, Ty closed the distance once again. I'd never seen anything like it, and couldn't tear my eyes away from the power and patience on display. After a minute, he stroked the horse's muzzle, soothing him the way I might comfort a nervous kitten. The horse endured his touch, but stood at an awkward angle, as if he might bolt away from Ty at any second.

You and me both, horse.

The horse took a few steps away from him, kicking out his hind legs in a clear *You're not the boss of me* move. Ty shifted right back into the animal's space, stopping him from going too far, and rubbed his muzzle again.

"You can kick all you like, you're stuck with me."

His firm but affectionate voice turned my insides warm and gooey, like a lava cake I hadn't expected.

Best to ignore that, too.

But how to let him know I'd turned up on his property? Shouting at a man's back seemed the wrong approach, but just watching him work didn't sit quite right, either. He had no clue he starred in the free peep show I was getting just steps behind him. I could wait at the fence watching him all day before he ever realized it. The idea appealed a little too much for comfort.

Before I'd sorted out how to best get Ty's attention, the horse noticed me. He jerked his head away from Ty's hand, taking several steps backward.

Ty followed, keeping himself directly in front of the beast. "What's the matter, Bullet?"

The time had come to announce myself, but I couldn't do it. I kind of liked being so close to Ty without the cloud of awkwardness that usually hovered over us. The moment he saw me, that shadow would fall.

And fine, I liked watching a well-built man work. Sue me.

Ty must have caught on that Bullet wasn't just being contrary, and he glanced over his shoulder. I swear the man did an actual double take. I didn't even breathe. He was just so...Ty. Six-foot-one, a faded blue button-down stretched tight over his chest, his dark eyes blazing in the shade of his Stetson. He stared back at me, confusion and something like pleasure flashing across his face before it tugged down into a familiar scowl.

All those sweet, gooey feelings swirling through me curdled in my stomach at that look I knew too well. I almost wished I'd stumbled on the murder cabin.

Bullet jerked away as if he might rip the lead rope from Ty's grip and run free. Ty tore his eyes from me, but before he could say or do anything, the horse spun in a circle, kicking his hind legs. Ty tried to lunge out of the way, but as quick as his name-sake, the horse's hooves lashed out and met Ty's chest, sending him sprawling in the dust.

"Ty!"

My stomach lurched, overcome with a sick ooze as I ran to the pen gate. I fumbled with the latch, my fingers almost too shaky to manage it, but I finally pushed my way through. Halfway to Ty, I realized I'd just doubled Bullet's potential targets, and kept one eye on the animal. He'd moved to the far side of the pen, standing still enough I figured it was probably safe to be so close to him.

I threw myself down next to Ty, my knees digging my pretty floral skirt into the dirt as I looked him over. One of his hands hovered over his chest, the other locked in a fist against his thigh. His eyes had shut tight, his face a white sheet of pain. The Stetson had landed a few feet away from his head, spinning slightly in the breeze.

I put a hand on his forehead, unable to shake the thick fear that grabbed my stomach in its grip, threatening to drag me into the dust alongside him. "Oh, Ty, are you all right?"

He drew in a breath like taking in oxygen was a new, totally unknown experience, wincing until the creases around his eyes became stark pale lines beneath the dusting of dirt on his skin. A ragged moan rumbled out of his throat as if he couldn't control it. When he finally opened his eyes, it took him a minute to focus on me. As recognition settled in, a grimace twisted his mouth.

"Hey, June," he groaned.

TWO

PAIN. Everything was pain.

All of my nerve endings must have been tied to my chest, and every single one of them flickered with flame. Bursts of light danced in my vision until I thought I might pass out. I couldn't even think straight, my brain just a tangle of the words *Oh hell!* and *Is that June?*

That couldn't be June Evans. She'd never been out to my place before—what was she doing here anyway? And why did she have to be here to witness the first time I'd ever been laid out by a horse?

"Ty, can you hear me?"

A thread of panic ran through her voice as she caressed my forehead. That soft touch had to be happening to someone else's body—so at odds with the misery gripping the rest of me.

"You're going to be okay," she continued in that soothing tone.

Still to be determined.

Words failed me as white-hot fire scorched through my ribcage, turning my insides to ash. I could only grunt in response, and even that took it out of me. I didn't know that horse had kicked me, I would have thought I was having a heart attack.

Breath searing my lungs, I turned my head to see where the animal had gone. Bullet stood at the edge of the pen, calm as could be, watching over me with mild interest. When I'd muttered under my breath this morning that Bullet's stubbornness would be the death of me, it hadn't been a request.

"What can I do?"

One of June's hands moved to the buttons on my shirt, her fingers brushing my chest. Each little touch came as a lick of fire on a body already engulfed in flames.

"Should I—? Something might be broken."

I raised one finger to stop her touching me, unable to hold in the way I groaned on every exhale. No question something was broken. The crack still echoed through my skull like a gunshot. But knowing it and being able to do anything about it were two different things. I didn't believe in out of body experiences, but I would have paid any amount of money to have one right now. I couldn't escape the agony. Moving, lying still, it all amounted to the same thing—a nonstop explosion of pain.

"Okay."

To my relief, she stopped tugging on my shirt. Did I just ask June Evans to stop undressing me? Did I have a concussion, too?

"Is there someone else out here?"

My thoughts were so crowded out by everything going on in my chest, it took a minute to remember. Aaron, my ranch hand, split his time between my ranch and another on the other side of town, but he'd already left for the day. She probably couldn't reach him on his cell out there, and even if she could, what would be the point? Just a kid barely old enough to drink, he wouldn't come out here and patch me up.

"Your parents, maybe?"

"Vacation," I ground out. They'd just left on an anniversary cruise, somewhere off in the Netherlands or France, or both, I couldn't remember. Thank the Lord for small favors. Only adding my mother hovering over me could make this situation worse.

"Isn't there anyone else I can call?"

Maybe she meant an ambulance. She sure sounded like she wanted to call one.

Worry furrowed a line between her eyebrows, her deep blue eyes filled with something close to terror. Her tender fear for me broke through a layer of pain, filling my chest with a whole new ache. Lying in the dirt, struggling to breathe—yeah, exactly the wrong time for me to think about any of that.

I shut my eyes again. If I could just breathe a minute, maybe I could get a handle on this. Only, I couldn't breathe, every inhale like pulling shards of glass through my lungs. My shallow breaths weren't enough to satisfy, but breathing deeply turned up the dial on the pain. Hopefully, my broken ribs hadn't gone and punctured anything vital.

"What can I do?" June asked again, as though maybe I had a little card in my pocket that would give her instructions. *In the Event of Broken Ribs...*

"What are you doing here?" I wheezed. Not at all polite, but lying miserable in the dirt, manners weren't my top priority.

"I just wanted to talk to you."

She spread her palms out as though that should be explanation enough. June wanted to talk to me? Made about as much sense as anything else right now.

I struggled to sit up, like a turtle on its back. She grasped my shoulder with both hands and pulled me upright. Curse words and misery filled my brain. All the jostling amplified the pain, like shouting into a megaphone, sending fresh torment across my chest, but breathing came a little easier now that I wasn't lying down.

June let go of me but kept her hands out near my shoulders as if she thought I might topple back into the dust. The worry lines around her eyes and mouth deepened as she watched me fight for breath. I had to look like I'd been run over.

Not the happy reunion I'd been planning on, I'll tell you that.

"I'm going to call Booker." She grabbed the purse slung over one shoulder and rummaged around in it.

"Don't call anyone." I just needed a minute. I shifted to try to stand, but spikes of agony shot from my ribcage straight to my brain, clouding my vision.

Okay, maybe I needed two minutes.

"I think we should get you to the Medical Center."

"I'm fine."

Why I was lying, I didn't even know. I couldn't take a breath without searing pain, and I'd been flat on my back for ten minutes. At least I hadn't lost my lunch to round out the indignities. Nothing like seeing a man hurl to impress a woman.

Not that I was looking to impress June. Lord, I needed to get a handle on this.

"You're not fine, come on."

She tugged on my shoulder again, sending fiery spasms through me as my muscles twisted and pulled over my ribs. An animal-like noise filled the air, and it took me a second to realize I'd made the sound.

"Don't," I hissed.

She released me, her eyes wide. "I'm sorry. Do you want me to call an amb—"

"No." I didn't need to be carted off my own property. I'd get my legs again here in a minute.

Any time now.

Soon.

"Isn't there somebody else I can call for you?"

"I don't have anybody else."

The soft look in her eyes lasted only a second or two before it turned to steel. "Then I'm going to take you to the Medical Center."

I lifted my hand, blocking her renewed attempt to grab me. The thought of moving again turned my stomach, and I wasn't interested in testing out how long the no-hurling part of this ordeal might last. "Just give me a minute."

"You want to wait and see if you get *better* first? It would take a miracle at this point."

"Pray for me, June."

She laughed a little, just a slight exhale of breath, but her smile did me in. It always had, since that first day I'd seen her on my younger brother's arm. Bret always had been a lucky, selfish jerk.

Thirty-one years old, and he'd never been faithful to a woman yet. His carelessness for the way he took and then discarded what he wanted should have crushed him under whole mountains of shame, but he didn't seem to feel it. He'd moved on from June easily enough, a feat I couldn't understand, since I hadn't managed to forget her and I hadn't even been the one dating her.

I squinted at her while she fretted over me. I hadn't thought I'd have to see her until Booker and Eden's wedding. I couldn't very well avoid her then if I wanted to—I was Booker's Best Man and June the Maid of Honor. We were pretty well destined to interact. In my mind, our reunion would be polite but distant. A nod between us now and then, a little meaningless conversation at the rehearsal dinner. Maybe even a slow dance or two at the reception.

But having her turn up out of the blue to watch me get kicked in the chest by Bullet? Hadn't seen that coming.

"You know your ribs are broken, right?" She kept her voice gentle, cushioning the blow.

"I've got a hunch."

"I know you're a man and all, but you still need to see a doctor. I'm no WebMD, but even I know a horse kick straight to the chest isn't good."

"You know I'm a man?"

She always did have a funny way of talking to me, pointing out the obvious and poking at my ego being her chief go-tos. Or they had been two years ago, back when I'd still allowed myself to talk to her. After a while, our closeness had become too much to bear, and I'd retreated to my ranch and kept my distance. Leave it to the universe to match up my best friend and her favorite cousin.

"You know what I mean."

"Yes." I groaned, shifting in the dirt as if I might magically find a comfortable position. "I'm a man."

"For the moment. I could call that horse over here and let him have another go at you."

I started to laugh, but the shaking in my chest dropped me into a new level of misery. I just managed not to shout. Had I yelled when I got kicked? I didn't even know. I couldn't rightly remember anything beyond the sound of my bones breaking. I glanced down at my crotch, but everything looked normal. You know you're having a bad day when not vomiting or pissing yourself is the high point.

"We really need to get you to the Medical Center. Come on, I'll help you up."

"Can't do anything for broken ribs but load up on pain pills." I had too much to do around here to spend a few days floating off to dreamland.

Dammit. I wouldn't be able to do anything around the ranch for the foreseeable future. If possible, my chest constricted even more as my brain pieced together what this would mean for my business.

I'd built up a nice clientele since I started working for myself four years ago. In addition to a few easy boarders, I had a steady stream of horses coming in for training. I wouldn't mind more, but I had enough for now. Mostly, I trained work horses, the occasional riding horse, and starting colts. Those wild, young ones were my favorite. Or they had been, right up until one landed a hoof on my ribs.

"Then let's get you those pain pills." June maneuvered so her shoulder was ready to slip under mine, but she didn't quite touch me. She seemed to be waiting for a signal this time.

I looked her over, doing my best not to linger as my eyes skated up and down. "I've got a hundred pounds on you."

"I'm not offering to carry you to my car."

I tried to take a deep breath, but the inferno in my chest stopped me. I'd just have to make do with shallow gulps of air. My lungs seared either way, from lack of breath or too much of it.

"On the count of three."

Where June got off bossing me, I wasn't sure, but I didn't mind. In fact, I kind of liked this take-charge side of her. I would have liked it even more if we weren't in a filthy horse pen.

Not the time.

"One...two...three."

Standing proved a special kind of torture. The blaze of anguish from my chest down my limbs made my legs shake and my mind spin. I thought for sure I'd finally pass out, and tried to shift away from June so I wouldn't collapse straight on top of her. She held on tighter, adding to the fire in my ribs, but I managed not to faint. Another win for this banner afternoon.

"You doing okay?" she asked, that worry line deep between her eyebrows.

"I've never been worse, June."

The few times I'd let myself get drunk off my ass, I'd had more coordination than I did now. I walked like a bow-legged cowboy, trying and failing to avoid the ripples of agony every step sent through me. She guided us across the pen, her body flush against mine for support. The sheer enormity of my injury refused to let my thoughts idle there, but I wasn't so out of it that I couldn't file that memory away for later.

"Should we do something about the horse?" she asked as we let ourselves out of the round pen.

Bullet had found a leftover clump of hay along the pen fence and stood chewing away on it. I was in no shape to turn him out, and wouldn't ask June to try in a million years. He wasn't an aggressive horse, just a young one with more energy than he knew how to use up, and no notion of what constituted good behavior. No way would I risk June taking that horse's lead rope.

"He'll be fine in the pen for a while." Lord willing.

She led me around the barn to a little car I didn't recognize. Great. On top of everything else, I would have to cram myself into a tiny hatchback. "What was it you wanted to talk to me about?"

"I just..." She moved the hand on my back to get a better hold, her fingers splaying as if me staying upright depended on her alone. "I wanted us to talk before the wedding. Make sure everything is going smoothly. I didn't want things to be awkward."

"Don't worry, June," I wheezed, my chest a crackling fire. "This isn't awkward at all."

THREE

june

THREE HOURS, two X-rays, and one prescription later, I drove Ty back to Victory Ranch. Pretty sure he'd grumbled the entire time. Oh, the excuses that poured out of that man's mouth.

I don't need a doctor, June.

There isn't anything to do about broken ribs, June.

I'm a man, June, I can take it.

He didn't say that last one, but he was thinking it. If he'd been in a little better condition, he might have bolted before I ever got him through Magnolia Ridge Medical Center's sliding glass doors.

I sat with him in the waiting room, where he met every word of consolation I offered with a dismissive grunt, like his injury had devolved him into a cave man. When they finally called his name and he hobbled off to the exam room— ignoring the wheelchair the nurse had pulled around, naturally —I couldn't decide if I found his stubbornness endearing or maddening. The nurse definitely thought it the latter. We shared a weary look behind his grumbling back.

When he came out again with the news the doctor said

there wasn't much to do but give the bones time to heal, the look he gave me had been smug as all get out. The man had broken ribs, but he still managed to gloat about it.

"Just say it." I pulled out of the Medical Center's parking lot, waiting for the *I told you so* that must surely be coming.

"I don't have to say it, June." His voice came out gravelly and hoarse. "We both know I was right."

"Very smooth." Glancing sideways, I looked him over. He sat at an awkward angle, holding the seat belt away from his chest with one hand, his face contorted into a deep scowl. His every word and breath strained from the effort of forcing air in and out of his lungs, yet he wanted to deny he felt any of it. My blood got hot just thinking about his repeated attempts to pretend the situation wasn't serious. "Three broken ribs is not nothing. People die from horse kicks, you know."

"So I've heard." His dry voice betrayed borderline amusement, as if my worry made me ridiculous. "And only the one rib broke. The other two are just cracked."

As if that made anything better.

"What would you have done if I hadn't been there? Just laid in the dirt until Bullet got hungry and ate you?"

"Horses are herbivores, and if you hadn't been there, none of this would have happened."

I sucked in a breath, guilt tangling with my indignation.

"That wasn't my fault." I'd been thinking it through the whole ordeal, but that didn't mean I wanted *him* to think it. "I didn't mean for that to happen."

"No. But you distracted the both of us."

"How could I distract you?"

The question bubbled out even though I couldn't deny he'd been distracted. I'd seen his reaction, his look of shock at seeing me on his ranch. The tiny flash of pleasure right before Bullet kicked him.

17

That hint of a smile stuck in my brain, like the afterimage of a bright light, flashing in my head every time I blinked.

He shifted slightly, groaning in the back of his throat. He'd balked over the heavy-duty pain medication the doctor had suggested to see him through the first few days. I'd guessed he would as soon as the word *sedative* was uttered in the Medical Center pharmacy. He'd condescended to let them fill a prescription for Percocet, but he hadn't bothered to take one. Instead, he seemed determined to get by purely on anger and bitterness. Any little movement he tried to make ended in an array of groans, grunts, and muttered curses. He had a rather larger repertoire of favorite swears than I did, even if he mostly kept them under his breath.

"I wasn't expecting visitors," he finally said.

Regret pricked at me for the spur of the moment social call. I hadn't made the horse kick, but I *had* snuck up on him. Horses didn't like surprises, even I knew that.

Still, I wasn't ready to take all the credit for his current condition.

"You haven't been answering my texts."

"I've been answering them."

I forced a laugh. "'*Got it*' is no better than a '*k*'."

He tried to turn to face me but didn't get very far before he stopped, stifling a tortured sound in his throat. "I haven't been answering your texts adequately, so you drove out here to check up on me?"

The ruffle of amusement in his voice annoyed me enough—the fact he was right just piled on the irritation.

"Saying it like that makes me sound like a stalker."

"You're the one who followed up on a text with a visit to my house."

I stared straight ahead, grinding my teeth. "Maybe you

should put up a *No Trespassing* sign if you're so opposed to visitors."

"I'm not opposed. I just like to have a little warning when a woman's going to show up at my place unannounced."

Did that happen often? He was certainly attractive enough to warrant female visitors. His bedroom eyes and chiseled jaw probably brought the ladies running. Ugh, not the point.

"That makes no sense."

"You still haven't explained the visit."

"I want to be sure you're actually doing all the Best Man stuff you're supposed to be doing. Blowing me off all the time isn't very reassuring."

A sound between a laugh and a groan escaped him. "How am I blowing you off? I told you I'm handling it, and it's handled."

My eyebrows probably shot straight up to my hairline. "Really?"

He gave a stout nod. "Really."

"The suit rentals, the groom gifts, the—"

He shifted his hand as if flicking away my questions. "June. It's handled."

The verbal equivalent of 'k'. I released a throaty exhale and rolled my eyes.

It didn't take long to drive back through town and into the countryside. With a population just over ten thousand, Magnolia Ridge's downtown boasted brick storefronts along Center Street, gradually giving way to the farms and ranches that surrounded it. A strange sort of longing tugged at me every time I visited, my home but not my home. I'd lived in Austin eleven years, ever since I'd packed up my boxes and moved down for college, and it still didn't hit me with that same sense of comfort as Magnolia Ridge did.

I passed the turnout to my pop's with a twinge of regret for ever leaving his place this morning. I'd driven up from Austin, dropped off my bags, and headed straight to Ty's. I should have stayed away from his ranch and left well enough alone.

I side-eyed him again. He was probably thinking the same thing.

"You're in town early," he said. "Wedding's two weeks away."

"There's a lot to do to get ready for a wedding."

"And you clearly don't trust anyone else to do it."

That amused tone again, like he might have laughed at me if his ribcage hadn't been destroyed this morning.

I shot him a glare that had no effect whatsoever.

"They're overcomplicating it," he went on. "Get your license, grab the preacher, find a field somewhere. Boom. Done."

I groaned at the image of the slapdash ceremony he'd conjured. "Don't ever become a wedding planner."

He tried to chuckle, but the sound cut off in his throat. "Don't worry."

"Don't you talk to Booker about this? There's the final dress fitting, the flowers, decorations, writing up a seating plan for the reception, finalizing the meal count for the caterer—"

"That's an awful lot of effort for the same outcome."

I turned up the ash-bordered lane that led to Ty's ranch. My first trip along it this morning might as well have been days ago.

"Some people are a little more romantic than you are."

He muttered into his hand, staring out the window. Arguing with him proved pointless. The man was about as romantic as the horse that kicked him, and just as stubborn.

I parked in front of the farmhouse and scrambled around to his side of the car to help him out. The hatchback's low height made for an awful lot of bending and maneuvering to get such a

20

big man in and out, and every move he made left him groaning and grumbling from pain.

I held a hand out for him at his open door, but he refused to take it, tightening his grip on the door handle instead.

"Mule," I said under my breath. I swear, I'd developed an eye twitch after just a few hours of his bullheadedness.

He climbed the steps up to his porch, stifling a ragged groan on each rung. He turned to me at the door, his grim face drained of its usual healthy color. Normally, the dusting of stubble on his chin made him look rugged, but now, it gave him the appearance of a man at desperate ends. I wouldn't want to see this Ty in a dark alleyway.

"Tell me about the other reason you're here. I missed that part."

"You know, the bachelorette party, wedding prep. Spend some time with my family."

It had been too long since I'd been in Magnolia Ridge for more than a weekend, not since my mother's illness just over two years ago. After she died, I thought staying away from home would help ease the raw grief that lived inside me. The unending busyness of my life in Austin had papered over that ache, but never quite healed it. Weeks had stretched into months, until I couldn't remember the last time I'd spent real, quality time with the rest of my family. Eden's wedding gave me a good excuse to take a semi-vacation and stay awhile.

"Not here in Magnolia Ridge, here at my house. You said you didn't want things to be awkward between us." He gazed down at me with those golden-hazel eyes that bored right into my soul. "Why would things be awkward?"

Right. In all the excitement at the Medical Center, I'd neatly avoided that talk, but I couldn't keep putting it off. The confidence that had driven me out to his ranch had faded somewhat after the whole horse-kick debacle. Nerves tossed around in my stomach like a ship on stormy waters while I tried to line up my thoughts.

Before I could answer him, Ty pushed open his front door and waved me inside. When I crossed the threshold, air conditioning stirred a draft around me, instant relief from the heat outside.

I stopped just inside the door, staring around. For some reason, I'd expected to find the interior matched the farmhouse's aging exterior, but everything had been updated. Crisp white Craftsman trim, bright silver-gray walls, oak floors newly refinished. Ty's brown leather sofa and huge flat screen TV suited the room just right.

"This is nice."

He narrowed his eyes at me. "The horses don't live in here."

"I know that. I was just expecting...doilies, I guess."

"I'm fresh out."

He stood with his arms crossed in front of his chest, his biceps straining against his sides. Looked to me like he was trying to compress his chest to ease the pain. While he'd been in the ER with the doctor, I'd spent my time googling horse kicks and broken ribs. The articles I read confirmed everything Ty had told me—binding and splinting ribs weren't recommended anymore. It eased some of the pain but did more harm than good. It looked like he would rather have small relief than none at all.

Gazing up at him, nerves skated through me all over again. Why did he have to be so big? Tall and broad, he made my perfectly average five-foot-seven feel tiny. His bunched eyebrows and deep scowl only added to his imposing aura. Filthy, too, covered head to toe in dirt, and he still managed to be the single most...

Breath stuttered in my chest, but I forced those thoughts to die out. My ex's older brother was not the man to be having *those* kinds of thoughts about.

My gaze caught on the little plastic pharmacy bag dangling from his fingers, spurring me to action. "You haven't had your pain pills yet. Let me get you a glass of water."

"June—"

I rushed past him to the kitchen. This had been remodeled, too, with gleaming white cabinets and a sleek faux-marble countertop. I ran my hand over the island's butcher block top. This whole house seemed designed to make my interior decorator's heart happy. Surely, this was too modern to have been his grandmother's taste, but I wasn't entirely convinced it matched Ty's, either. It sure suited me, though.

Remembering my errand, I found a glass, filled it with water, and brought it out to him.

"June." He gazed down at me, his eyes gone steely. "What are you doing?"

I held the glass in front of him until he took it, then swiped his pharmacy bag and read the instructions on the pill bottle. Percocet wasn't exactly a heavy hitter, but it should ease his pain. I shook out two capsules and handed them over. He popped them into his mouth and swallowed them down in one swift gulp, his eyes never leaving mine.

"When was the house updated?" I asked.

"Recently."

"Who did you bring in to do it? Madison's?" Kurt Madison was the best small contractor in Magnolia Ridge, or so I'd heard. I kept up on local businesses in my field, even if I never had call to use them in Austin.

"I did the work."

"You?" I glanced around, taking in everything from the smooth floors to the perfectly mitered corners on the Craftsman trim. Homeowner-completed renovations usually gave themselves away with sloppy seams and spotty finish. This work reflected an eye for detail I would have expected from a pro. "But it's so good."

One eyebrow ticked up. "Kick me when I'm down, why don't you."

I cringed over my backhanded praise. "I'm impressed, is what I mean. Most people think they have a good eye for stuff like this, but you actually do."

He winced as if my revised compliment had the opposite effect. "I had some help."

"Really? Magnolia Ridge doesn't have many interior designers. Who did you hire?"

He set his jaw, his mouth tensed into a straight line. "We're getting a little off track. You were going to tell me what you're doing out here."

"I told you, I wanted to make sure you're doing all the Best Man stuff."

"And I told you I am. What about the other thing?" He shifted his feet, crossing his arms over his chest again, squeezing himself in a one-person hug. "Why would it be awkward between us?"

"Right. That." I shoved away my questions about Ty's perfect-looking house and our hometown's small selection of professionals in my industry. Time to get this over with. "Eden's not just family, she's my best friend, and it's important to me that her wedding is perfect. I want everything to go smoothly."

"Okay."

From the unchanged expression on Ty's face, that explanation hadn't illuminated anything.

"Don't you want to sit down?"

Maybe it would be easier to talk to him if I didn't have to

crane my neck to stare up at him. How could a man with a crushed ribcage leave me so twitchy with nerves?

"I'm fine."

Sure he was. His casual words rang completely at odds with the tension in his voice and the lines in his face. He needed to be sitting down at a minimum—preferably in the hospital—not standing here in his living room arguing with me about how fine he was.

I blew out a sharp exhale. "Look, I don't want there to be any tension between us during the wedding, that's all."

One of his eyebrows twitched. "Why would there be tension between us?"

I made a sound of disgust. He wanted me to spell it out? Fine.

"Because of everything that happened between Bret and me, obviously. I'm not thrilled to see him again, but I'm not going to wreck the wedding over it, either. I'm past all that. I won't have a problem with him. I want to make sure you and I won't have a problem, either."

His mouth pulled at the edges, but resulted in a grimace, not a smile. "I don't have a problem with you, June."

Gah, this man! Every conversation today made me want to rip my hair out. Or his. But considering the trouble that had come from my efforts to get to this point, I would have to take him at his word.

"Great. Good. All I want is for us to be friendly for Eden and Booker's wedding, okay?"

He nodded, but at this point, he'd probably agree to anything if it meant I'd leave.

"Okay. Friendly it is."

"I'm also going to want some proof you've got the Best Man stuff covered."

"You've got a real Type A thing going on here, June."

I flashed him a cheesy grin. "Type A as in Awesome at Handling Weddings?"

He shook his head at me. "I'll send you my plans, receipts, the works. It's been great seeing you, but I've got to order a *No Trespassing* sign."

FOUR

FRIENDLY.

June wanted me to be friendly. I could do polite, I could even do cold, but I couldn't do friendly with June Evans. I'd proved that well enough when she dated Bret. The woman was all sunshine and enthusiasm, and I'd never quite been able to shut up the voices that clamored for so much more than just *friendliness* with her.

I watched as she drove off in that little car of hers, the tires kicking up dust behind her. When she disappeared from view, I finally sat down in my recliner. Standing hurt like the devil, but I wouldn't let her watch as I grunted and groaned myself into a sitting position like some ancient man climbing into his death bed.

Not that she hadn't already seen me at my worst. That had to be one for the record books, a woman pulling up to my property and promptly watching me get my ass handed to me by a four-year-old horse. In all my time working with horses, I'd never been kicked like that, not even as a stupid, reckless kid. I'd been bit a time or two, sure, and had plenty of little injuries, but nothing like this. I'd started a lot of green horses that didn't

27

know what they were capable of, but I always stayed in charge of the situation. I never took my eyes off them when we were in the pen together, never got distracted by anything around me.

Until June turned up on my ranch.

If it hadn't been for Bullet, who knows how long I would have stood there gawping away at her like an idiot. She'd just appeared out of nowhere, a vision of everything soft and beautiful and completely out of reach. I'd sworn to myself I'd keep her that way, no matter how much it tore me up inside. And she thought I had a problem with her? Well, that was probably better than the alternative.

I had to focus, and fished around in the pharmacy bag for my cell and wallet. The one saving grace of the day was that June hadn't barged into the ER with me to make sure I was being adequately cared for. I'd rather get kicked again than let her witness me having to be undressed by a nurse because it hurt too much to take my own pants off. Couldn't say which had been worse, the red-hot poker in my chest, or the searing humiliation.

I thumbed in Booker's number on my cell. He had grown up on a ranch and knew his way around flighty horses, even if he didn't do anything with them these days. With Aaron out of reach until tomorrow morning, I didn't have a whole lot of options for getting Bullet taken care of for the night. The rest of the horses would be fine out to pasture, but I didn't like to leave Bullet in the small round corral with nothing to do. A horse like that would find his own amusement, and that would surely end in trouble.

"What's up?" His deep voice rumbled on the other end of the line.

Booker Robinson had been my best friend since second grade. We'd been so tight, we had legitimately thought we were twins, our seven-year-old selves too innocent to see my white skin and his black skin as a barrier to blood brotherhood. That bond had stuck fast through school, with only a short pause when we went off to different colleges. When we both rolled back into Magnolia Ridge, we'd picked up right where we'd left off, and our friendship had seen each other through the last dozen years of highs and lows.

Didn't mean he wouldn't give me crap about this particular low.

"I need to ask a favor."

In theory, Booker's job as Magnolia Ridge High School's P.E. teacher and basketball coach left his summers free. In practice, he wound up almost as busy mid-summer as in fall. Basketball clinics took up most of his time, and he was trying to finish his continuing education course before the wedding so he could have the last of the summer to enjoy being a love-crazed newlywed.

Not that I was jealous. Booker deserved every bit of happiness with Eden. Still—nothing like your best friend getting everything he ever wanted to make a guy see all the gaps in his own life.

"That's not how this works," Booker said. "You're my Best Man, you're the one at my beck and call."

"Not today, man. Any chance you could come by and turn out a horse for me?"

"You mean you found one you can't handle?"

"Not exactly." Lord, how to explain? I hadn't thought about all the questions I'd have to answer, not one of which I wanted to discuss. "I've had a slight complication."

"A complication? Do tell."

I rolled my eyes to the ceiling. I would never hear the end of this. "I got kicked."

"The Unbreakable Ty Hardy got kicked?"

I sure hadn't started it, but that nickname did bring out a

29

surge of pride. Kicks were part of life in my field, but I had a reputation for avoiding them. I was in charge, and no horse had ever got the drop on me.

All of that changed this morning. I'd just have to hope and pray the story didn't spawn any new nicknames. "Not unbreakable now. I've got a few cracked ribs that say otherwise."

"Who got you?"

"Bullet."

Booker's laugh rang through the phone. "Bullet? That sweet little thing?"

"Yeah, and that sweet little thing is still standing in the pen where I left him when I went to the Medical Center. I wouldn't ask you to let him out into the pastures if I was in any shape to do it, and Aaron won't be back until morning."

"Sure, I'll swing by. But you know I have to ask—how did it happen?"

The vision of June standing by the pen came back to me. I wasn't sure I'd ever forget it. Flowers danced over her knee-length skirt, and the sleeveless top she'd worn had been just tight enough to mesmerize. I had no idea how long she'd been standing there watching me work. For a few glorious seconds, I thought she'd come to me for something other than the wedding.

Instead, she'd come calling to make sure I wouldn't be an ass to her.

My stomach kicked again over this whole mess.

"I got distracted by a woman."

Booker hummed a low note, sounding pleased as could be. "I am loving this story already. Who's the woman?"

I hesitated but couldn't see much sense in trying to hide the truth. We would all be together in a few weeks, anyway. "June Evans turned up on my property."

"June? What for?"

"She wanted to check up on me, make sure I'm fulfilling my wedding obligations." I couldn't tell him the rest, how she'd wanted to clear the air between us, her request for *friendliness*. Everything would be easier the less I said.

"Huh."

That one little syllable told me plenty. A little too thoughtful, a little too curious. A little too *You're full of it.*

I'd never shared my interest in June with Booker. Just admitting my feelings for her to my best friend felt like crossing a line, inching closer to giving myself permission to act on those forbidden feelings, so I'd kept my mouth shut. I didn't have many secrets from him, but I'd held onto that one. Still—we'd known each other going on thirty years. The man knew me better than anyone.

"So you'll come turn him out?" I said before he could ask more questions.

"Yeah, you got it. I'll be there in about thirty minutes."

"I appreciate it."

"Oh, and Ty?"

"Yeah?"

"Is Glass Ribs a good nickname, or—"

"Just get your ass over here."

31

june

OKAY, so that had been a disaster.

I walked into my parents' house, amazed at how perfectly wrong everything had gone at Ty's. I'd driven over there specifically to smooth out potential wrinkles, and instead, I'd created about a hundred new ones. The kick, running him to the Medical Center, my feeble explanation that I just wanted us to play nice for a few hours at the wedding. I couldn't have designed a worse mess.

My father walked out of the kitchen with a piece of toast slathered in jam in one hand. He ate jam made from the fruit of our orchards like he was under doctor's orders. That probably should have fattened him up a little more after all these years, but he didn't look very plump for mainlining sugar that way.

"Hey, Junebug, how did—" Whatever else he might have said got swallowed up as he took in my filthy condition. "What happened to you? Are you all right?"

"I'm fine. I just went to Ty Hardy's."

He looked me up and down. "Uh-huh. Ty do that to you, or the horses? Because one I'd have to shoot, the other, it's just their nature."

"It was both, kind of."

Slipping off my dirty heels, I sat down at the old kitchen table and explained how Ty had been kicked, glossing over most of our conversations. Being in the wedding party together provided enough of an excuse for me to go see Ty, but hopefully, my pop wouldn't ask questions. Long experience had proved I was no good at lying to him.

"Ty Hardy got kicked?" Pop took a big bite of toast and chewed a minute. "I didn't think I'd live to see the day."

"Well, today's the day."

"You know what they call him, don't you?"

A few choice names swam through my mind.

"*Unbreakable*. He works with a lot of wild ones out there, but he's always managed to avoid getting injured. I guess that winning streak's over."

"He's got three cracked ribs and an utter refusal to accept it. He didn't even want me to take him to the Medical Center in the first place."

The fact he thought broken ribs was something he could just wait out drove me a little insane. I still didn't like that the doctor had done nothing more than give him pain pills and a breathing device to try to keep his lungs strong. He needed to be in a hospital bed somewhere under a physician's care, not hobbling around his house making his injury worse. I doubted he would have even taken his pain meds if I hadn't been there to see that he did.

"Sounds normal to me. When I hit that deer and busted my ribs, your mother wanted me to go to the doctor, too, but I didn't see the point."

Seriously? I blew out a breath. "I wasn't looking for you to take Ty's side in this."

"There's no side, there's just nothing to do about it. Like a broken finger or a toe."

"And why can't you straighten out the ring finger on your right hand?"

He curled his right hand into a fist a couple of times, one finger not quite matching the others. "It's not so bad."

I shouldn't have expected my pop to get worked up over an injury. He could fall out of a peach tree, get a concussion, and still finish the rest of his chores in the orchard without so much as stopping to get an ice pack.

"His injury's a lot worse than a finger." The sound of Ty's ribs breaking would haunt me for the rest of my life. He had been so vulnerable lying there in the dirt, like a completely different man. The confident, in control rancher had been replaced by a man who'd simply needed help. He'd needed *me*. The desperate look in his eyes hadn't lasted long, but I couldn't shake the memory. "I guess his parents are out of town. Does he have anyone else to help look after things?"

"I don't have anybody else."

His words kept rolling around in my mind. Running his training business all by himself was one thing, but having a busted-up chest with nobody to take care of him? The idea hurt my heart. No one deserved that, much less Ty.

Pop massaged the finger that couldn't straighten. "I figured he'd have a ranch hand or two out there, but I don't rightly know."

"One, and only part-time." The question nagging at me didn't have anything to do with Ty's paid staff. I ran my fingers over the grooves of the old wood table, playing this as casually as I could. "Is there anyone else who might take care of him?"

"You mean like a girlfriend?" Pop's keen blue eyes always saw right through me. "I used to see a blonde with him around town, but it's been a while now. Probably even since before you and—" He waved his hand around in the air as if gesturing at a pile of trash. "*Bret*."

Pop had never quite been on board with Bret, even when things had still been fresh and new. A small-town farmer, he didn't trust big corporations, and he trusted their lawyers even less. The fact that Bret had started out in Magnolia Ridge didn't change things. As far as my pop was concerned, he had betrayed our town's values. Betraying me had been the final nail in that coffin.

"Don't worry about Ty," he said. "If he says he's got everything under control, he does. His word is better than most."

"It's not Ty's word I'm worried about." The man was more likely to grow another head than cheerfully follow doctor's orders, even when those orders were *Take it easy*. Maybe especially then. I'd like to believe he was lying in bed right now, getting some rest, but I wasn't that naive.

The back door opened, and my older brother slunk through. Even dirtier than I was, he looked completely wrung out, but grinned when he caught sight of me.

"Well, hey, Junebug!"

I leapt into Jed's arms, and he caught me in a generous hug. I still hadn't gotten used to the idea he'd come home for good after being overseas nearly half my life. He'd enlisted in the Army straight out of high school, and I'd only seen him sporadically for more than ten years. After our mother's death, he had finished his tour in Afghanistan and applied for an honorable discharge. I still felt like a kid cheering my big brother home on leave every time I saw him.

He'd grown his dark curly hair out a little more since the last time I'd been in town and sported a dusting of whiskers across his chin. He grinned through the dust caked on his tanned skin, but then his mouth dropped into a frown.

"Eden's wedding isn't this weekend, is it?"

"No, a couple more weeks. I just wanted to spend some time with you all."

"Darlin'," he drawled, "I don't know what kind of fanciness they've been teaching you down in Austin, but around here, we say *y'all*."

I swatted his arm and rolled my eyes as we moved farther into the kitchen.

"And what happened to you? You wrestle a pig?" he continued.

"One of Ty Hardy's horses," Pop said.

"It's a long story," I said in response to Jed's raised eyebrows. "And not important."

"Wrestling a horse is not ladylike," Jed said. "A pig, maybe, but a horse? That's a bridge too far. " He filled a glass of water and downed half of it in a gulp before turning piercing eyes on me. "What were you doing out at Ty Hardy's?"

Why didn't I just say I fell in the driveway at home? It would have been such a simple lie, and would have saved me all kinds of hassle.

"I just wanted to talk to him before Eden's wedding, make sure he's got the Best Man stuff covered. And I didn't want things to be weird between us because of everything that happened with me and Bret."

Jed looked me over. "How'd that go?"

"Not so hot," Pop said. "Ty's got broken ribs now."

Jed's mouth dropped open in theatrical indignation. "You injured the wrong brother?"

"*I* didn't do it! It wasn't my fault."

Not really. Sixty-forty, at most.

"You are oozing guilt, Junebug."

Not surprising. Olive branches weren't supposed to come with a swift kick to the chest.

"You're still planning on staying until the wedding?" Pop asked, and I nodded. "That vacation time, or working from here?"

"Some of each."

"Online decorating," he said, shaking his head. "I don't get it."

He'd voiced no such confusion during my five-year stint at the big Austin design firm I'd signed with right out of college. But ever since I'd hired onto internet-only consulting firm Domestic Bliss, my job had become less straightforward. More than once over the last two years, he'd asked me, "How do you decorate through the internet?" I'd never quite succeeded in explaining how my virtual job worked.

The fact that it had been a definite step down on my career ladder didn't help anything.

"Must be nice," Jed said. "I've got to find myself a plum job where I can work from the comforts of my bed. There's always the obvious."

My brother the ladykiller. "The problem there is you'd have to have a skill women actually want."

He mock-gasped. "That was brutal. As God as my witness, I've never left a woman disappointed."

I snorted. "Never?"

"Granted, it took me a while to get the hang of things in high school. Ever since then, though—"

Pop cleared his throat, obviously not a fan of Jed's inability to settle down. "What about your plans for yourself, June? Have you made any headway there?"

I'd rather go back to talking about my brother's skills with women than discuss my job situation. I didn't have anything concrete to report. "I'm still working on it."

"Awfully thoughtless of your friend to cut loose on your plans like that."

"It was a good opportunity. I can't really blame her." It had stung plenty, but I understood her decision. Even if her new plans had devastated mine.

Jed threw a filthy arm across my shoulders. "June, when someone screws you over, it's okay to blame them for it. Some might call it healthy."

"She didn't screw me over; she just got a really great job offer. I would have done the same thing if it had been me."

He leveled me a hard look. "No, you wouldn't."

My stomach twisted in confirmation, and I gave him a thin smile. "No, I wouldn't."

Kim and I had been friends since our days in design school. We'd followed similar career paths, moving up from internships to become full-fledged designers at our respective firms. After years of dreaming and months of planning, we'd intended to launch our own design firm. *Heartwood Home* would put our personal stamp on Austin interiors and propel our careers to the next level.

Instead, Kim took off with barely a moment's hesitation, and *Heartwood Home* dissolved into nothing. Based on our increasingly sporadic conversations, she was happy out in Houston. Meanwhile, I'd been left treading water, unsure which direction to swim. In truth, I was *not* okay with it. I wouldn't have abandoned our friendship and those big plans for the safer bet of a furniture chain. But blaming Kim didn't do much to change my situation. I'd spent the last few months trying to figure out what to do next, with no clear answer in front of me.

For now, I would put all that aside and focus on making Eden's wedding a librarian's dream day come true. I could sort out all the rest later.

"How are things out in the orchards?" I asked.

"Better than Kandahar."

"I'm getting a little tired of you saying that," Pop said.

"Sorry, Pop." Jed's face lit with a grin. "Say, since June's in town for a while, we should have a big family dinner. Have Wade and his crew over. How about tonight, what do you say?"

My oldest brother and his wife had two little boys, with a third baby on the way. Another thing I'd missed in my long stretches without visits home—quality time with those two rambunctious little guys. In all honesty, though, they wore me out even in small doses.

Pop didn't glance up at Jed as he pulled a jug of milk from the fridge. "We'll do it another night."

Jed's excitement deflated, but he seemed to take it in stride. "Should I order pizza?"

"Sounds good to me. I'm going to go get cleaned up first." I slipped out from under his arm, even dirtier than I'd been pre-hug.

"And stick me with the bill?" he called after me as I climbed the stairs. "I see how it is."

I paused on the landing as the old familiar sensation of being home sank through me. The comfortable feeling left an ache behind it, a hollowed-out place where my mother belonged. Being here was like remembering another life, memories I could almost touch but couldn't hold. As much as I loved the old house, it would never be the same without her in it.

I peeked into my parents' bedroom. Pop hadn't changed much in here since Mom's death, but I still noticed the difference. No stack of books on her nightstand, no basket of knitting by the bed, no fluffy purple bathrobe thinning at the elbows hung over the bathroom door. Even my mother's scent had faded, the smell of Dove soap and lavender lotion that used to follow her everywhere she went.

That ache inside me grew and swelled until I had to swallow it down, fighting off tears. I missed her something fierce.

Pop's footsteps on the stairs jolted me back into the present. I hurried into my old bedroom and shut the door, changed out of my filthy top and skirt, not even bothering to dust them off for fear I'd only grind the dirt in deeper. A shower would be in order soon, but I slipped into a tank top and shorts first and sprawled on my bed, feeling very close to and yet nothing like my long-ago teenage self. I'd had a few bumps and bruises in the eleven years since high school graduation, but I'd come through stronger. Some days not much wiser, but still. Stronger.

I pulled my phone from my purse and thumbed in Eden's number.

"June, are you in town yet?" she said after one ring.

"I am currently in my childhood bedroom, wondering why I've never pulled these awful boy band posters down from the walls."

No less than fifteen heartthrobs stared down at me from their posters, the carefully curated outfits they wore making them ridiculous by today's standards.

"You love them too much to ever do that."

I harrumphed, considering them. "Only Justin. He looks way better now than when he had that afro."

"Yeah, don't ever mention white guys with afros to Booker, it will start a whole *thing*."

"I've been duly warned." A tall, hilarious, thoughtful Black man, Booker probably had some interesting opinions about Justin's faux-fro, but I would refrain from bringing it up before the wedding. Maid of Honor duties, and all. Maybe it would be safe to ask at the reception.

I couldn't imagine a more perfect match for my cousin than Booker. Where Eden could be a little fussy sometimes, he took things in stride. His impulsiveness balanced out her need to research and plan. Together, they made up a romantic super-hero duo worthy of sighing over, which I'd done a time or two. The only real surprise was that they were about to get married less than a year after they'd started dating. But I guess the old saying proved true: When you know, you know.

I toyed with the tassels on the pink and purple afghan laid across my bed. "So...I have to tell you something."

"That doesn't sound good. As long as it's not about my wedding, shoot."

If she could only see my face. "Eh, it's not really, but it does kind of affect it a little."

"A little?" Eden's voice rose an octave already. "What happened? Did the books get mildewy? I was afraid they would. I knew you should have kept them in climate-controlled storage—"

"No—"

"Are the deliveries delayed? Which one? I've been tracking the packages. Did you send me all the tracking numbers?"

I should have known better than to open up the floodgates of her wedding worries. Best to get straight to the point.

"It's not that, either. The books are fine, and all your orders are being delivered this week." I'd been thrilled when she'd asked me to decorate for her wedding. I'd never staged a wedding before, but so far, everything was going to plan. All except for the one little snafu. "It's just that I kind of broke Booker's Best Man."

She sucked in a breath, and I could imagine her eyebrows crinkling in the middle. "You did what now?"

I shut my eyes tight but couldn't erase the vivid, slow-motion picture of Ty being thrown backward, landing shocked and broken on the ground. My stomach churned with fresh guilt over the image I couldn't shake.

"I went out to Ty's and I sort of distracted him from this horse he was working with and the horse kicked him and now he has broken ribs and can hardly move." I blurted it all out in one breath, as though that would make the story less awful.

"Broken ribs? Is he okay?"

The impressive assortment of swears he'd muttered this morning echoed through my mind. "He's okay in the sense that an injured bear is okay."

Eden sighed. "What did you go out there for anyway?"

My turn to sigh.

"I don't even know anymore." In hindsight, it all seemed ridiculous now. As usual, I only had perfect clarity *after* I'd made the wrong decision. Had I actually gone and *poked* the bear? "He wasn't really giving me wedding information. And I wanted to call a truce, I guess."

"I didn't realize you were ever at war."

"You know what I mean. We've got tricky history together, and I didn't want your Maid of Honor and Best Man to ruin your wedding with dirty looks and snide comments."

"Ty can be a little taciturn—"

A sarcastic laugh barked out of me. "A little?"

"But I have a hard time imagining him being anything other than polite. Aloof, maybe, but a gentleman."

"He was." And there lay the problem. I still thought about the conversations we used to have when I'd been dating Bret, all the little talks that somehow made me feel more known than I had in ages. Maybe ever. Until that closeness had fallen apart and Ty had disappeared. "But we've barely seen each other since then. I wanted to make sure there were no hard feelings."

"It sounds like Ty had some hard feelings today."

"Funny." The thread of guilt I'd been trying to squash wove itself into a whole sweater. Ty never would have been injured if I hadn't barged in on him like that. Who just shows up without a warning text?

"What about Bret?" Eden asked. "Are you going to call a truce with him?"

The guilt blasted apart, turning to lava in my gut. We hadn't dated long, but the whole *cheating on me* thing had made an awfully big impression.

"It's on him to stay out of *my* way. If I know Bret, he'll plaster on a huge smile and act like nothing ever happened between us. If I'm really lucky, he'll pretend he doesn't even know me."

"But then you run the risk of him hitting on you, you beautiful stranger."

I sighed, imagining just how that scene would go. Seemed unlikely he'd forget we'd dated, but considering he'd started seeing someone else while we were still together, who could say? It might not have been all that memorable for him. "You're right. Better he remember me and feel like the sorry piece of crap he is."

"I'm sorry about how awkward this is going to be for you, you know that, right?"

I knew. Eden had apologized as soon as she'd addressed Bret's invitation, and several more times since he'd accepted. But my history with the Hardy brothers aside, Booker had his own history with them, and I couldn't expect my feelings to overrule his at his own wedding. I didn't love the idea of seeing my most recent ex-boyfriend again, but I would just have to suck it up and deal.

"It's going to be fine. I'm past that."

"There's still time to add a plus-one and rub it in Bret's face."

I laughed, thinking about the string of first dates I'd had in the last several months. No one man stood out among them as someone I would ever want to see again for coffee, let alone bring to a family wedding.

"I don't think so."

"What about that guy you met at trivia night a couple months ago?"

"He texted a truly unfortunate photo." I'd wanted to disinfect both my phone and my eyeballs after that one.

"Ew. What about the musician?"

I had to think back a second to remember. "He thinks monogamy is an unnatural construct foisted upon us by religion."

"What about—"

"Unless the next name out of your mouth is Justin Timberlake, the answer is no. Nope, I'm just going to be like Switzerland and stand alone. Neutral."

She made a little sound of amusement. "You're not exactly known for neutrality. You're more like France, all heartfelt emotion and judgmental looks."

All that heartfelt emotion had always been my Achilles heel. If I hadn't been so caught up in my feelings for Bret, maybe I would have realized he hadn't had any for me. Almost thirty years old, and I'd been played by a player.

"Then I need to be like Germany." I sat up on the bed in a burst of inspiration. "I'll be cool and calculating, and totally unemotional."

"You're thinking of robots, not Germans," Eden said with a laugh. "And I love you, but you couldn't be unemotional if your life depended on it."

I sighed back onto the bed. This was probably true.

SIX

"YOU DON'T LOOK SO GOOD."

Aaron had just turned the last of the horses out to pasture for the day, and he now watched me with a wary expression. He'd been sneaking looks at me all morning, like he thought I might either pass out or spontaneously combust, and wanted to be sure he witnessed it.

"Sit down, at least," he continued.

"I'm fine."

I couldn't lift so much as a jug of milk, standing under the shower spray that morning had been unbearable, and walking from the house to the barn felt like a herculean task, but I was fine. I'd spent the morning trying to find at least one chore I could still handle, but so far, I'd only managed to hover around the barn, groaning whenever Aaron was out of earshot.

He secured the pasture gate and brushed off his gloves. Finishing up his equine management degree, he was young, but he'd been around horses since he was a kid, and hard work didn't faze him. He'd helped out around the ranch since just about the day I started my business up. I wasn't sure what I'd do once he graduated and moved on to bigger things.

45

"You look like you're going to faint."

That would be better than spontaneously combusting, but not by much.

I moved closer to the low, rough-hewn bench spanning one barn wall, not liking the prospect of trying to sit on it. Not at all. Too many muscles in my chest pulled in sitting down and getting up again, as I'd learned many times over the last twenty-four hours. Wasn't worth the effort. I leaned against the wall instead, but that didn't bring any relief.

Aaron laughed as he walked by me to examine the tack. "You are something else. Broken ribs, man—you should be in bed at least a day or two. Get some rest."

Easier said than done. I'd hardly slept last night—lying down strained my chest in ways I never imagined it could, and every restless movement had sent a fresh jolt through me. The pain meds had dulled the ache in my ribs, but they'd also left me light-headed and dizzy, with strange thoughts swimming in my brain. Thoughts about a certain pretty distraction I'd tried to put behind me a year ago. They took away the barrier I put into place every time I thought of her, and I didn't like that. Sleep stayed just out of reach.

"Maybe later. Do you think you can take over the training of those two riding horses for a while? They still need plenty of lead practice."

"No problem, I'm happy to do what I can to pick up the slack. Want me to see if I can rearrange my schedule a bit and spend an extra hour or two here to get some of the daily maintenance done?"

Those tasks stacked up in my mind, my gut twisting harder with each one. The most basic part of my job, and I couldn't do it. "I hate to ask you to do that."

"Who else is going to? You?" He dragged a gloved hand

across his forehead, leaving a streak of dirt on his copper skin. "If a butterfly landed on you, it would knock you over."

I gritted my teeth. The kid was right, of course, but he didn't need to crow about it. "I'll be able to ride again in a couple of days."

"A couple of days? When I was in high school, a guy I know got clocked just like you did, only cracked one rib, and *he* couldn't ride a horse for a month without crying. I wouldn't think it would be any easier on an older dude."

I grimaced. The doctor had said six weeks at a minimum, but I didn't have that kind of time, *older dude* or not. The horses I boarded for the extra income wouldn't be much trouble, but the others needed to stick to a daily training schedule. Beyond that, I had a few that still waited to be started, including Bullet. I would just have to heal a mite faster than expected, that's all.

"Maybe I'll call around, see if some FFA kids can come in for the little stuff." There were only so many favors I could call in from my friends. Anyway, Booker had laughed his ass off when he'd showed up the night before to turn out Bullet, and I wasn't eager to relive the experience. "Even with your help, I'll still be behind on all the real work."

Aaron raised a shoulder. "It happens, man."

"Not to me."

He pulled a halter and lead rope down from the wall for one of the riding horses. "Sucks to be human like the rest of us, doesn't it?"

He disappeared again before I could respond.

He thought the whole situation funny, but my clients wouldn't find it so amusing. Eventually, I would have to call them, let them know there would be a slight delay in their horses' training schedules. My stomach crawled thinking of the inevitable conversations. Circumstances were out of my control, but I didn't make excuses. In a field that was all about reputation, this injury could seriously damage mine. If my clients started jumping ship, word would get around.

I made my slow way back to the house, playing through scenarios of how I could possibly stay on top of work, when gravel crunched in the drive. I looked up in time to see June park her car next to my truck. A stupid kind of elation like I'd felt when I saw her yesterday washed through me, a tidal wave I wanted to rush into when all sense told me to run the other way.

I had no business feeling anything where this woman was concerned.

She got out of her little eco-friendly car and walked straight toward me. I couldn't decide if I should laugh or cry. The woman had no clue about ranch-appropriate attire. A cute little skirt and top yesterday, denim shorts and flip-flops today. Flip-flops. On a horse ranch. Heaven help me.

"What's this? Returning to the scene of the crime?"

Her smile stalled, and a little line formed between her eyebrows. "Well, good morning to you, too, Mr. Sunshine."

I grumbled in the back of my throat. It must be possible to keep her at arm's length without being an ass about it, but I hadn't figured that one out yet. I tried for something a little more welcoming—but not *too* welcoming.

"Good morning, June. Nice to see you again."

Her raised eyebrows said my tone had landed on patronizing.

"How are you feeling today?"

Like I'd been hit by a truck. Not that she didn't know. "Peachy."

"Did you sleep all right?"

"Not really." I didn't think she needed the run-down on my night. Once again, she'd come out to see me for reasons I didn't quite understand. I'd told her I had the Best Man stuff covered.

I'd told her I would be *friendly* at the wedding. What did she want, assurances in writing? "Did you need something?"

She pressed her lips together, glaring like fire. So I was still being a surly ass. My ribs were broken, and I'd barely slept all night—I'd earned today's bad attitude.

"I came to check on you, see if *you* needed anything."

"I'm doing just grand."

Her laugh cut into the sultry morning air. Still early yet, but already eighty degrees out—not that I minded, considering how she'd chosen to dress. *Those legs.* I pulled myself away from wholly inappropriate thoughts of everything from her flip-flops to her Daisy Dukes.

"You're not *grand*. Why are you even out here? I thought you'd be taking it easy for a few days, at least."

With Aaron on task for the morning, I'd been headed to my house to try do just that, but I cut a wide circle and walked back toward the barn instead. "Thanks for your concern, but I'm fine."

She kept pace with me. "I'm not sure you are. You're all gray around the mouth. You should sit down for a little while, take a break."

This again.

"I don't think that would make much of a difference." Nothing did. My muscles throbbed in my chest like my ribcage might bust apart any minute—just a matter of not doing anything to make it worse. Walking around didn't help, but lying in bed, wishing for sleep that wouldn't come, proved no better. I didn't know what to do with this restlessness I couldn't shake. If I let it, it'd swallow me whole.

"What could it hurt to try?"

"Just my pride," I muttered, striding past the empty stalls, trying not to think about all the work I'd normally be doing right now. I could scrape by for a while with a little extra help from Aaron, but I didn't have a contingency plan for this kind of situation. Nothing like it had ever come up before. Solo operations like mine were common, but maybe I'd put too much stock in my *unbreakable* reputation.

"Did you have breakfast?"

I laughed but cut off the sound with a grunt when the pain shocked through me.

"I did." If she considered toast breakfast—which I didn't. But anything more would have been too much for me to manage. I'd been defeated by fried eggs. An all new low.

She walked through the barn aisle beside me, her flip-flops slapping against the concrete floor. "Is there anything I can do for you? Anything you need?"

Nothing she could provide. Nothing realistic, anyway.

"I'm not sure exactly what you're offering here, June."

She splayed her hands, glancing around. Apparently, she wasn't sure, either. "I feel kind of responsible for the state you're in—"

"A bit, yeah." A little advance warning of her impromptu visit would have been nice.

She glared again, but there might have been a speck of humor to it.

"I just wanted to see if I could make it up to you somehow."

Hundreds of ways she could make it up to me spun through my head, but I shut them all down one by one. That would never happen. Not now, not ever. I'd already been left once by a city woman with big plans—I wouldn't sign up for the same heartache with June.

"It's just ribs, June. I'm fine. Unless you're offering to muck out stalls and water the horses, there's really nothing I need."

Her face lit up, and she took an eager step closer. "I could do that."

I leveled her a hard look. "Since when?"

The line between her eyebrows returned. "I grew up on a farm, you know."

"Remind me again how many horses your dad has out on his fruit farm."

She pressed her lips together in a look of irritation. Too bad for her it was cute as could be.

"I know how to muck out stalls. Your grandmother taught me right here."

Now that stopped me. "Gram taught you? When?"

"At a Girl Scout merit badge trip."

My brief laugh fanned the flames in my chest, igniting the embers in my lungs. My temples ached from all this walking around, and a cool sheen of sweat had broken out on my forehead. I needed her to get gone so I could collapse and not think about leggy brunettes for a while.

"What, twenty years ago?"

She held her head a little higher. "Seventeen."

"My mistake. While I'm sure that badge looked awfully nice on your Girl Scout sash, I've got fourteen horses here that need to be tended."

"I've got nothing but time until Eden's wedding." She bobbed a shoulder. "More or less."

Even if my injury had been directly caused by my brain short-circuiting when I saw her yesterday, her offer to help out around the ranch smacked of pity. I was in no mood to be fussed over and coddled, especially by June. Bad enough having Aaron listen to me moan and groan as I moved around—I didn't need to add her to that audience.

"Don't you have houses to decorate?"

She smiled a little as if she'd already won the argument. "I'm with an internet-based firm, so I'm pretty flexible."

When we talked about her work last year, she'd made the internet thing sound like a stop-gap solution on her way to starting her own business. I almost asked her why she hadn't moved on yet, but caught myself. I didn't need her hanging around any longer than she already had been. I needed to get her on her way, off my property, and out of my thoughts.

"It's a nice gesture, but you don't know what's involved here."

Her chin lifted higher. "I'm sure I can handle it."

"I'm sure you can't." She wasn't cut out for this, and I didn't have the heart to have her around all the time.

A fire sparked in her eyes as she glared up at me. "There's no reason for you to be this stubborn, Ty. You need help around here, and I'm going to do it. You can complain all you like, but you're stuck with me. Now sit down, you're too pale."

"I don't need to sit—"

She pointed a finger in my face. "Sit. Down."

I planted myself on a barrel under the tack wall. Wasn't easy to do, and I groaned like an *older dude* in the process, but the throbbing in my temples eased as soon as I sat down.

"Now." She stood over me so I felt like a kid brought before the principal, shrinking under her shadow. "You need help. I'm offering to give you that help, at least until the wedding. I believe there's a phrase about gift horses a man in your trade would know."

I would have laughed if it weren't for the misery in my chest.

"I appreciate your offer, I truly do, but there's nothing in your life down in Austin that makes me think you're a good fit for this."

She swung a hand around, gesturing at the stalls. "It's not rocket science. It's literally shoveling horse crap."

"And it's hard work. I bet you'd regret all your promises before two weeks were even over."

A light sparked in her eyes. "You're on."

"What? No, that wasn't an actual *bet*—"

"If you win, fine, I'll walk away and admit I'm just a city girl who can't keep up. But if I win..." She paused, obviously at a loss for a good prize for proving she could shovel horse crap. "If I win, you have to admit I proved you wrong. Publicly."

I shook my head a tic. "Those are the worst stakes I've ever heard."

She flashed a sugar-sweet smile I wished weren't so obviously fake. Her true smiles worked a kind of magic trick on my heart, opening up what I'd intended to shut down for good. Not that I needed any more incentive to cave to her right now.

"You could always throw in a ride on one of your horses."

"Not happening."

She crossed her arms and jutted out one hip. "Ty Hardy, are you afraid of losing?"

This whole thing was asinine, but her little challenge dug at me. My bones were broken, my professional reputation was surely sliding toward shaky ground, and I couldn't even take a shower, but I still had a sliver of pride left.

I stood, swallowing down the groans. "I'm not afraid of watching you fall on your pretty little behind."

One of her eyebrows twitched, and I wished I hadn't said it quite that way. Probably still the effects of last night's pain meds making me talk like a fool.

"Challenge accepted." She held her hand out.

I shook it, her hand soft and warm in mine. I held it a beat longer, and the air seemed to crackle between us. I had blinders on, everything around me narrowed down to just June. A fire that had nothing to do with my busted ribs uncurled in my chest, spreading outwards until I seemed to fill with it. Awareness flickered in her eyes, her fingers twitching against my palm.

I dropped her hand and turned to leave the barn, stamping out that hopeful fire.

"There's just one problem," I said as I passed her.

"What's that?"

I looked down at her feet, taking in the shiny violet toenail polish that did something dangerous to my heartbeat.

"You can't muck out a barn in flip-flops."

SEVEN

june

THIRTY MINUTES LATER, I returned to Victory Ranch. I'd gone to my pop's and changed into jeans, a plain T-shirt, sneakers, and had pulled my hair into a quick bun. Thankfully, Pop and Jed were out in the orchard, so I didn't have to explain what I planned to do at Ty's property for the next few weeks.

Not that I fully understood it myself. Ty was absolutely right, I had no clue what I was getting into, and every sign pointed to my biceps failing after a day, let alone weeks—but I hated him thinking so little of me. He thought I couldn't even shovel out stalls? I would prove to him I could do something useful, even if it was just cleaning up after his horses. A crazy way to soothe my pride, but once the idea took hold, it wouldn't let go. If nothing else, it would help erase some of the guilt that flooded my stomach every time I thought about the hand I'd had in that awful kick.

I found Ty leaning at a strange angle against the back pasture fence, watching the horses graze. Over in a dirt pen, a younger guy worked with a horse, guiding it with a long stick. Happily, the horse wasn't Bullet. Frankly, I didn't want to see that menace horse again.

Ty turned around as I approached, and my breath snagged in my throat. Completely unfair that even looking that unfriendly, he still managed to be the handsomest man in a fifty-mile radius.

"Is that your ranch hand?" I asked, shaking away those thoughts.

He nodded, looking me over. Heat prickled up my neck as I waited to see if my new outfit passed the Ty test. Emotions I couldn't name flared to life in his eyes as his gaze drifted down my body, and my stomach threatened to do a little swoop in response.

Finally, his gaze rested on my feet. He cocked his head to one side. "Those shoes still aren't going to cut it."

I wiggled my toes inside my gray sneakers. "They're the closest thing I've got to work shoes."

Considering what I would be working in, I hoped this little act of penance wouldn't destroy my favorite pair of running shoes.

"Come on." He crooked a finger and led me into the barn. "I'll get you hooked up."

I followed him to a supply area where a few pairs of tall rubber boots stood beneath a shelf. Even though I could guess what he used them for, the boots didn't have a trace of *muck* on them. The man might have a dirty job, but he must have been meticulous about cleaning up afterwards.

"Try one of those."

I picked up one of the rubber boots, but it was heavier than I expected. "This is never going to fit. Your feet are huge."

"Your feet are tiny. Put the boots on over your shoes, then."

It took plenty of tugging, but I managed to pull both boots on. I stomped around, getting the feel for walking in such large shoes. Small wonder he didn't trip over his own feet every day.

"You done, or do you need another lap?" he asked.

"I'm ready."

He nodded to a far corner. "Bring that wheelbarrow to the first stall. I've got all your tools lined up and ready. And here," he said, holding out a pair of thick work gloves. "You'll need these."

I slipped my hands into the gloves. Flexing my fingers, they swam in the smooth leather. "These are huge, too."

"What can I say? I'm a big guy."

Heat unfurled across my skin.

Nope. I wouldn't let my thoughts go *there*. This was Ty. Perfect male specimen or not, he was still my ex-boyfriend's brother. I pushed all considerations of his size away, reminding myself I needed to be a robot. Unemotional. Logical. Not thinking about how cozy I felt standing next to him.

I brought the wheelbarrow over to the stall as instructed, and he handed me a pitchfork, which I lifted straight up in the air. "I feel like a peasant about to rush a castle."

He didn't even crack a smile. "Hilarious."

"I guess Frankenstein jokes are out."

He cocked an eyebrow. "First, you sift out the waste."

"So serious." I glanced into the stall. "Right. The waste."

Mucking stalls turned out to be just as awful as I remembered it from when Abigail Hardy had showed me how as a Girl Scout. I hadn't been around manure in years, but the smell brought those memories back full force. I didn't remember the waste falling apart quite so easily, as though every little ball of crap wanted to hide itself from me in the bedding. I fussed and fumed, digging at pieces until I totally decimated a pile without ever getting any into the wheelbarrow.

Ty made a clucking sound in the back of his throat. "That is unfortunate. Try to get all the way under it next time, so it doesn't fall apart."

A small smile tugged at the edges of his mouth. For a man

who claimed he wanted nothing to do with this bet, he sure looked like he got a kick out of it.

Huffing a breath, I moved on to the next clump. I'd only been at it fifteen minutes, but gaining Ty's respect by shoveling his horses' manure didn't seem like such a hot idea anymore.

"Make sure you leave any clean bedding behind," he said as I dumped a large forkful into the wheelbarrow. "We don't want to waste it."

I tried to scoop more carefully, but picking up the manure and leaving the bedding in the stall wasn't as easy as he made it sound. A clump of manure fell between the tines of the scoop, landing with a soft thud on the cement floor outside the stall.

"Whoops."

"It's okay. You can sweep the floor down after you're done."

My shoulders sagged. "Great."

"Now," he said, handing me a broad shovel. "Find the urine spots. You need to get rid of all of it, so check for any discolored bedding."

"How do I find the urine spots?"

He nodded toward the floor of the stall. "You look for it."

I sighed and started poking around in the straw with the shovel. It didn't take long to find the first soaked area, and I learned that shoveling wet bedding was harder work than shoveling clumps of manure. It smelled worse, too, a thick, acrid smell that burned my nose and stung my eyes when I exposed it to the air.

"That's a stallion's stall," Ty said from behind me. "He usually has a few episodes to find."

"Episodes? I'm standing in his urine, you can call it what it is."

His brief laughter turned into a groan. I whipped my head around, but he watched me without expression, like both the laugh and the groan had been my imagination.

"You could sit down while you supervise, you know."

"I need to make sure you're doing it right. A dirty stall can lead to all kinds of disease."

Great. Just what I needed to hear. Not only was his estimation of me on the line, now I had the threat of sick horses looming over me, too. I searched more diligently through the bedding.

"So, you have all the groomsmen's suits figured out, right?"

I heard a quick exhale over my shoulder.

"June."

"I'm just curious. It's kind of my job."

"Funny, I thought it was my job."

I waved my hand in a so-so motion. "My job is to double-check your job."

"What is the point of the Best Man, then?"

"Science is still trying to figure that one out."

After digging out all the wet spots—the stallion had left four—came sifting to make sure the last traces of waste were gone, followed by trucking the manure to the waste collection shed. Finally, Ty showed me the huge pile of fresh bedding out in the hay barn, and I carted load after load to replenish the cleaned stall. He walked me through every step, offering dry commentary on my shoveling style, and pointing out dirty areas I'd missed. By the time I finished, the stall shone, ready for the stallion to come water it down again.

"Pretty good, right?" I said, grinning over my work.

"Pretty good." Ty twisted his wrist to check his watch. "And it only took you thirty-five minutes. With thirteen stalls to go, you just might be out of here by eight tonight."

My pride whooshed out of me along with my breath as I looked down the row of empty stalls. This was only the first task of many I'd agreed to tackle every day for the next two weeks.

I'd had smarter ideas.

"You'll go faster now that you know what to do. I want every stall to look as good as this one." He paused, his eyes narrowed on mine. "Unless you want to go ahead and admit right now that you're a city girl who can't cut it."

Staring right back at him, I straightened my spine, moved the wheelbarrow to the next stall, and started the whole process over again. Like I would ever give him the satisfaction of saying *I quit*.

But he was right, at least where the improvement was concerned—I did make quicker progress after that. The work wasn't any easier and didn't smell any better, but it didn't take thirty-five minutes to clear out another stall.

After I'd completed my third stall under Ty's watchful eye, he brought me a red Solo cup filled with water from a huge thermos that sat on the shelf above the rubber boots.

"You can take a break whenever you want," he said as I downed the water in one long go. "You're not on the clock."

"I'm fine." I handed him back the empty cup. Taking a break would just prove I couldn't handle it. Plus, if I sat down, chances were good I wouldn't want to stand up again. "Thanks."

His mouth twisted, his expression no more pleased than when I'd showed up this morning. "You don't have to do this at all, you know."

"I know." I went back to my shoveling. "Hey, what do you have planned for Booker's bachelor party? Or do I want to know?"

"What does that mean, exactly?"

I rolled my eyes at how difficult he had to make everything. "You know. A strip club. One last crazy night of bachelorhood before Booker settles down."

"You think a lot of me, don't you, June?"

60

I shoveled a large clump of manure into the wheelbarrow, ignoring the growing ache in my lower back. "I'm not judging. Pole dancing lessons is one of the most popular options for bridesmaid parties right now."

A weird, strangled sound came from behind me.

"Pole dancing lessons? You doing that?"

I shot him a saucy look over my shoulder. "I'm not giving anything away."

The young man who had been out in the round pen popped his head through the barn door.

"I've got to get going." His eyes lit on me. "Oh, I didn't know you got one of the high school girls out here."

I had filthy spots on my clothes, flyaway locks of hair stuck to my sweaty face, and my back felt every one of my twenty-nine years, but I grinned at him. "I like you already."

"June, this is my ranch hand, Aaron Ortega," Ty said. "Aaron, this is June Evans. She's a...friend."

His mouth twisted over the word as if he didn't like that explanation any better than I did. But outing me as his brother's ex-girlfriend wouldn't have been a more acceptable title at this point.

Distracter extraordinaire, maybe.

Aaron walked over to shake my hand, grinning all the while. "Nice to meet you. Are you going to handle all of this while Ty is on the mend?"

"No," Ty said at the same time I said, "Yes." We glared at each other a beat. He could be as irritated as he liked, but he wouldn't get rid of me that easily.

I broke the stare-down and turned to Aaron. "I absolutely am."

"You must be a good friend. Not many people are willing to muck stalls out of the kindness of their hearts."

"I kind of owe it to him. I'm sort of the reason he's all..." I gestured vaguely at Ty's chest. He stared down at me like he didn't appreciate the reminder.

Aaron glanced between the two of us. "You made Bullet kick him?"

"Not intentionally. I turned up unannounced, and I don't think Bullet liked it too much. He got a little panicked."

"He wasn't the only one," Ty muttered.

"You must have really shocked both of them, then," Aaron said. "Ty's the most focused man I've ever met. Dude can't be moved when he wants something."

Ty cleared his throat, and Aaron caught the subtle signal to carry on.

"Anyway, nice to meet you. I'm here for a few hours most days, so I'll probably see you later." He waved and left the barn.

My gaze skated over Ty's rough features, ignoring his ever-present scowl. What was he like when he really wanted something? *Dude can't be moved.* Sounded about right to me. So what *did* he want?

"What?" Ty growled when I stared at him too long.

I scowled back. "Absolutely nothing."

I went to work, mucking, cleaning, and spreading fresh bedding. My time improved with each stall, but it still took the rest of the afternoon to get through them. When I finished, sticky sweat covered me from head to toe, my hands ached from blisters across my palms, the stench of manure clung to my clothes, I had a wet spot on my jeans from accidentally kneeling in a stall, and questionable dark patches marked my exposed skin.

But I'd mucked all the stalls.

I rinsed off the rubber boots with a hose before tugging them off. I hadn't spent a day doing real, manual labor in years, not since my summers working on the family farm during college. An exhausted sort of triumph thrilled through me as I stood before Ty, filthy but proud of my work.

He shook his head at me. "You can stop grinning like that."

"Like what? Like someone who proved you wrong? Why would I stop doing that?"

His eyebrows tugged closer. "You didn't prove me wrong. Our agreement was two weeks."

"You said I couldn't handle it. I think I proved I can."

His mouth twisted, fighting back a smile. "I'll give you that."

I grinned even wider. "I'll take it. You need me to do anything else tonight?"

Please God, no. All my muscles ached, and if I had to lift anything else right now, I might cry. On top of that, I was supposed to meet Eden in less than an hour to make wedding decorations. Despite everything I'd said to Ty, given the choice between shoveling horse crap and making paper flowers, I would choose the paper flowers every time.

"I'm good. Aaron fed and watered the horses out in the pastures before he left. Didn't think you'd have strength left to do it tonight."

An argument rose up inside me at the casual slight, but no sense voicing it. I *didn't* have the strength left tonight. "Should someone bring the horses in to, you know, mess up all my hard work?"

"They'll be okay turned out for the night. Horseflies haven't been bad this season."

"Okay, then." I pulled off the leather gloves, wincing as I exposed all the wounds my work had left on my hands. Angry, open blisters stretched across the tops of my palms just below my fingers, with another covering the pad beneath the first knuckle of my right hand. The smarting had numbed with each scoop of the shovel, but taking off the gloves seemed to have switched the pain back on.

Ty loomed next to me, my hands suddenly held in both of his as he inspected them. "Dammit, June, why didn't you say something?"

"I didn't think it was this bad." It had hurt, but I'd thought that just came with shoveling stalls all day. Working on my laptop didn't really compare to working with my hands on a ranch.

He gave me a scorching look, then took me by one forearm. I could have slipped out of his light grip if I'd wanted to, but I let him lead me to the wall with the rubber boots. He rifled through a small plastic bin for antiseptic tubes and Band-Aids. Minor injuries must be a common thing out here. Judging by all the gauze and athletic tape, blisters were probably the best-case scenario.

"I should have known better." He held my hands beneath the water jug's spigot and twisted the knob. Fresh water washed away the worst of the dirt that had collected in the blisters' raised edges, stinging over the open wounds. He found a clean rag and gently patted my palms dry, scolding us both the whole time. "I never should have agreed to your little scheme. I knew you were too delicate for this, but I didn't think you were so stubborn you wouldn't say anything when your hands were bleeding in your gloves. I'm not trying to work you to the bone, June."

"I'm not delicate." And my hands weren't bleeding, but that didn't seem the right battle to pick.

I tried to focus on his caustic tone instead of the gentleness of his hands, but it proved impossible. He applied the antiseptic cream to my open wounds with feather-light touches that sent shivery tendrils rippling up my back.

He stopped, worry etched in the creases around his eyes. "That hurt?"

"No." I'd never admit the shiver had nothing to do with the blisters.

He finished smoothing out the cream, his touch even lighter than before. My heart raced, my skin practically glowing with delight from every little brush of his fingers. I barely breathed for fear of giving away how much he affected me. His big, calloused hands that kept horses in check worked as carefully as possible while he applied a series of bandages over my palms and fingers.

When he'd finished, my hands still ached, but the sting of the open blisters had eased. Now, if I could just stop thinking about his gentle touch and what it did to me, I might be able to walk out of here with a shred of dignity intact.

Ty put away the tube of antiseptic and snapped the plastic drawer shut. "I don't want you coming back tomorrow."

I blew out a breath. All the tender little feelings that had been swirling through me broke apart. "I've had blisters before, Ty. I'll be here tomorrow."

"You'll just wind up doing yourself a worse injury, you're so stubborn."

I laughed in his face, deepening his scowl. "You really want to talk about stubborn? I think you win that award. You should be resting."

"I won't have you hurting yourself any more out here. It's not worth it."

"I'll bundle up the blisters, I don't care. I'm not giving up on this bet."

He exhaled through his nose like an angry bull. "There is no bet. We're done here."

A white-hot fire lit in my chest at how easily he'd dismissed me. "We are not!"

"This proves you have no business being out here."

I might have pointed out his total inability to do the work I'd done today, but even I knew that would only make him slam the door on me completely.

"All this proves is that I'm stronger than you think." I wasn't beaten down after one day of hard work. After being unceremoniously dumped by my boyfriend and watching my job plans vanish before my eyes, a few Band-Aids were nothing. "I said I would do this for you, and I will. I don't go back on my word."

He glared a full minute, as if he thought I might run crying from the barn if he stared long enough. I stood even straighter, waiting. I could see him warring with himself behind his eyes, but just which emotions were in conflict, I couldn't say.

Finally, he shifted, shaking his head as if he thought I was nuts. "Fine."

That fire in my gut cooled down, but I resisted the urge to gloat. "I'll be back tomorrow, first thing."

"Not first thing. Aaron's usually here in the mornings, and with the horses out all night, there won't be anything to muck."

"Okay, so noon?"

He did another one of his little exhale-groans that I suspected were subtle laughs cut off by the pain in his ribs. "Noon it is."

I nodded agreement, tallying up my win. I should not have been so satisfied to keep mucking out his horses' stalls, but I gloried in my victory all the same.

* * *

"This feels so wrong." Eden looked over the sheaf of loose book pages in her hand as though they were a puppy she was about to barbecue. "I've dedicated my whole life to my love of books, and here I am destroying them."

66

Out of all of Eden's literary-themed wedding decor, the paper roses for the bouquets were the most labor-intensive, but the payoff would be worth it. Finished flowers littered my cousin's dining table, where we'd been furiously cutting, curling, and gluing paper roses for the last couple of hours. After leaving Ty's, I'd had a quick shower at my pop's, but it hadn't brought much relief in anything other than smell and the sticky feeling of sweat. My shoulders and back ached, and the blisters on my hands throbbed, but I still had enough left in me to curl paper flowers.

"You're turning discarded books into something beautiful." I carefully rolled the cut pieces of a page. "That's ecologically responsible *and* frugal."

She ran a fingertip down one of the pages as if admiring a precious gem. "*Pride and Prejudice*, though."

I stopped rolling the petal in my fingers. "That's what you told me to find."

"I know." She started cutting out petals again, her scissors moving slowly as she traced each shape. "I still feel guilty about it."

"There's a lot of that going around," I muttered.

She cut a glance to my bandaged hands. "I can't believe Ty's got you doing chores."

I'd turned up at her apartment with four copies of *Pride and Prejudice* I'd salvaged from Austin thrift shops and a bottle of rosé, but all she had noticed were the bandages.

"He's not exactly happy about it."

Pausing her cutting, she absently read the book page she held. "I'll have Booker call Ty. I'm sure he can talk some sense into him."

"Don't do that. He needs the help, and I don't mind doing it." The man drove me crazy, but he couldn't handle those chores on his own, bet or no bet.

That brought Eden out of her classic book fog. "You don't mind shoveling manure for hours, and ending the day with your hands all bandaged up?"

When she put it that way, I did mind a little. It wasn't how I'd planned to spend my time in Magnolia Ridge. My body ached, I needed a nap, and I already dreaded the next two weeks of work—but the day had been exhilarating in its own way, too.

"It's not that bad," I said. Eden bobbed her eyebrows at my hands again. "Okay, yes, it is that bad, but I kind of liked being out there today, doing something physical and real. Most of my work lately has been of a virtual nature."

The biggest downside to working for an internet-based company was that I never met my clients anymore, and never saw their homes. I missed the giddy excitement of going through another person's house, listening to their vision for it, and finding ways to make that vision an even better reality. I missed heading out to stores to find the perfect accessory, handling bolts of fabric, and test-driving furniture. Nowadays, I mostly spent my time on email, scanning photographs, and clicking around in my design program. I only saw the *Before* picture, never the *After*. I had no way of knowing if my clients even did anything with my suggestions.

At least today, I could see the results of my labors, even if it had just been clean horse stalls.

"So you're having a reverse vacation," Eden said.

"Something like that."

"Enjoy it then, I guess. Myself, I'm looking forward to a real vacation. On the beach. With my husband."

I made a face. "Don't rub it in."

She grinned across the table. "Five days in Key West with my man. It's going to be the best vacation ever."

"I think it's called a honeymoon."

Her grin turned sly. "I bought a thong."

"Swimsuit or underwear?" Honestly, I couldn't imagine Eden in either.

"A swimsuit, but I don't know if I'll have enough courage to wear it."

"I'm sure not wearing it would work for Booker, too."

We laughed over that, the rosé making everything sound both more risqué and more hilarious than usual.

"I think the wine was a bad idea," I said, surveying our stash of paper flowers. "We're not making as much progress as I'd hoped. We should have invited the girls."

The girls being Harper and Eliza, Eden's younger sisters. Both women lived in Magnolia Ridge, and both would have been willing to help make wedding decorations. More or less.

"We would have had fewer roses done with their help, and less wine," Eden said. "I'm familiar with Eliza's work."

The youngest and wildest of the Webb sisters, Eliza had always seemed to go out of her way to do the opposite of whatever was expected of her, from her liberal arts degree to the bright aqua hair she'd sported the last time I visited town.

"You know, I'm surprised she's still here. I thought she would have headed back to San Antonio by now."

Eliza had barely unpacked her bags in her city apartment before she'd come home again. It sounded like her internship hadn't gone to plan, but I'd figured she would try again eventually. Instead, she'd stuck around to try just about every job Magnolia Ridge had to offer in the last few years.

"Don't talk up the joys of big city life. You'll give her ideas."

I frowned over my paper flower. My life in Austin wouldn't do much to draw Eliza in. Sampling the city's nightlife had been fun for a while, but now, I found the crowds and noise claustrophobic. Lately, most of my *big city life* centered around my cramped apartment, where they raised the rent the maximum the law allowed every year.

"I won't talk up the joys," was all I said. Eden knew all about my Austin woes, and now wasn't the time for a pity party.

"Dad's a little ticked they paid for four years of college for her to make soap for a living, but I think Mom's just glad she's stuck around. She likes that we're all close by."

Her comment struck a nerve, a little needle finding its way home with a sharp pinch. My pop couldn't say he had the same benefit of me living close by. Only forty miles separated Austin from Magnolia Ridge, but the short distance didn't mean much when I rarely traveled it.

Coming back and being reminded in a thousand tiny ways that my mom was gone just pushed again and again on that bruise, keeping the ache fresh. The city couldn't magically bring her back, but it didn't confront me with her loss quite so viscerally, either. Yet, whatever my motivation, it still meant I didn't see my pop or brothers nearly enough.

"Eliza makes soap now?" I asked before the shimmer of guilt tossing around inside me could turn into something tangible and trample my night.

"She's become the belle of the central Texas farmers' market ball. I guess she's doing pretty well with it. She hasn't asked to borrow money lately, anyway."

I couldn't really imagine Eliza as a business owner. I wasn't sure I could even imagine her as a pet owner at this point in her life. Twenty-five, all flirty impulsiveness—Eliza didn't exactly scream sensibility.

"What?" Eden asked, curling her fingers open and shut, stretching out the ache I felt in my own fingers from all the intricate work. "It's not that shocking. They're really good soaps."

"I believe you. I'm just surprised. Starting your own business isn't easy."

"You know Eliza. She jumps into everything she does with both feet, no looking back. She might regret it the next day, but you can't fault her enthusiasm."

I'd had a toe in my own business the last few years, but I hadn't yet fully jumped in. In theory, I did freelance work on the side of the online job, but in practice, I hadn't put enough effort into it to get more than a few bites. Even my plans to start a firm with Kim had been more like wading in the shallow end, holding someone's hand. I kind of envied my younger cousin's ability to throw herself into new things. I wasn't sure I'd ever really jumped into the unknown with both feet like that.

Stupid bets with grumpy ranchers not included.

EIGHT

"I'M SORRY ABOUT THIS, TY," Seth Jenkins said as he secured Cisco in his trailer. "You know how it is."

"I understand."

I couldn't rightly say anything else. I'd called my clients that morning to let them know their horses' training had been put on an indefinite hold. Aaron could help with some of the lighter training tasks, but I wouldn't make promises I wasn't sure I could keep. All commitments were off the table for the time being. Bullet's owner had apologized repeatedly for the kick and had already sent over a bottle of whiskey 'to help with the pain.' Everyone else had been some degree of sympathetic to my situation.

Everyone except Jenkins. He'd showed up within hours to collect his horse.

I had expected more disappointment than the rest of my clients had shown, but watching Jenkins claim his horse gnawed at me. Would my other clients be so accommodating if I still couldn't manage their horses in a few weeks? How many more horses would be carted away before I healed up? And *when* would I be healed up? These questions without answers were like slivers under my skin.

Jenkins locked up the trailer and held a hand out to me. "No hard feelings. I just can't wait around the next couple of months."

I shook his offered hand. "I understand."

As the truck and trailer rattled away down the lane, I mentally checked Cisco's training routine off my list of to-dos. I should have had everything crossed off my list by now, but part of my brain hadn't yet accepted I couldn't do the work. Every hour of every day brought some mental reminder of my regular tasks—time to get Ransom started under saddle, time to do ground work with Opie, time to bring the horses in—but I couldn't actually *do* any of it.

This morning, I'd tried a little experiment just to see if I was really in such bad shape as all that. I'd called my horse, Bonanza, to me from the pasture. He had come and waited while I opened the gate. I'd held the lead rope out, thinking maybe I just needed to get used to working around the pain; maybe I could find some way to avoid tugging at my chest. But just tossing the halter over the horse's neck had nearly knocked me to the ground.

That settled it. As much as I hated it, I wasn't ready.

Waiting around for my ribs to heal wouldn't be easy on me, but it might be hard on my business. This little setback probably wouldn't put me under financially—my insurance would cover some of the lost income, and I wasn't likely to burn through what money I had socked away in the short-term. But the possible long-term effects had my gut clenching these last two days. Horse training like I did relied on a strong reputation, and Jenkins would be sure to let folks know he'd taken up a new trainer to start his colt. I might have to make inroads with ranchers all over again.

Just my luck, the dust had barely settled behind Cisco's trailer before June pulled down the lane. I'd figured her insistence on helping me around the ranch would have died out after she went home covered in sweat and with her hands ripped to shreds, but here she came again, eager to prove me wrong two days in a row.

She hopped out of the car and walked right over to me, all breezy and lovely.

"That horse trailer that just pulled away, did someone drop off another horse for you to train?"

I almost laughed at her optimism. "Not dropping off, taking away. He didn't want to wait for me to heal up."

Her expression crumpled. "Oh, Ty, I'm sorry."

She moved her hand as if she wanted to touch me on the arm but thought better of it. Probably for the best, since any soft gesture from her would likely hurt one way or another.

"It's just business."

"What about the other owners, are they comfortable with a little delay?"

The question of the day. "Seem to be. For now. I can't predict no one will change their mind in a few weeks."

She gazed at me a minute, and something soft and tender stretched around inside me. That was one thing I couldn't have.

"Don't," I said, turning to head back into the barn.

"Don't what?" she asked, keeping pace at my side.

"Don't look at me like that."

"Like what?"

I stopped to face her. "Like that. Like you're feeling sorry for me. I'm not the first trainer to get injured by a horse, and I won't be the last. It happens. It's not the end of my career."

"I'll try to look at you differently, then."

She had a way of sounding perfectly innocent when she got her sass in.

74

"Come on. Are you ready for today's set of chores?"

"Absolutely."

I led her to the hose on the outside of the barn, where I tried to casually lean against the wall without looking like I needed the rest. I'd done too much to help Jenkins collect his horse and tack, and the effort left my chest aching.

Done too much, that was rich. I never thought the day would come when standing around watching while another man did all the work would be too much for me.

"Before we bring the horses in from turn out, we've got to get their stalls ready with feed and water."

"Sounds great."

"I thought you'd say that." Her rosy optimism charmed me, even if it proved just how naive she was about what I did. "You pull the water bucket off the stall wall, bring it out here, dump it, scrub it out, and hang it up again. Then drag the hose over and refill it, and don't get any water in the bedding."

"I can do that." She moved away, ready to get started.

"Wait." I pulled a small bundle out of my back pocket and passed it over to her. "You need these."

She took the black and tan women's work gloves like I'd given her a bundle of flowers.

"You bought me gloves?"

I tried to shrug it off but couldn't move my shoulders like that anymore. "They need to be the proper size if you don't want your hands to get torn up all over again."

First thing this morning, I'd gone into town to get them. I'd bought a few new pairs for myself, too, hoping Mike Torres at Ranch and Home wouldn't notice the smaller pair among the rest. Of course, Mike had noticed, and I'd had to explain that yes, I'd bought them intentionally. For a friend.

A friend who was currently looking up at me with doe eyes.

"That is really...decent of you."

The praise this woman doled out. "Stop, you're too kind."

"I would have said sweet, but I didn't think you'd like it."

Oh, I'd like it, all right. Too much. "How are your blisters this morning?"

"They're not so bad. I changed out the bandages, so I think they'll be all right." She pulled the gloves on over her hands, flexing her fingers a few times to test them out. It pleased me more than was reasonable to see they were a perfect fit. "Thank you."

You would think I'd given her diamonds instead of work gloves, she looked so grateful. Surprise shone in her eyes, too, like she couldn't believe I'd been that *decent*. Just what kind of man had I led her to believe I was? And was breaking that image really the best idea?

"You ready?" I finally said before the moment could drag out any longer.

"I'm ready."

I nodded and sat down so I could have a clear view of her as she tackled the chore. Toting a five-gallon bucket filled with water wasn't nothing, and doing it thirteen times would be a harder task than she seemed to think. Her arms strained as she sloshed the half-empty bucket from the stallion's stall, and she smiled to herself as she scrubbed it out, taking way too long to inspect the quality of her work.

After emptying, cleaning, and replacing three more buckets, I could see her enthusiasm fading. No, it wasn't rocket science, but that didn't make it easy work.

Watching her lug the buckets back and forth, thoughts of Delia flitted through my mind. I wasn't sure why, since they were nothing alike. I couldn't have picked out two more different women if I'd tried.

Delia. Now there had been a woman with mistake written all over her—I'd just been too blind to see it. A few years back,

I'd been at the Mother Lode, and Delia had slunk up out of nowhere to challenge me to a game of pool. Her job managing Texas's second-biggest wine broker had sent her to a nearby winery for the summer to gain some first-hand experience in the wine-making process. She'd been in a mood for a few other first-hand experiences, too. Delia had enjoyed riding my horses in the afternoons and spending time with me at night, but it had all been just playing at being a cowgirl, I saw that now.

I'd been foolish to think Delia and I could have been more than a momentary fling. What business did a two-bit horse trainer have with an executive in heels? Humiliation still burned through me when I thought about how far gone I'd been. I wouldn't have called it love, but I'd thought it was on the way to something real. That I'd been so overthrown by someone who hadn't felt a thing for me still galled me.

As much as she'd cooed over the horses, she had never so much as glanced sideways at a pitchfork in the months we'd spent together. I never would have asked for her help around the ranch, but watching June scrub every last inch of the water buckets, indignation crawled around in my stomach that Delia had never had enough interest to offer.

After she left, I'd been determined not to make the same mistake twice. Career women and ranchers didn't mix. But then, I'd met my brother's girlfriend, and I'd started thinking about making all new mistakes. Terrible, awful, tempting mistakes.

Caring for a woman who was already taken had been bad enough, but caring for my *brother's* girlfriend? Guilt ate me up six ways to Sunday. Oh, I'd tried to fight it—first my feelings for June, and then when that didn't work, the guilt—but I'd thrown myself on my sword in every battle. I'd wanted her, and I'd hated myself for it. So finally, I left her be, hoping more than believing Bret would straighten up and treat her right.

Would have been smarter to bet on a dead horse.

"Okay, what am I doing wrong?"

June's voice pulled me out of my sad-sack thoughts.

"What?" I snapped. She knelt in front of the hose bib, paused mid-scrub, with a bucket in one hand and the brush in the other.

"You're staring at me and you don't look happy about it. Am I not getting the buckets clean enough?"

"Buckets are fine."

She pointed the scrub brush at me. "Then why do you look like you're thinking about murder?"

Maybe because I was thinking about how my brother cheated on you like a fool?

"This is just how my face looks, June. You're doing great."

Her eyes lit up. "Really?"

"Yes, really."

She smiled her delight, and that tenderness curled through me again.

I shoved those feelings away before they could dig in and take hold. I'd been down that road before and knew what waited for me at the end of it. I wasn't about to let myself feel something more for June, only to watch her drive away when her visit to Magnolia Ridge came to an end, carting my heart off with her.

june

I ALMOST LIKED Ty better the day before when he'd micromanaged my work in the barn. This afternoon, he watched my progress with shuttered eyes, making little conversation as I moved between the stalls. His stormy mood reminded me of those last visits I'd spent at the Hardy house last year, before he stopped joining in altogether.

When we first met, we'd been friendly, companionable. Comfortable. For a while, I'd been totally at ease with Ty. Something about that ease, though, had left me with a shade of guilt, considering I'd been his brother's girlfriend at the time. Soon, that guilt had been swallowed up by confusion as Ty grew more distant, until finally, he didn't come around anymore at all.

Maybe he'd started dating that woman Pop had mentioned. I wondered what type of woman Ty was attracted to—in the six months I'd dated Bret, he'd never brought a date of his own to the barbecues his parents held. He liked blondes, apparently. Probably ones savvy on a horse, and with sense enough not to wear flip-flops to a ranch.

"Looks like you're ready for the hay," he said after I'd filled the last water bucket on its hook. "Grab that black feed cart at the end of the barn aisle and follow me."

He led me past the two round pens he used for training to the open-sided hay barn. I'd made countless trips out there yesterday for fresh bedding, and it looked like today's duties would make round two. Small comfort my legs were getting as good a workout as my arms when I really just wanted to lie down in the hay and snooze.

Ty stood in the hay side of the storage shed, cutting the twine on a bale with a pocket knife.

"The bales come apart easy enough," he said, tipping a chunk from the end like slicing off a pat of butter. "Each section's called a flake, and each horse's stall gets a flake in each hay feeder on either side of the stall door."

It sounded easy, but I'd already learned that word had an all-new definition on Ty's ranch. He stepped aside while I pulled the bale apart and tossed the 'flakes' into the heavy-duty cart. It didn't take much to fill the feed cart to the top.

"One in each hay feeder," I confirmed over my shoulder, turning the cart in a wide circle.

"Spread the hay apart some as you fill the feeders. Makes it easier on them."

Easier on them? They were already getting room service courtesy of my aching muscles. But I trudged the cart back to the barn and did as he said, spreading the hay in each corner feeder, and doing my best to ignore the steadily growing sweat-stains on my T-shirt. I returned the empty cart to him in the hay barn, wondering what kind of industrial-strength anti-perspirant it would take to make a dent in my sweat out here.

I went through the process again, piling half the bale of flakes into the cart and trotting it over to the barn to spread in each feeder. On my second return to the hay barn, Ty watched me with raised eyebrows. I had decidedly less pep in my step.

"Isn't there an easier way to do this?"

The corners of his mouth twitched. "Yes. Usually, I stack two whole bales in the cart and just make the one trip."

"Now you tell me. Let's do that." I tugged at a bale but didn't lift it an inch.

"Bales weigh fifty pounds."

I shot him a glare and went back to piling flakes into the work cart. This time, I filled it past the top, since the hay seemed unlikely to topple. Double-checking my count down to the last feeder, I finally turned the fully-loaded cart back toward the barn. Ty walked beside me, apparently satisfied I had enough hay.

"You're enjoying this," I grumbled at him.

The trace of a smirk ghosted his features. "It has its moments."

I distributed the rest of the hay in the stalls, thankful my trips to the hay barn had ended for the day. Probably.

"Now on to the grain," he said after I'd put the feed cart back in its spot. "Bin's over here." He knocked on the lid of a large green metal storage container in one corner of the barn. "See the whiteboard outside each stall? It's got their grain amounts listed beneath their names. You just measure it out."

Doling out the horses' grain proved the easiest task he had given me so far, despite the tediousness of trotting back and forth, and I finished pretty quickly. "Now we bring the horses in?"

"If it were just my horses, and a few hours later in the day, I'd say yes, but I don't trust these young colts with you. Aaron's going to come out for an hour or so this evening to stable them."

Even if it wasn't quite the attitude I'd hoped for, his concern for my safety was sweet. And considering what I saw Bullet do to him, entirely sensible. "So what next?"

His lips quirked to one side. "You're going to love it. Mucking."

Everything inside me wilted. "But the stalls are all clean."

"The pens aren't." He hooked a thumb toward the line of rubber boots behind him. "Best put on a pair."

I sighed but squared my shoulders and tugged on a pair of rubber boots. When I straightened up, I followed him out to the circular pen where I'd first encountered him and Bullet. That day echoed in my mind, not just the sound of his ribs cracking when he got kicked, but the way he'd looked at me right before it happened. In a flash so quick I couldn't be sure it had really been there, he'd looked at me like I was a present he had never expected to receive.

That small spark of pleasure had awakened an awareness of Ty I couldn't shake, but wasn't entirely sure I should encourage.

"This round pen and that one behind it need to have the manure picked."

He raised one arm to point at the far pen but winced and dropped it again. He tried to make it all look natural, as if he'd totally meant to swing his arm at nothing, but I saw how much he had to adjust to the limitations of his new normal.

"Wheelbarrow and pitchfork are where you left them yesterday."

His mouth pressed into a bleak line, his eyes dark in the shade of his Stetson, his breathing shallow. Rather than take it easy even for a few minutes, he kept soldiering on, fighting upstream against the pain.

"You really should go lie down. You don't look good."

I didn't think it was possible, but his mouth flattened even more. "Gee, thanks."

"I mean you look miserable. How's the pain?"

His eyes cut away. "I've been better."

"Isn't the Percocet taking the edge off?"

"It did," he admitted. "Did a few other things, too. I didn't like it, so I didn't take any more after that first night."

That just figured. Mr. I'm Too Big and Strong to Take Pain Medicine topped the list as the most stubborn man I'd ever met. "So you're just going to grit your teeth and bear the pain?"

"Along with a steady stream of Ibuprofen."

My eye twitched at his sheer audacity. "If Ibuprofen was all you needed, that's all the doctor would have prescribed."

"So you're a ranch hand *and* a doctor now?"

"Does it matter? You wouldn't listen to me even if I were. If you go on taking shallow breaths like you're doing, you'll wind up with pneumonia. That's why you're supposed to take your pain pills, to help you breathe easier."

His eyebrows quirked. "Where'd you hear that?"

"I looked it up."

He cocked his head to the side, examining me like I sat on a shelf in a museum of curiosities. "You looked it up?"

"I know how to Google. Pneumonia's the number one complication after broken ribs, usually because stubborn men refuse to do what they're told."

"That's why we're called stubborn."

"It's not funny. If you get pneumonia, you'll be out of commission even longer than you're going to be already."

That at least seemed to get through to him. He worked his jaw as if readying his next retort, so I cut him off. "I can pick manure out of the pens by myself. You go inside, do about a hundred jumping jacks, and definitely don't do the breathing exercises you were told about at the Medical Center."

His eyebrows pulled down, deepening his scowl. "I regret how much you know about my medical history."

I laughed. "I'm sure you do. Now go be a stubborn man and don't do a thing I just told you to."

Praying he'd listen for a change, I went back to the barn to fetch the wheelbarrow, giving him a chance to return to the house without a witness. While I gathered up the tools, his footsteps crunched through the gravel and faded toward the farmhouse.

Good. He needed to get off his feet and rest a little, whether he wanted to admit it or not. Everything I'd overheard in the Medical Center and looked up in the days since said that if he kept with his current activities, he could wind up in Intensive Care. I could just imagine how that would go.

Ty Hardy, lying in a hospital bed, cursing out the IV tube in his arm and demanding to see a *real* doctor who would release him. I laughed to myself over the idea.

A big, tough guy, he wasn't used to being looked after, that much was plain. When I turned up yesterday, I'd half expected to find he'd put a lock on the front gate to keep me off his property. Or that *No Trespassing* sign he'd threatened to find. He wanted to prove his point that ranch work was too hard for me, but not at the expense of actually letting me do the work. Now, I suspected he was starting to enjoy bossing me around, having me muck out stalls, and watch me cart horse manure around.

It wasn't awful work. Certainly a different world from picking out color schemes and furniture styles for other people's houses, but not as miserable as I'd thought I'd be when I agreed to it. I was hot and sticky and smelled a delight, but I liked seeing the immediate results of every completed task, even if just a pen clean of manure. Not exactly an accomplishment to share on my interior design website, but an accomplishment just the same.

Ugh, my website. I needed to stop licking my wounds over Kim's sudden departure and sort out my future. The online work wasn't bad, but it didn't have my heart. I wanted real clients again, wanted to have a hand in every stage of a house remodel or a room refresh. The question was, could I handle striking out on my own? The idea of doing all my own marketing and promotional work made me shudder, but the freedoms my current job afforded me wouldn't be matched by a corporate position. That left me at the same crossroads I'd been stuck in for the last few months. Which way to turn?

An hour or so later, I'd picked through both pens and had a nice little mountain of manure in the wheelbarrow to show for it. I dumped it on the heap and put the tools away, careful to return everything exactly where I'd found it. Clean work boots, every tool in its place, meticulous notes on each horse's stall— for being a rough and tumble rancher, Ty sure could be a fussy one.

Mr. Fussy found me hosing off my boots outside the barn.

"You get it all?" he asked, gruff as ever.

Whatever rest he'd got hadn't done much for his cheery attitude.

"Every last bit." I adjusted the hose spray to get a clump of dirt between the boot's treads. I would pretend it was dirt, anyway.

He cocked an eyebrow. "Every last bit?"

"You can always check for yourself if you don't trust me."

He inclined his head a touch, relenting. "I'll take your word for it."

I pulled the boots off and rubbed my neck, letting my fingers knead deep into my muscles. I could hear a nice, warm bath, preferably with a fizzy lavender bomb and a glass of wine, calling my name. Closing my eyes, I released a long exhale. When I opened them again, Ty stared at me with a shuttered expression I couldn't read.

Heat bloomed in my stomach, but I shoved that spark aside before it could catch fire. I dropped my hands, too aware of how my shirt clung to my sweaty chest and stomach. "Anything else today?"

"Nope, you're good. You can even take tomorrow off."

Gazing up at him, I scrutinized every line in his face. "Is this a trick? I'm not done out here."

"What do you take me for, some kind of ogre? The bachelorette party's tomorrow. I figured you'd want extra time to—" He waved his fingers in the air. "Get ready."

"I could take offense at that. You think it takes me all day to look nice?"

Given the circumstances, he wouldn't be entirely wrong. Still.

He opened his mouth but shut it again. If anything, his gaze darkened even more. "Most people would jump at a day off."

"You really don't need me?"

He looked torn, and I wished for the hundredth time he could just admit when he needed help. I knew he wasn't used to relying on other people, but he wasn't in any state to refuse help when it was offered, either.

"Aaron's coming in for a couple of hours. Horses will be fine."

I wouldn't bother asking how *he* would be. He didn't seem to appreciate the question, and wouldn't admit to needing anything anyway. "The next day, then?"

"Unless you've had enough."

I just laughed. "I'll see you then, Ty."

TEN

june

AS FAR AS bachelorette parties went, this was the best one I'd been to. Yes, I'd planned it, but still, it worked out to be a pretty great evening.

Eden and her bridesmaids lounged on plush couches while our feet soaked in copper tubs of warm water dotted with rose petals. I cupped a mug of herbal tea in my hands, a soothing neck wrap warmed my shoulders, and the scent of lavender and roses wafted all around us. Nature sounds and birdsong drifted down from hidden speakers, sinking into our bodies and unwinding our tension. I could almost see the strain of the last two days on Ty's ranch fading from my muscles.

"You have all the best ideas, June," Eden's middle sister, Harper, said. "So much better than a pole dancing lesson." She shot their youngest sister a significant look.

"It would have been *fun*," Eliza said. "And it would have been a gift for Booker, too." She bobbed her pale eyebrows, dancing in her seat in mock seduction.

"I would have died of shame." Eden took my hand and gave it a squeeze. "Thanks for not putting me through that."

"I think Eliza's the only one who was on board with pole dancing," I told her.

"It's good cardio." Eliza continued to wiggle, undeterred. "If it leads to more cardio, so much the better."

"Do not make me think about my brother doing *cardio*," Chloe said. "I'm trying to enjoy myself."

Eden leaned back against the couch. "Mmm, cardio with Booker."

Chloe tossed a rose petal at her. "You are disgusting," she said, flashing Eden a saucy grin.

Chloe radiated Booker's same confidence and charm, her ease making me feel we were old friends even though we'd only connected a few hours ago. She lived in Austin, too, but our paths hadn't crossed.

"I've been in here a few times for facials." Harper chose to avoid the cardio innuendo. "But I've never been in this room for foot massages."

"I thought it would be a good break from the stress of the lead-up to the wedding." I'd spent weeks researching the *perfect* bachelorette party before deciding on this. Eden wouldn't have been on board with some of the wilder ideas out there, and no matter what I told Ty, pole dancing had never been a contender. But a spa day followed by fancy cocktails? Couldn't miss with that.

"It hasn't been so stressful," Eden said over her teacup.

Eliza and Harper hooted laughter.

"You are a gigantic ball of stress," Harper said. "You just can't tell because it's not that different from how you normally are."

Eden took a prim sip of tea. "I like things to be done right. That's normal."

Her sisters laughed harder.

"June, you've checked on all the books for the decorations, right?" Eden asked, ignoring their glee.

"See what I mean?" Harper said around a giggle.

I tried not to laugh at the implication I might have accidentally misplaced two hundred old books. "They're all still in their boxes in my pop's garage, don't worry."

"We're all agreed everyone will understand the books are because I'm a librarian, and not because Booker's name is *Booker*?"

"She just can't stop," Eliza said with a grin.

Eden made a face at her youngest sister, but I was pretty sure she'd been serious about the question.

"So are weddings for nerds your side hustle or what?" Chloe asked me.

"Maybe it should be. I'm an interior designer."

Her face lit up in the soft glow of the massage therapy room. "Which firm are you with? I'm an architect at Reid and Waters. Maybe I've heard of it."

"Oh." I hedged, tiny waves of not-quite-shame washing through my stomach. "Domestic Bliss."

She seemed to try to connect the words in her mind. "Is that in Austin?"

I sipped at my tea. "It's online-only."

The smile on her face altered slightly, just a drop of her mouth, a change in her eyes, but I noticed it. Probably the best response I could hope for from people with more traditional careers in my field. If Kim and I had started our partnership, that would have been something to brag on no matter how poorly we were getting on, but working for a big, faceless internet company? I might as well have said I decorated prison common rooms for a living.

"That sounds interesting." She'd opted for diplomacy, at

least. Some people didn't. "I've always wondered what it would be like to work for an internet-based company like that."

I curled my toes against the smooth stones that lined the bottom of my copper tub. "The work isn't that different from the firm I was with before. There are always requests coming in, so I keep pretty busy, and I like that I can work from home."

Chloe circled her ankles in the foot soak like she was trying to think of how to say *Bless your heart* without actually saying *Bless your heart*.

"It's good that places like that are making interior design accessible to people who don't have a lot to spend."

That still sounded like a *Bless your heart* to me. Times like this? I really wished I had something to brag on. *Anything* to brag on. "I kind of like working these smaller bids for people who don't have an unlimited budget."

She laughed, but it wasn't unkind. "Honey, there's a lot to be said for an unlimited budget."

A spa employee came in to top off everyone's foot baths and check on our neck wraps before she disappeared again. I slumped deeper into the plush couch, drawing in long, slow breaths of the heady lavender scent that clouded the air.

Even if I didn't work for people with unlimited budgets these days, my job wasn't that bad. Not really. Most of the contracts I got through the site were one-offs, a single room the owner wanted to freshen up or repurpose. Small changes could have a big impact and transform a home without breaking anyone's bank. And yes, I could work my day job wearing pajamas in the comfort of my own apartment. It wasn't glam-orous, but it paid the bills.

"So," Eliza said, her eyes keen on Eden. "Did you finally decide how you're pairing us up with the groomsmen for the ceremony? Please say you put me with Travis."

"I did, only because you wouldn't stop texting me about it," Eden said.

"Good." Eliza sighed, long and low. "He's so hot."

"And ten years older than you are."

"I don't care, he's a gorgeous man."

"Who has a girlfriend." Eden wagged a finger Eliza's way, and I got the feeling they'd been through this before.

Eliza smiled like a perfect saint. "You'll never know in the pictures of us together."

"It's not prom, we're not doing couples' poses after."

"Just let me have this, okay? As *my* groomsman, he's legally obligated to dance with me during the second song, and I'm going to make the most out of that dance."

Oh. I hadn't thought about my obligatory dance with Ty. How would that even go? Maybe he'd hold me close on the dance floor, his big, strong hands wrapped around mine, swaying in time to the music. I'd lean in and put my head on his shoulder. His hand at the small of my back would pull me close... My stomach did a little swoop just picturing it. But I refused to indulge in the stomach-swooping, imagining instead the scowl he'd have plastered on his face the whole time.

"I don't care who you pair me with," Harper said. "I'm just looking forward to talking to a man under seventy, for a change."

Chloe cocked an eyebrow. "You what now?"

Harper waved a hand. "I'm a physical therapist."

"You're the one who chose to work in a retirement home," Eliza said. "You should have gone into sports therapy. You could be rubbing down sweaty athletes instead of wrinkly grandpas."

"I didn't choose my job for the dating opportunities. Anyway, you make soap. What kind of men are you meeting?"

Eliza grinned. "Dirty ones."

Chloe and Eliza roared with laughter, but Eden looked like

91

she struggled not to roll her eyes. She probably would have had a better sense of humor over the whole thing if it weren't her baby sister making the saucy jokes.

She turned to me. "How's Ty doing? I hope he'll be up for all the excitement next week."

I wore my own little scowl, well aware it echoed Ty's usual look. "He'd never let on if he wasn't."

"Why?" Harper asked, looking from Eden to me. "What happened to Ty?"

Everyone's eyes fell on me, waiting for me to spill the juicy gossip. Ty would hate having anything said about him behind his back, especially something about his injury—but he wasn't keeping it secret, either. Eden had left me too close to the edge to just refuse to elaborate. *Nothing* would be a blatant lie, and they would all find out at the rehearsal dinner, anyway.

"Ty got kicked by one of his horses. He's got a couple of broken ribs."

"No way," Eliza said. "I'm surprised his bones can break, he's so—" She mimed caressing something in front of her. "Hard."

Chloe made a sound of savoring something delicious. "I had such a crush on him growing up. He was cute when he was younger, but good Lord, what a man."

Something hot and greasy squirmed around in my stomach. Chloe was gorgeous, with rich dark skin, high cheekbones, and sexy hips, plus she was apparently a talented architect at a sought-after firm. She probably knew how to ride a horse, too.

I should not care who had a crush on Ty, or when. I should not.

But I so did.

Was it smart? Not a bit. Didn't mean I could magically make the distress disappear.

"Half the town has a crush on him," Harper said, heaping

more awkwardness onto my secret discomfort. "Every time I see him in town, all the women get thirsty."

"Too bad he's married to his horses."

Chloe's dismissive tone immediately relieved the squirmy sensation in my stomach, yet also made me want to defend him from the mild insult. He didn't deserve that kind of scorn for being dedicated to a job he loved. That ranch meant everything to him, and he worked hard out there, even when by all rights, he could have dialed his duties down to zero. Seeing his commitment to his business firsthand only made me admire him more.

"His brother, though—he's a keeper. Sexy *and* a corporate lawyer," she continued.

The warring feelings in my stomach hardened over. My cousins took turns casting furtive glances at each other, avoiding me. Apparently, town gossip hadn't reached Chloe's social circle in Austin. That brought me some comfort. With any luck, the only people at the wedding who would know about Bret's little indiscretion would be my family and Ty.

Sensing the shift in the room, Chloe looked around. "What?"

After some hesitation, Eliza took it on herself to explain. "June used to date Bret. Before his current girlfriend. Like, *right* before. And a little bit during."

Chloe looked as if she wanted to disappear into the couch cushions. She watched me with big eyes, as if I were about to fly off the handle. "I didn't know that. I mean, I knew he dated around, but I didn't think he was a cheat, just a player." She cringed. "I'm not making this better, am I?"

"Don't worry about it, I'm over it." I didn't like having to replay the low points of my recent love life, but I didn't wish Bret back. Not even on my worst day.

"But you're both going to be at the wedding?" she asked. I

tilted my head in confirmation. She let out a low whistle. "Small towns, man."

"I don't really think of Bret as being part of Magnolia Ridge."

"He grew up here just like the rest of us," Harper said.

"I guess I've compartmentalized."

"Compartmentalized," Eliza repeated. "That's a strange way of saying you want to throat-punch a guy."

I laughed at the image. My days of wanting to do bodily harm to Bret were long over. Then again, I hadn't seen him in almost a year, so...

"I mean, I only really knew him in Austin. We only came to town for dinners at his parents' house."

In hindsight, that whole scenario had been weird. Bret took me out in Austin sometimes, but he'd bring me back to Magnolia Ridge almost every weekend to have dinner with his family. At the time, I'd thought it illustrated his deep family bonds, but now, I suspected it was so we wouldn't be seen together in the city.

Apparently, I had a faulty red flag detector.

"Still," Chloe said. "Nobody wants to run into their ex at a wedding."

"You used to date Shaun." Eden flipped her neck wrap over, settling deeper into the couch. "Is that going to be awkward for you?"

Chloe made a face. "That was more of a friends with benefits type of thing. I don't mind seeing him."

"I could use a few benefits right now." Eliza's lament prompted another round of laughter over our mugs of tea.

At the suggestion of *benefits*, Ty sprang into my mind again, all ruggedly gorgeous, looking out for my well-being on the ranch.

I almost laughed at my brain's stupidity. A ridiculous

thought, and not just because of the whole ex's brother thing. What had hurt most in my relationship with Bret wasn't even the cheating revelation—although that had been a neutron bomb at the time—but how he'd never really let me into his heart.

It had taken time and hindsight to see it, but everything with Bret had been on the surface, a veneer of affection that didn't go all the way down. I'd promised myself that the next time I got involved with someone, it would be with a man who was just as willing to share his heart as I was.

If any man kept his heart under lock and key, it was Ty Hardy. As great as the *benefits* of a relationship with him would likely be, I had no intention of risking my heart with someone whose emotions were just as shallow as Bret's.

ELEVEN

IN ALL MY THIRTY-FIVE YEARS, I'd never been asked to plan a bachelor party before, but I thought it turned out all right. Dinner at Antojito's Cocina, followed by a couple of bourbons at a new distillery in town. No weekend trip to Cabo, but nobody needed that kind of trouble. Booker had suggested we drop by The Broken Hammer for beers to round out the night, and even though I'd been spent since dinner, I didn't complain. How could I? I'd sit through just about anything to keep my best friend happy.

Still, The Broken Hammer was a terrible choice on a regular night, let alone for a bachelor party. It reminded me of college, when drinking still held excitement, and I could hang around with Booker and our buddies for hours, clinging to the hope that obnoxious relentlessness would get us a woman's phone number. Now, I just wanted to have the one last beer and go home. I wasn't sure if that made me mature, or just old. Since the other guys didn't seem to mind doing a little more carousing, it probably just made me old.

The five of us crowded around a corner table, taking turns buying pitchers and talking way too loud. I nursed my beer, barely listening to their stories, my thoughts on one thing only —getting out of there. This late in the evening, the pain pulsing through my ribcage on every breath left me on edge, and the crowded bar only made it worse.

At least at Antojito's and the distillery, I'd had a little personal space. We hadn't been in The Broken Hammer an hour before a drunk guy stumbled into me on his way to the restroom. The pain had sent me reeling, made that much worse when the guy clapped me on the shoulder to apologize. But I stayed for Booker's sake, even if I had to grit my teeth through a whole evening of listening to guys talk about their cars.

"I blew out a rod," Shaun said. "I either have to do a complete rebuild or get another engine." He seemed to consider. "Or get another car."

"My BMW's still going strong." Isaiah's smug smile hadn't won him new friends tonight. "No complaints at five years."

"That's nothing." Booker pointed his glass of beer at me. "Ask Ty how many miles are on that old Chevy he drove us here in."

Isaiah did as he was told.

I glanced up. "Two-fifty."

He almost dropped his beer on the table. "Two hundred fifty thousand? That can't be right."

Any other time, I might have been up for a lengthy discussion on my vehicle maintenance routine, or how Shaun shouldn't be surprised his truck needed an overhaul when he cared more about how it looked than anything under the hood, but tonight was not that night. I took another long pull from my glass, calculating how early I could leave a party when I was technically the host.

"Oh, it's right." Travis slipped his phone into his back pocket. He'd been fielding texts from his girlfriend all night.

"It's because he's running an engine that isn't dependent on computers."

Shaun groaned. "Can we not start that?"

"I'm just saying, all I do is repair machinery whose tiny little computers are on the fritz, while thirty-year-old tractors and harvesters without all that run just fine."

A heavy equipment technician with a grudge against computer chips, Travis never passed up an opportunity to get a dig in against them with tech guru Shaun.

"Call the help line next time you're stumped," Shaun said with a grin. "My rate is fifty dollars an hour."

Travis shook his head. "What a racket."

Isaiah looked between the two of them. "Is that good money around here?"

Travis cut a glance to me. A big shot out in San Antonio, Booker's old college buddy Isaiah had looked down his nose at Magnolia Ridge all night. Guys like Travis and me, who worked with tractors and horses, didn't seem to rate with him.

Travis leaned an elbow on the table, ignoring Isaiah's question. "I want to know how the Unbreakable Ty Hardy finally got kicked. There has to be more to that story than you said."

I'd given them the bare-bones, three-point story at the restaurant: Kick, pain, hospital. They'd laughed a little, commiserated a little more, and then the whole subject had been dropped, for good, I'd hoped. Unfortunately, the more they drank, the more interesting my injury became.

"I got distracted. Bullet spun away and kicked out before I could do a thing. It happened so fast, I'm not sure I could say exactly what happened."

Just a blur in my memory, like an old videotape paused mid-action. The only thing I remembered with any clarity about the kick was the sound of my bones cracking. Well, that and the pain. Couldn't forget that, since it still rattled around inside me.

"You got distracted?" Travis said. "I didn't think you ever got distracted."

I didn't. Part of the reason I'd always done so well working with horses was that I let them know I was in charge, but I never forgot they were still powerful beasts with minds of their own. Aside from a few wild ones I had to reform, horses weren't naturally aggressive, but they could get dangerous in a blink. I always kept my eyes on the animals, watching their responses so I could adjust my methods, making sure the both of us were safe at all times.

Except when a beautiful woman turned up out of the blue and made me forget every last thought in my head.

"It happens." I glanced at Booker. He had his eyes turned up to the ceiling, a little too intent on counting the rafters to look entirely natural, proving he had his suspicions about June. Just what did Booker suspect, and how long had he suspected it? Was I that obvious?

"How long are you going to be laid up?" Shaun asked.

"A month or more."

"Must be nice to have that kind of time off work."

Sitting around with my chest on fire, the idleness driving me crazy, didn't count as a vacation. The only bright spot were the visits from June, even though I'd told myself from the beginning I should put her out of my mind entirely. I hadn't been able to so far, but I hadn't exactly been trying.

"So what happens with your business?" Isaiah asked. "Do the horses just twiddle their thumbs while they wait for your bones to heal up?"

"Pretty much." I wasn't about to tell them how Seth Jenkins had jumped ship at the first opportunity, or how every time my cell rang, dread coiled through me at the thought it might be another client ready to do the same. Nobody wanted to hear that, and I sure didn't want to share it in the middle of a party.

"Did you find some high school club to come out and take care of the daily chores like you said you were going to?" Booker asked.

I took a long drink from my beer. "Something like that."

I didn't want to mention anything about June to this table of guys. She was green as all get out, but she worked harder than I'd expected her to. I thought she would quit in the first two days sure as anything, but she hadn't. I'd been waiting for her to complain about the work, grouse just a little, but she hadn't done that, either. She tackled every chore I threw at her, no matter how much it hurt or stank. The woman knew how to push all my buttons, but I couldn't fault her determination.

"Excuse me, can I buy you a drink?"

While we'd been talking, Eden had slunk up behind Booker to purr in his ear. All five of us goggled up at her, a blonde angel gracing our table.

"Honey, you can do anything you want." Booker sprang up to wrap her in his arms, giving her an enthusiastic kiss that dragged on and on.

He didn't need to show off like that. Everyone knew they were getting married.

My gaze drifted from the PDA over to the women clustered behind Booker and Eden until I found June. A slight smile touched her mouth as her eyes met mine, and my fool heart kicked to life like it'd just been waiting around for her to show up. The guys found extra chairs for the women, and before I knew it, she'd scooted up right next to me. The smell of flowers filled the air every time she moved. Roses, maybe. Something soft and feminine, just like her.

I should have left this party when I'd had the chance.

Chloe bought another pitcher of beer while Eliza refilled the guys' glasses with the last of the one on the table. Conversations buzzed around as new acquaintances were introduced and old friends reconnected. In a town this small, everybody knew pretty much everybody else one way or another.

My attention got stuck in sideways glances at June. Her hair was a little tousled, her smile relaxed, her eyelids just softly drooping. She looked ready for bed, or like she'd just rolled out of it, I wasn't sure which. The whole effect made her absolutely delectable. My heart ached against my ribcage, urging me to scoot my chair even closer.

"Hi." She blurred the single word into multiple syllables.

Well, that was new. She was a little tipsy. Maybe more than a little.

"Hello." On the other hand, I sounded like an uptight idiot.

She leaned as close to me as she could without actually touching my arm, and I had the feeling she was about to say something wicked.

"Do you want to know a secret?"

Did I ever.

"What's that?" I wished she would let her fall of dark hair play over my arm. It would have killed me, but I would have thanked her with my dying breath.

"Bachelor parties are supposed to be fun." Her mouth quirked at her little jab.

I decided to play it innocent. "You're not having fun?"

"*You're* not having fun." Thankfully, her voice came out too low for Booker to hear. Then again, with Eden planted firmly in his lap, he wasn't likely to be listening in on what June had to say anytime soon.

"I'd guess you ladies have been having enough fun for all of us. What was your first stop?"

"Driftwood Day Spa."

"I've never been to that bar."

Her breath hitched in her throat, sending all sorts of delicious thoughts through my mind.

"That was a joke," she said, sounding genuinely impressed. "Maybe you're having a little fun, after all."

"Maybe a little." The night had picked up, that was for sure. Getting caught up in June's smiles and hushed conversation was dangerous territory, but like she said, the night was meant to be fun. So I would have fun.

Within reason.

"We had foot soaks, and leg and scalp massages until we were all blissed out," she went on.

Imagining June blissed out wasn't helping me keep to my *within reason* parameters.

"We had paraffin dips, and my hands are so smooth. Feel." She held one hand out for me to inspect.

I didn't know what a paraffin dip was, but I knew how to follow instructions. I ran my fingers over the back of her hand. Touching her velvety skin only kindled a desire to feel more of it. All of it.

Lord, I couldn't keep my head on straight around her.

Instead of exploring any more of that soft skin, I put my hand back on the table.

"Smooth," I confirmed. "How are the blisters?"

"Not so bad." She turned her hand over to show me the damage, and touched the fresh bandages across her palms. "After that, we went to Sidecar."

"And I reckon you had one or two."

"Just one, but it was a doozy. Their sangria doesn't mess around."

"The hallmark of a good sangria."

She smiled, open and free, and I had to clamp down tight to stop my heart opening up in return. It had always been this way with June, from the first time Bret brought her to our parents' over-the-top Fourth of July barbecue two years ago. There was just something about us that clicked, something about her that got under my skin and stuck with me long after she was gone.

Memories of that day still wandered through my mind when I least wanted them to. I'd been near the grill, listening to one of my mom's friends talk business I didn't care a thing about. June came out the sliding glass doors onto the back deck, a gauzy dress flecked with red, white, and blue stars swaying around her in the bright summer sun. When she looked at me, I'd thought my heart stopped—I was that far gone in two seconds.

And then Bret had come out and snaked his arm around her waist, and my heart really had stopped.

I'd meant to play it cool with her, but never quite managed it. Instead, we settled into an easy friendship as if we'd known each other for years. She made me laugh, a spark of sunshine breaking through the gloom Delia had left behind. She didn't make anybody guess where they stood with her, either. Utterly transparent, her heart shone out like a beacon, on display for all to see. Whatever indifference I'd tried to fake, that openness had drawn me in and taken over my rational thoughts. No matter how many times I told myself my friendship with June was innocent, I'd known my side of it was anything but.

She scowled at the beer in front of me. "You're not supposed to mix alcohol and ibuprofen."

Nurse June, at the ready to diagnose, treat, and scold.

"It's not a problem."

"That can be really dangerous, you shouldn't—"

"It's not a problem because I didn't take the pain pills this afternoon." I'd probably regret my decision tomorrow, but I could have a couple of beers, at least.

Her scowl shifted into something far too tender for my liking.

"Are you in too much pain?" she asked so low, I could barely hear her.

"Define too much."

Her smile hit me square in the chest. I should have headed for the door right then. I could have made any excuse to leave early—I could have just admitted to everyone my busted-up chest couldn't take it anymore.

But this completely relaxed side of June seemed to ease some layer of the ache that consumed me, and I wanted to enjoy it, even if I knew it couldn't last.

So I stayed.

june

I HAD to admire Ty's tenacity. Out on his ranch, he prowled around out of sheer stubbornness to keep his business going, and tonight, he stayed at the bar long after he wanted to leave, all for the sake of his best friend. I could respect that, even if it drove me straight up the wall.

He should have been tucked up in bed, sleeping with the help of some pain meds to soothe his aches. Instead, lines strained at the edges of his mouth, and one eye twitched now and then in a stifled grimace. His color wasn't the best, either, but at least he was sitting down—about as close to resting as I figured he would let himself get. Sitting still was probably too much inactivity for a man like him, all action and movement, as wild and rugged as the horses he trained.

"What's the diagnosis, Nurse June? Is it pneumonia?"

His question jolted me out of my contemplation. I'd been goggling at him. Sitting a foot away from him and staring right into his face like a teenage girl mooning over her celebrity crush.

"I think you'll live." I tried to look more normal, and less dreamy. "You're too stubborn to get pneumonia."

He nodded. "Got that right."

Eliza came over and bent forward to put her head down between ours like an overeager waitress. "How are you doing, Ty? I heard about your accident."

"I'm doing fine."

He took another sip of beer, his expression closed. Oh, he hated talking about his injury. This must be the worst for him, everyone fussing over him and asking after him, and nothing he could do about any of it. His pride must bruise all over again every time someone brought it up.

Eliza took her time looking him over, but that seemed to be the end of her conversation with him. She turned to me. "Come play shuffleboard with us. It's bridesmaids versus groomsmen, and we need you."

I looked at Ty. "I guess you're not playing?"

"I wouldn't do them any favors."

"Like they need an extra guy," Eliza said.

"Sure, I'll be right there," I told her.

She skipped off to the shuffleboard table where the others had already gathered tossing out trash talk. Eden and Booker sat together at the far end of our table, apparently left out of the bridal party competition. From the looks of things, they hadn't noticed. Their foreheads touched as they murmured low to each other, their fingers intertwined, alternating pale and dark skin locked together. Even in the middle of Magnolia Ridge's premier dive bar, they looked altogether blissful.

I glanced away before I could get too heart-eyed over them like a weirdo.

"Do you need anything?" I asked Ty. His look could have cut glass. He'd apparently had enough of that question. "Right. Got it. You're grand. I'll just—"

I darted away to the wedding party, my heart jackhammering away.

"We're down a man with Ty out of commission." Travis stood in front of the long shuffleboard table, tossing a puck back and forth in his hands. Eliza had called it—the man looked like a walking Ken doll, with tanned skin and wavy-blond hair. He didn't do all that much for me, though.

I peeked over my shoulder at Ty. He avoided looking at either his overly-affectionate table mates or the group of us huddled near the games, but stared off somewhere in between the two. He took a long, slow drink of beer. The movement of his throat as he swallowed was weirdly hypnotic. Who knew throats could be so...interesting.

"Are you boys afraid of a little competition?" Chloe asked.

Remembering I hadn't come here to stare at Ty, I snapped my head back to face the rest of the bridal party.

"You want to put a wager on the game?" Shaun asked, sidling closer to Chloe.

She bumped him with her hip. "What are we talking?"

From the look on his face, he had a few specific things in mind.

"We don't need to bet on it," I said. Already knee-deep in one iffy bet, I didn't need another, no matter the stakes. "I probably even things out anyhow."

We played a few rounds of shuffleboard punctuated by occasional shouts of approval and cries of shame. My ability to aim improved the longer I went without alcohol, but my game was still atrocious. I'd never liked bar games. The whole point was to prove how drunk you were, and then drink a little more to celebrate.

I leaned over the table, my puck in hand, hoping I wouldn't prove myself disastrously drunk.

"Here." Isaiah suddenly stood right next to me. "You just have to finesse it."

He put his hand over mine, leaning against my shoulder as

he guided me to release the puck. His tutorial didn't go as planned, and my puck went off the lane halfway down the board, landing with a *thunk* in the gutter.

"I could have done that much on my own," I told him.

"I don't want to overwhelm you all at once."

Isaiah stood close, looking down at me with deep brown eyes full of mischief. I bet he overwhelmed a lot of women. He reminded me a bit of Shemar Moore, if Shemar Moore ever played a San Antonio commodities broker with a killer shuffleboard game.

He reminded me of Bret, too—heavy on the casual flirtation and light on sincerity. Not exactly a ringing endorsement.

"We definitely should have bet on this," Shaun said.

I slid my last puck down the board, just knocking Isaiah's off the lane, but taking my other two off in the process.

"I think you let me win." Isaiah slipped one hand to the small of my back in a sort of consolatory half-hug. "You had that shot, easy."

I rolled my eyes at his obviousness. "That's a stretch."

Over his shoulder, I saw Ty watching me from across the room. He looked away, draining the last of the beer from his glass. Eden and Booker had deserted the table, leaving him by himself. Still scowling, burly Ty, but sitting alone, he looked forlorn and forgotten.

"Are you ready to make quick work of me at darts?" Isaiah asked, the caress of his fingers on my back coaxing me to say yes.

"I'm going to admit defeat and bow out now." I eased away from his embrace, knowing half the women in this bar would have killed to trade places with me. He looked like he might try to convince me to stay, but Travis had already started herding the group over to the dartboards for the next phase of the bridal party competition. With a last glance back at me and a shake of his head over what I was missing, Isaiah joined them.

I returned to the table and took my seat next to Ty. "I'm not that great at bar games."

His eyes flashed to the group at the dart boards. "Looks like you've got a willing teacher."

"That's why I hate bar games. They're just in here so guys can coach the girls."

"You've found out our secret."

I faced him fully. "How bored are you?"

"A fair bit."

"You could go home, you know."

"Right when you're making me feel so welcome?"

"You need to rest." I whispered the suggestion, hoping not to dent his pride any more than it already had been.

"I'm doing fine."

"So you keep saying." I glared at him, trying to hypnotize him into confessing he was anything but fine. When he didn't break down, I stared at him in earnest.

He was so handsome, it was criminal. The phrase *rugged good looks* didn't do him justice. With his broad forehead and broody eyebrows, he deserved a whole new expression devoted just to him. *Ty Hardy good looks.*

So. I was still a little drunk. Good to know.

Sometime while I'd been playing shuffleboard, the pitcher of beer on the table had been transformed into a pitcher of water in a reverse miracle. I poured myself a glass and drank it down, willing it to rescue my slightly muddled brain. If I could just stop staring at Ty, that would be enough. But not staring right now was so, so hard.

"So where are your parents?" I asked. He had never said where they'd gone on vacation, and the whereabouts of William and Rebecca Hardy seemed a safe enough topic of conversation. Otherwise, I might blurt out something about his great hair or broad shoulders, and I needed to keep a lid on drunken June tonight.

"Europe." He said it like the word itself didn't interest him. "An anniversary cruise."

"Oh, that sounds romantic."

He shifted a little like that word didn't interest him, either. "If you say so. I'm not sure I'd want to be cooped up on a boat with a few hundred other germy tourists, but I'm sure they're having the time of their lives."

"Don't you find anything romantic, Ty?"

The words escaped me before I could think them through properly, but I wanted to know the answer. Did a man like him think of romance at all? Or was he just work, horses, business?

No, with his Ty Hardy good looks, romance had to factor in there somewhere.

And now, I'd probably started blushing. *Note to self: next time, lay off the sangria.*

He stared at me, likely readying some gruff, sarcastic response. His mouth worked, drawing my entire attention to the movement. He had luscious lips, full and soft, but angled slightly off-center. I realized he couldn't avoid his perpetual smirk, a permanent twist of his mouth whether he intended it or not. So maybe he *wasn't* always thinking I was a ridiculous know-nothing city girl. A bright little wave of satisfaction—and was that *hope?*—swirled through me.

"Watching the sun set over my pastures," he finally said. "That has its romantic moments."

"Oh." Ty's sweet honesty surprised me. Something soft and warm seemed to fill me up, his confession turning my insides up to high heat. "That does sound nice."

"And it's free."

I cooled right down again. "And now you're back to being unromantic."

"What? They shelled out thousands for that cruise, easy. I'm just saying, I can watch the sun set over my pastures any night I want."

"All you're missing is a woman to share it with."

His jaw pulsed. "Right."

The moment between us shifted. I'd hit a sore spot, but I wasn't sure exactly how. My thoughts drifted to the blond woman, the Amazonian goddess of my imagination who could rope and ride with the best of them. For the first time, I wondered how that relationship had ended, and what had gone wrong. Who she'd even been to begin with.

Blondie had probably fallen for him with everything she had, but couldn't get past his stony outer shell. His heart was buried so deep, she had never been able to reach it, and she'd finally had to leave, heartbroken by his rigid stoicism. He'd been too proud to beg her to stay.

Ty narrowed his eyes on me like he knew I was sifting through imaginary versions of his past. Or maybe I'd just been staring too long again. That seemed to be a real problem tonight. Still couldn't draw my eyes away, though. The moment dragged on, moving from awkwardness, to something almost tangible. My gaze fell to his lips again, and the kiln in my chest I kept trying to turn down cranked up to high again.

Eden and Booker returned to the table, shattering the moment. The rest of the bridal party joined them—the games had apparently ended in a draw, leaving both sides disappointed. I shifted slightly away from Ty, who gave away nothing of whatever he'd been thinking before the interruption.

"We're calling it a night." Eden spoke too loudly, in trademark drunk woman style. "Booker's going to come home with me, Ty."

"None of you are fit to drive," he said as we stood from the table.

Huh. So he bossed around people who weren't me, too. Good to know.

"I haven't been drinking." Harper's petulance said she hadn't been a totally willing designated driver.

"She lost at rock paper scissors." Eliza threw an arm around her sister. "You're so responsible. I love that about you."

Harper crinkled her nose. "Okay, you're not going to throw up in my car, right?"

Eliza rolled her eyes. "That was one time."

"It's going to be a tight squeeze. You'll have to sit in the back between Eden and June until we drop off the lovebirds."

"I could drop June somewhere."

Isaiah's heated look would have flattered me any other time, but tonight, I just wasn't feeling it. Not with my body still on fire from a little sustained eye contact with Ty.

"Oh, that's okay—" I started to say, when Ty cut in.

"I'll take June. I'm going that way."

My pop *did* live close by him on the other side of town. Ty was just being practical. The curl of fire crackling through me? Completely unrelated.

Outside The Broken Hammer, Eden called out to everyone not to forget about the rehearsal dinner the next weekend, as though anyone in the bridal party would forget our duties. I said my goodbyes and followed Ty to his old red truck. He unlocked the passenger door with his key and gestured toward it but didn't open the door. Even through my lingering sangria-haze, I could still put two and two together.

"It hurts to open it?"

His jaw ticked again, and I imagined his molars being ground into dust.

"You can stop asking me that, June. It hurts to do everything."

"Here, then." I darted to the driver's side.

"I'm not going to let you drive." He walked around the front of the truck to me. "That sangria's still doing a number on you."

I rounded on him. "In what way?"

"You keep drifting away in your thoughts. I can see you checking out, spinning your secret yarns. You get on the road, it won't end well."

All true. I'd been staring at him lost in thought all night, but I didn't like that he had noticed. "I never offered to drive. I'm just going to open the door for you."

He stared at me until I had a feeling he was rethinking his offer to take me home. I snatched the keys out of his hand, anyway. Unlocking the driver's side door, I understood why he'd been reluctant to open mine. Old-school heavy on its creaky hinge, it took a good yank to get it open wide. Without another word, I gave him back his keys and walked around to climb in the passenger side.

Using a little artful maneuvering, Ty managed to climb up onto the bench seat with a minimum of winces and groans. He started the engine, and soon we were out on the main road back through town, windows cracked to let the hot summer air blow through the cab.

The truck smelled like him, a swirl of leather mixed with hay, and something entirely Ty. Warm and inviting, like curling up by a fire, or lying on a blanket in the sun. I closed my eyes, breathing it in.

"You okay?" he asked.

My eyes flew open again. "I'm fine."

"Don't pass out on me."

"I'm not drunk."

"You were a little."

Too dark to see it clearly, but I could hear the smile in his voice.

"*Were* being the operative word. You were drinking, too. Should I be worried about you?"

He said something under his breath that sounded like *not about that*, but I couldn't be sure. Louder, he said, "I had one beer in the last two hours. I'm good."

"Well, you're being a real gentleman to drive me home. You're a good man, Ty."

"Some might even call me the Best Man."

I could imagine. His rancher hands might be rough, but he'd been achingly gentle when bandaging my blisters. No telling what else those hands could do.

Whoa. It didn't take much for my brain to veer straight off the rails tonight. Steering my thoughts back to safe territory, I said, "You and Booker go back a long way, don't you?"

"Since we were kids. I'm closer to him than I am to Bret." He glanced sideways at me, as if maybe he expected me to get bent out of shape at the mention of my ex.

"It's okay, Ty. It's not like I forgot you're brothers."

His mouth twisted, and even in the dim light from the dash, I could see he didn't appreciate the reminder of their connection. I'd never had any reason to suspect bad blood between them, but I hadn't suspected a lot of things about Bret.

"It makes sense, though," I said, soothing him for reasons I didn't quite understand. "You and Bret aren't very alike."

They were both driven, laser-focused on building their careers, but the similarities ended there. Bret was all charm and charisma and did his best to impress everyone he encountered. Ty was reserved, as though holding back the best part of him for the people who mattered most. Bret was the life of the party, but Ty was the one who had done all the work to make the party happen. Bret talked, Ty listened.

Bret had lied to me, but Ty was straightforward. He could be a grouch, but at least he was an honest grouch.

"I would hope we're different." His low voice practically came out a growl. "What he did to you was unforgivable."

I stiffened in my seat, little whirls of embarrassment bubbling through me. "I guess he had his reasons."

He stopped in front of my pop's house, threw the truck in park, and turned to face me. The porch light slanted across his face, shadowing half his features. "Never do that, June. Don't ever justify him cheating on you. You deserve better than that."

Ty so rarely showed any emotion at all, the vehemence of his words seemed to light me up like glowing neon. *You deserve better.* I knew it, but hearing it from him hit differently, somehow.

Not thinking too hard about it, I unbuckled and slid across the space between us on the bench seat. "Thank you for saying that."

He watched me with wary eyes as I leaned toward him. I closed the distance, finally brushing my lips against the warm skin of his cheek. For just a moment, I closed my eyes and breathed in his comforting smell up close. Soap. Leather. Hay. All Ty. I only had a shred of sense left, but enough to spare me from pressing my nose against the skin on his neck.

Pull yourself together.

As I drew away, he exhaled a soft groan and then stilled, frozen in place. I scooted back to my side of the seat, careful not to touch him again.

"I'm sorry. Did that hurt you?"

Something flickered through his eyes, and a muscle in his jaw pulsed. "It's fine."

Except it wasn't. His voice strained from the tension coiling through him, like he might snap any second. But it wasn't pain that made him groan like that—it was *me*, the kiss. The heat in

115

his eyes seared my soul for all its longing, and the fire deep inside me roared back to life.

My stomach flipped over, the breath stilled in my lungs. How had I read everything all wrong? It wasn't dislike of me that kept his hands gripped tight around the steering wheel, but something so far the opposite, I questioned everything I thought I knew of him. The realization hit me like one of Bullet's sudden kicks.

Ty was attracted to me.

Ty, who seemed determined to keep me at arm's length and get me off his ranch, was attracted to me? How long had he been hiding *that*?

I blinked hard, emotions clouding my thoughts until my head swam. Picking up my purse from the floor of the truck, I tried to act as normal as possible after seeing that flare of desire in his eyes. A tall order when his delicious scent filled the air, and my lips still tingled from where I'd pressed them against his stubbly cheek.

"Thanks for the ride home." My voice sounded strange in the cab of his truck. Too loud, and too strained. "It would have been cramped in the back of Harper's car."

"No problem."

I made the mistake of meeting his eyes again. His features looked tortured, so torn between desire and despair, I ached for him. I tugged on the door handle and climbed out before I could do something stupid like slide back over and kiss him again.

THIRTEEN

EVEN THOUGH MY every thought centered on her, I did my best to keep my distance from June. I walked out to greet her when she arrived in the morning and gave her a few instructions before holing up in the house again. Between her and Aaron coming and going all afternoon, I would have been better off to just stay out in the barn, sitting on the bench and keeping an eye on things, but after last night, I couldn't face her.

Truth was, I couldn't resist her.

Everything would be easier if she thought I didn't like her. Probably anything was better than her realizing it had taken every ounce of strength in me not to pull her into my arms and kiss her senseless right there in front of her father's house. When she'd leaned up close, that scent of flowers washing over me, I'd nearly lost my mind. If she'd gone for my mouth instead of my cheek, it would have broken the last thread of my control. Her sweet, warm lips brushing over my skin had been full of such tenderness, doing absolutely nothing in return had knocked me out with a whole new kind of pain.

But indulging in that impulse would have been worse. Bret

was the one who took what he wanted without thought for the consequences, not me. Everything I valued in myself—trustworthiness, loyalty, honesty—would blast apart in a single kiss.

But good Lord, I wanted that kiss.

Again and again, I told myself what I'd seen in her last glance had simply been pity. She considered me a friend, and nothing more. Or if not a friend, friendly. Sort of. But I couldn't walk that slippery slope with June. Her small kiss left me tortured with fevered dreams of her dark hair and soft mouth until I woke up in the morning aching for everything I couldn't have. Actual *friendliness* just might kill me.

The sound of a truck rattling into the yard startled me out of my thoughts. I went to the front window, and my stomach sank as a horse trailer rolled in. Adam Wright. Might have guessed that man would be the next to come by.

Wright ran a cattle ranch a few towns away. He brought his horses to me to be started and trained, but he made a point of mentioning how far he had to drive to get here, how he sure would like to have someone more convenient to his ranch. Apparently, my injury had been the push he'd needed to find that someone.

I walked out to greet him as soon as he climbed out of his truck. We shook hands, and he looked me over, a satisfied expression on his face.

"How are the ribs doing?"

"Working on healing."

"You know, I got kicked like that once about a dozen years ago. Left a nasty bruise, but didn't break any bones."

He smiled as if maybe I would congratulate him on his ribs of steel.

"Wish I could say the same. I see you brought your trailer."

"I have to collect Ladybird," he said, looking me dead in the eye. "I'll settle up with you, of course, but I've made other arrangements to finish her training."

"I understand."

And I did. She was destined to be a working horse, and Wright wanted her ready for the range as soon as possible. I couldn't fault him for handling his business the way he thought best. I just wished it wouldn't hit my own business so hard.

We walked into the barn to collect Ladybird's tack. June looked up from mucking stalls, casting a curious look on Wright before glancing at me. Her expression changed, and just like that, she understood. She went back to her work, but I'd seen the tug at her mouth, the twitch in her brow. How she could read a situation like that so clearly, I couldn't guess. Or maybe she could just read *me*. That would be a problem all on its own.

After Wright had the bulk of Ladybird's tack loaded into the trailer, he grabbed a halter and lead rope and headed out to the pasture to call her in. I watched from the open barn door as he struggled to reach the horse. Ladybird didn't pay him much mind, jumping away whenever he got too close. Not sure what he'd expected from an untrained horse. I might have helped him a little more if he'd asked, but as it was, I just watched his attempts.

June came up beside me as Wright crept closer to his mischievous animal.

"He's taking her?" she asked, her words soft and gentle.

"Somebody else will finish her training."

"Oh."

She hesitated, and I thought she might say something more, but after another minute, she turned and went back to the stall. I wouldn't have asked for it, but I could have used a few words of encouragement from her. I needed to cling to the hope that everything I'd built wasn't about to fall apart.

Wright finally led Ladybird out of the pasture and loaded

her up into the trailer. He turned to me, holding out a check. "Here's the training and board rates through today."

I took the check and slipped it into my pocket. "I appreciate it."

"It's nothing personal. I need another horse for the ranch this fall."

"I understand." If I never had to say those words again, I would be a happy man.

Once the truck and trailer rattled away out of sight, I went back to the pasture gate. A few of the younger horses pranced around in the excitement of losing one of their companions, but most of the others just grazed in the summer sun.

Two clients had jumped ship, and I had no way of knowing how many would follow, or who they would call when their next horse needed to be trained. Would Jenkins or Wright come back to me after I healed up? Or would their new trainer hold their allegiances better than I had? I wanted to smash my fist through something, but the pain wouldn't have been worth it. Even shouting any number of curses would have sliced my lungs to ribbons. Like so many other things right now, I had to just sit back and take it.

June leaned her elbows against the fence railing next to me. For a few minutes, she didn't even look at me—she just gazed out into the pastures, watching the horses. Soon, it would be hot enough I'd have to bring them in to the barn during the heat of the day, but they had another week or two of long hours outside to roll and wander before the mid-day heat became a hazard. I was in no shape to tend a horse flagged from heat stroke.

"I never liked that horse, anyway," she finally said.

I exhaled a laugh that burned my lungs. "She's a trouble-maker. Like you."

At June's smile, the tension and anger inside me broke

apart. Maybe I didn't deserve her sweet smiles and attention, but I didn't have the strength to keep pushing her away, either. Not right now.

"What are you going to do?"

She meant my business plans and lost clients, but my mind fixed on something else entirely. What was I going to do about her? "I don't know."

"You still have the other clients, though, right?"

"For now. But I can't charge them regular training rates when I can't so much as lead the horses. Aaron's doing his best, but I'm strictly a boarding operation for the next few weeks."

"I'm so sorry about all this," she said softly. "How hard is this going to hit you?"

Her lingering guilt, though touching, was completely unfounded. She'd more than made up for any blame she bore for my situation. "I should come out okay. This line of work is all about reputation and word of mouth. Clients will come back."

My optimism was more for her sake than anything else, but I found comfort in the sentiment. Clients *would* come back. Eventually.

"I'd think they'd be glad you were honest with them and admitted you can't keep training their horses right now. Another guy might have hidden the truth for his own benefit."

Guilt cut through me, a hot knife slicing my insides. That honesty I prided myself on only went so far when it came to June. If she knew all the truths I'd hidden from her, she would walk away right now and not look back.

"I always loved this ranch." She watched the horses as they grazed. "Coming out here to do Girl Scouts with your Grandma was like going to Disneyland for me."

"I was pretty fond of it, too."

She turned to me, all gentle curiosity, and I gave in to the impulse to answer the questions she didn't ask. "When I was little, I'd spend whole summers out here with Gram and Grandpa, doing chores and learning the ropes."

"Mucking stalls?" she asked with a sly smile.

"Mucking, feeding, cleaning tack, rounding up the horses at the end of the day. Dad thought seeing what actually went into tending horses would cure me of my interest in them, like it had for him."

"He doesn't like horses?"

"There are two kinds of people, June. Those who just like to ride horses, and those who love them with everything they have. My dad is the first."

"There's probably a third category of people who don't like horses at all."

"We don't talk about them."

She laughed, banishing the bleak mood that had settled over me. After a pause, I said, "He didn't like that I went into Ranch Management in college."

"You have a degree?" Her eyes grew wide, as if hearing the insult too late. "I mean, in ranching?"

"Yes, I have a degree. It's not the Old West anymore. You can't just walk onto a ranch and get a job."

She twisted her lips together, clearly regretting her remark. She hadn't offended me—people were always amazed a Ranch Management degree even existed. Anybody who didn't work with horses thought of it as a hobby, not a career people hung their whole lives on. But it had always been the only career for me, and now, my whole life hung on this ranch.

"So your dad doesn't approve of your career choice?" she prompted.

Bonanza loped through the pasture, searching for longer grass. I'd never gone this long without riding him before, and we both missed our old routine.

"I don't think Dad sees it as a career. To hear him tell it, I'm just running around like a kid playing cowboy, wasting time until I get a real job."

"Your Gram must not have agreed."

I smiled at that. "In a twisted way, I lucked out when Gram left Bret and me this old place. Dad didn't like that so well, either, but it was out of his hands."

"Wait. The ranch belongs to you *and* Bret?"

"He never told you?"

Her gaze darkened. "There were a lot of things he didn't bother telling me."

If Bret had suddenly materialized in front of me, I would have endured any amount of pain to punch that fool in the face. "Gram left the ranch to both of us, but Bret never wanted it. I've been buying him out the last four years."

Her eyebrows popped up. "The property must be worth a lot."

Inheriting Victory Ranch from my grandparents had been the luckiest break I would ever get in a career like mine. Most guys couldn't afford their own acreage and barn for years down the road, if ever. I'd spent the first eight years after college working as a trainer at the same big outfit Aaron worked for now, establishing my reputation and improving my technique. Five years ago, my Gram had passed and left the ranch to me. I'd worked doubly hard to earn my reputation since going out on my own, so no one could ever say I'd had my business handed to me. The land and the buildings, maybe, but I'd put plenty of work into those, too.

"I should have Bret paid off in another year. It will be a relief. Every time he gets ticked off with me, he'll say maybe he wants to share the ranch, after all. Starts talking about turning it into a dude ranch."

I shuddered to think of strangers crawling all over this land

I loved. Those threats spurred me to buy Bret out faster than I needed to, paying as much as I could each month toward his share. I didn't like having that question mark hanging over me, that worry of *What if Bret changes his mind?* I would rest easier once the ranch was mine outright.

"I'm sure that's just talk. Bret would never give up his lifestyle in the city to live out here."

"He could still make things tough for me if he ever wanted to."

Like if he knew how I feel about you. Neither of them could know that, for too many reasons to count.

"That's another way you two are different," she said.

"What do you mean?"

"Bret's job is all about finding out information and turning it to his advantage. That's who he is. But you aren't like that."

No, I wasn't. But sometimes, I sure wished I was.

FOURTEEN

june

POP AND JED found me in the kitchen when they came in from the orchards. Hot and sweaty, neither one seemed to mind the trail of dirt they left from the back door to the kitchen sink.

"You're leaving footprints."

"Sorry, honey," Pop said.

I grabbed the broom from beside the refrigerator. "What a mess. You're reverting to your bachelor ways."

Jed gave him a significant look, but he didn't seem to notice. Guilt swished around in my stomach for my little jab about my dad being a bachelor. *Too soon.*

"You're doing just fine, Pop." I stepped closer to kiss him on the cheek before sweeping up the trail he and Jed had left behind.

"Leave that for your brother." Pop winked at me and trundled up the stairs.

"What is that delicious smell?" Jed peered at a casserole dish wrapped in aluminum foil I'd set on the counter. "You're cleaning up *and* making dinner? You should visit more often."

"It's just lasagna and garlic bread. And Pop told *you* to clean up."

He opened the oven door a sliver, and the strong scent of garlic and marinara wafted through the kitchen. "You made two? It was sweet of you to think of me and my bachelor ways."

"I didn't," I said, passing the broom to him. "The other one's for Ty."

"Ty," he repeated deadpan. "Ty, Mister Working You on his Ranch Hardy? Sure, I can see why you'd make him dinner."

It might not have been the best idea. The tiny little kiss I'd given him had left us on shaky footing. He'd avoided me most of the day, until I had almost convinced myself I'd imagined that tortured look of his in the truck. But this afternoon, when Ladybird had been bundled up and carted off, he'd let me in again. I'd wanted to do something for him in return.

"Working on the ranch is about something else," I finally said.

"And that would be?"

I still hadn't explained about our stupid bet. Winning Ty over and soothing my wounded pride wouldn't sound like the best of reasons to muck out a guy's horse stalls where my father was concerned, and Jed would intentionally misunderstand no matter what explanation I gave.

"The working on his ranch part is really for me, and the lasagna is purely a pity meal. A mission of mercy. Like they do through the church. He *is* incapacitated."

"I'll bet. So you're just doing the Lord's work?"

I gave him the most pious smile I could muster.

"I've got a question for you," he said, leaning a little on the broom. "Bret's going to be at the wedding, right?"

I turned back to the counter and wrapped the cooling lasagna in one of my mother's casserole carriers I'd found in a drawer. No matter how over him I might be, Bret wasn't my favorite topic. "So Eden says."

"How come you went out to Ty's to make sure everything was all hunky-dory between you two for the wedding, and not Bret?"

I paused as I bundled up the garlic bread. Trying to work things out with Bret had never crossed my mind. Ty was the one I wanted to make amends with, the one whose good opinion I'd been so desperate to win. Ty was the one I wanted to talk to, wanted to see. After everything with Bret turned out to be fake, maybe I'd just wanted to reassure myself the friendship and honesty I'd once found in Ty hadn't been part of the show. But saying any of that felt like too much of a confession.

"Bret cheated on me." As though Jed needed the reminder. He'd offered to bloody the man's nose plenty of times. "I'm not eager to see him again."

"But you were eager to see Ty."

My mouth dropped open—to say what, I didn't quite know —when Jed's pointed look stopped me. Anything I said would only prove the point he was dancing around.

"Take out your lasagna when the timer goes off," I said, shooting him a final glare. "I'll be back in a little while."

"Don't expect us to wait for you," he called as I walked out the door.

* * *

I pulled up to Ty's farmhouse, wondering for the hundredth time just what I was doing there. Turning up unannounced again was probably a bad idea. He would take it like a grouch, and complain about me fussing over him. Maybe he didn't like being tended, but he didn't have anyone else to take care of him. With his parents out of the country and Bret disinterested, he had to fend for himself. The man couldn't even open his truck door without pain—he wasn't likely getting four-star meals while he recuperated. He needed someone to help him out.

That's all this was, I reminded myself as I climbed the steps to his porch yet again. Just being charitable. It had nothing at all to do with the way he'd looked at me after I kissed his cheek, like he'd wanted to devour me in the best possible way. No, this was just me doing the Lord's work.

I rang the doorbell and waited in the falling twilight. Crickets chirped in the sultry evening heat, little snaps breaking up the peaceful quiet. I'd just thought I might have to round Ty up at the barn when he opened the door.

"June," he said, surprise plain in his eyes. "The horses are all put to bed for the night."

"That's okay, I'm here for you." I winced, lifting the casserole dish to distract from my awkward phrasing. "I brought you dinner."

"Oh." He frowned as his eyes fell on the bundle in my hands. "You didn't have to do that."

"I know, I just..." Really, I had no good explanation for my urge to make him dinner. Nothing that made much sense, anyway. *Thanks for sharing with me about your childhood, here's some food!* wouldn't cut it. "I just wanted to."

"That was good of you. Thanks."

He held one hand out as if he intended to cart the casserole dish back to the kitchen himself. This late in the day, weariness lined his eyes and mouth, and his stiff posture proved just how much his muscles ached. He could no sooner carry this casserole dish one-handed than he could do a cartwheel. I wouldn't give up the goods quite that easily. So to speak.

"I can take it in for you."

"I don't want to trouble you." He edged over to put himself

between me and the living room like a bouncer who'd spotted a fake ID.

"It's heavy, you shouldn't carry it." I took one step across the threshold, but he didn't move, wedging me in the doorway for a moment. I stared up into his face. "Are you going to let me in?"

He sighed until the sound cut off with a low grunt and a grimace. His look of pure apology had me bracing myself—for what, I didn't even know. Finally, he moved aside and let the door swing open wide.

"Oh. My. Goodness."

Wreck wasn't a strong enough word to describe the house. Clothes were strewn across the floor, dirty dishes littered the coffee table, and I could see the pile growing in the kitchen sink even from the door. His recliner peeked out from beneath a tangle of blankets and pillows like he'd been sleeping in it since his injury. The worst-case scenario when visiting a guy's house come to life, only missing a pyramid of empty beer cans on the side table.

Ty was neither careless nor a slob. He would only live like this if his pain made it impossible to manage the simplest everyday tasks. The man rinsed his rubber work boots after he wore them—it must be killing him to let things get this bad.

Three steps over the threshold, I made up my mind.

"Okay." Walking past him, I avoided a shirt on the floor, and set the casserole and garlic bread beside the stove in the kitchen. "First things first."

I moved through the living room, gathering dirty clothes into my arms.

"What are you doing?"

"I'm helping." I sifted through the blankets on his makeshift bed before moving on to the piles on the floor. "Is your bedroom upstairs? Hamper up there?"

I didn't wait for an answer before I started up the stairs.

"You drop those right now, June."

His voice rumbled with stern authority, the same one he used when he talked to his horses. Too bad I wasn't any more inclined to listen than Bullet was. Two footfalls creaked on the stairs behind me, followed by another groan. I turned to find him paused at the bottom of the staircase, one hand hovering over his chest as he scowled up at me.

Stairs didn't seem to be his friend these days.

Even at this distance, his glare scorched. "You get back down here."

I gave him a quick smile and turned to assess my surroundings. Four doors led off from the landing, and they all stood open. One bathroom, two virtually empty bedrooms, and finally, Ty's room. The bed had been neatly made up with a quilt that his grandmother had probably sewed, although the pillows had been stripped for his nest downstairs. The closet doors stood partially open, revealing an assortment of button-down shirts and jeans, with a neat row of cowboy boots and work boots lined up at the bottom. A faint scent of dust and age lingered in the house, but mostly, it just smelled like Ty.

Maybe it was weird to stand around smelling the man, but since he wasn't here to see me do it, I indulged. I breathed him in, letting the scent transport me back to his parents' house more than a year ago, standing on the back deck watching him grill hamburgers. I had teased him about his meticulous flipping pattern—back to front, left to right—and he had teased me about my drink choice of hard cider. I'd tilted the bottle toward him, goading him to try it. He finally had, his eyes locked on mine as his throat worked.

The moment had seemed to freeze, comfortable and perfect, with just the right amount of sexiness—until the thought of

Bret had barreled into our cozy togetherness. I'd darted back into the house, as guilty as if we had kissed.

After that, things had changed between us. Our coziness disappeared, and his lop-sided half-smiles had been replaced by deepening scowls. I'd thought he'd been unhappy with me, and maybe he had been—just not in the way I'd expected.

My gaze drifted to the old blue shirt Ty had been wearing the day he got kicked, crumpled on the bed. Remembering what I was meant to be doing, I snatched it up. I guessed he hadn't spent much time in here since his injury, but a few dirty clothes dotted the room. Nosing around just a little, I found a mesh hamper in the closet and stuffed all the clothes inside.

I lugged the hamper downstairs where Ty waited for me, scowl firmly in place.

"You put all that down. You don't just barge into a man's house and do his laundry."

"I'm pretty sure that's exactly what I'm doing." I eased past him. "Is the washer this way, or—never mind, I see it."

The utility room on the far side of the kitchen had been renovated to match, with sleek front loaders beneath pristine white cabinets. I opened a cupboard and found laundry detergent on the first try. Kismet.

"June, if you even think about doing that laundry, I will take you over my shoulder and drop you outside on your behind, so help me."

I tossed his clothes into the washer. "I'm intrigued by the offer, but given your condition, I think that's pretty unlikely."

"It would hurt like the devil, but I'll do it."

I pushed start, and the washer chimed to life. When I turned to face him, heat rippled through me like I'd walked into a furnace. Irritation and bitterness made Ty an imposing sight, but I didn't feel a trace of the unease a person should feel under a gaze like that.

The undeniable attraction threw me. How could he look so gorgeous standing there blazing with anger in a rumpled button-down? A dozen other ways he could put that intensity to use flashed in my mind until a soft fluttering filled my chest.

We stayed that way a moment, staring each other down.

"Well?" I finally said, feigning a confidence I didn't quite feel, what with that zing of awareness pulsing through my blood. "Are you going to toss me over your shoulder or not?"

One of his eyes twitched. "It's still an option."

"Let's table it for now." I pulled his dishwasher open. Clean. Good.

"You don't have to do that," he said when I opened all the cupboard doors to more easily put away his dishes. "I'd really rather you didn't."

"Get used to it." I didn't know where this cavalier attitude over risking Ty's wrath had come from. Maybe if I acted as contrary as he did, my heartbeat would slow down, and I'd stop thinking how much I'd *like* him to toss me over his shoulder. "When you work yourself into the hospital, you'll have a whole team of people taking care of you. Doctors, nurses, someone to turn you so you don't get bed sores."

He crossed his arms while I collected the dishes in the living room, but he didn't get in my way. A plastic breathing tube sat on the side table next to his recliner. "Are you doing your breathing exercises?"

"Do you want to take my temperature, too?"

"Why, are you feeling feverish?"

"I'd say I'm a little hot under the collar."

I smiled to myself while I started the dishwasher. When I came closer to stand in front of him, a little of his irritation had dissolved. His forehead wasn't etched quite so deeply, and his gaze had lost that murderous glint. Whether he'd finally decided to accept my help, or was just glad I finished, I'd have to take it as a win.

"There, that was painless, wasn't it?"

His mouth tugged at the edges. "Painless isn't the word."

"Now, do you want me to serve up some of this lasagna?"

The beginnings of his smile disappeared. "About that..."

Before he could explain, gravel crunched in front of the house as a car pulled up. We both glanced toward the front window, and then at each other. He looked almost furtive. Guilty.

Oh, Lord. *Crap, crap, crap.*

"You had other plans tonight." I wasn't sure I succeeded in keeping my voice casual. My skin crawled as I replayed the evening. No wonder he'd been trying to shoo me out from the moment I barged through his front door. He really had been trying to get rid of me, and I'd been completely oblivious. I'd even started thinking—

Oh, I'd been ridiculous.

I flashed a fake smile. "I'll leave you to it."

Only, leaving would mean walking out the front door and facing whoever Ty was expecting. Maybe the blonde ex-girl-friend had turned up to tend him in his hour of need, after all. Maybe Chloe—she had known him all her life and flat-out admitted to having a crush on him. An old one, but hey, things happen.

The doorbell rang, its cheery chime loud in the stillness. I took a step toward the kitchen. Sneaking out the back door could work. Through it all, Ty watched me with an odd look on his face.

"Should I not be here?" I whispered.

"Depends on who you ask."

He went to the front door. I stayed frozen on the spot, dreading the idea of meeting Ty's date-slash-caretaker, but unwilling to simply disappear out the back. I hadn't done anything wrong, and besides, I sure hadn't seen any blonde hottie helping him around his ranch the last week.

He paused, glancing over his shoulder at me again. I looked away, suddenly interested in the bottle opener magnet stuck on his fridge.

Sam Adams. Good brand.

"Hey." Ty sounded as casual as anything when he pulled open the door.

"Hey, I've got a large meat lovers pizza with extra cheese."

I spun to face the door. A young man in a bright uniform stood in the doorway holding an insulated bag. A pizza guy? *Thank you, baby Jesus.* Relief washed through me, followed by a surge of embarrassment for all the crazy assumptions I'd let fly through my head. Not that it was crazy at all to think Ty could have a girlfriend out there somewhere that he had never mentioned. The crazy part was how quickly the idea had gotten under my skin. Jealousy still circled around in my stomach, churning anxiety in its wake like a demented little motor boat.

Ty pulled a few bills out of his wallet, and the delivery driver was soon gone again. He set the pizza on the kitchen table, watching me with a strange light in his eyes. Curiosity. Maybe amusement. Well, I had acted like an idiot tonight. Somebody should get a laugh out of it.

"I didn't know I'd be getting a delivery from you, so I ordered my own."

"You can have the lasagna tomorrow." I grabbed it off the counter and tucked it into the fridge so he wouldn't have to. "I'll just get going."

I needed to get out of here and go cringe myself into a coma.

"Wait," he said before I could sidestep him. "Are you hungry?"

FIFTEEN

MY IMPULSIVE DINNER invitation hung in the air between us. June looked up at me with a sort of startled curiosity.

"If you don't like pizza, I've got a lasagna in the fridge."

She laughed, and the tension that had radiated from her these last few minutes disappeared. Her shoulders relaxed, and when she spoke, she sounded like herself again. "Pizza sounds great."

We worked together to put out plates and glasses on the table, June doing most of the work due to my *condition*, before we sat down to share the pizza. Even if she didn't seem as wound up anymore, she was careful to avoid my eyes as we started in on our simple meal. I would have sworn her momentary panic had been borne out of a misguided jealousy, but that didn't quite add up. She thought I had some *other* woman doing anything at all to care for me? And that agitated her?

After a few bites, I said, "It's not lasagna."

"It was my mom's recipe, so you're right. This stuff isn't even close." She ducked her head, looking sheepish. "Not that I'm complaining, I appreciate the offer. It's nice."

135

"Well, I am a nice man."

"So I'm learning."

Regret needled me for how hard I had pushed her away, both during her relationship with Bret, and these last few days. She'd never done anything to deserve my rough manners and short comments, but I couldn't very well explain I was just trying to protect my own fool heart.

"So," she said, dabbing at her mouth with the edge of a paper napkin. "*Are* you doing your breathing exercises?"

My harsh exhale seared through my chest. "You can't let a thing go, can you?"

"Pneumonia is serious, Ty, and if you were hospitalized, what would happen then?"

"I'd imagine you'd turn up at the hospital and hound the doctors, asking them if they'd really given me enough antibiotics to do the job."

She tried to look stern, but too much playfulness filled her eyes to pull it off. Nothing like her fierce show of willfulness when she'd tidied up my house. I'd been steamed, but I'd been more attracted to her than ever, too. Meeting me toe-to-toe, taking charge—she had a way about her that left me wanting her at the most inconvenient moments.

Like all of them.

"I *am* doing my breathing exercises, June. I might be stubborn, but I'm no fool. I don't want to deal with pneumonia any more than you want me to catch it." I felt ridiculous every time I blew into that stupid tube and watched the little ball inside it float to the top, but I still did it. Maybe not as often as I should, but I could only take so much.

"Good." Her smile lingered so long, she was probably imagining me using the thing. "Nurse June approves."

"Do you always worry this much?"

She stiffened slightly and rolled her bottom lip against her teeth. "I guess I do, after everything we went through with my mom."

I groaned over my thoughtlessness. Her tone wasn't scolding, but it should have been.

"That cough stuck around for weeks, but we all thought it was just a cold. It would pass, you know? By the time she finally had it checked out, it was too late to do anything about the cancer."

A long pause stretched between us, June seemingly lost in memories of her mother, me wondering how I could have been so cruel. I kept close enough with Clint and Carol Evans to know cancer had hit her fast and hard. Sometimes, cancer came and lingered for years, chipping away at a person little by little. Other times, it sprang up and grabbed them before they even knew what was wrong. It didn't make sense.

"I'm sorry. It must be tough, losing your mother." My own mother found fault in most of my life choices, but I still couldn't picture being without her. "She was a real good woman."

June's expression softened, her eyes all sweetness. Pleasure swelled inside me, the joy of saying the right thing to a woman entirely by accident.

"It's been so hard," she said, her voice just above a whisper. "At first, I was..." She shook her head as if pushing away those thoughts. "I'm doing better now, but it's always there. I'll think I'm doing fine and then something reminds me of her, or I wear one of her necklaces, or *something* hits me...and it's like it starts all over again."

Anything I might say would be empty, so I did the only thing I could think to do. I reached over and took her hand in mine. A small gesture of comfort for a woman whose heart so clearly still hurt. Watching June's emotions play across her face, my heart ached right along with hers. I let her hand go again in a moment, but her smile returned.

"Thanks. Pop says I'm paranoid now. He thinks I fuss over him too much."

"You don't say."

"I guess I do worry over little things. Little things can turn out to be big." She flashed me that stern look again. "Not that three broken ribs are a little thing."

"Only one's broken." The two cracked ones were just collateral damage.

"The semantics aren't the point." She wagged a finger at me again. "This is serious, and if you're not careful, it could get a lot worse."

Even through her teasing, the genuine concern that shone in her eyes made me ache. "You don't have to worry about me. I'm doing my breathing, and I'll even do my physical therapy."

"Physical therapy?"

I could have kicked myself. I'd just handed her one more thing to harass me about.

"They're just shoulder exercises so I don't hunch over. But I'll do them." Anything so she wouldn't fear for me. I sort of liked her fussing over me, but I didn't want her thinking I was about to be hospitalized, either.

A smile curved across her lips. "See that you do."

After polishing off the pizza, we cleared the table. Or rather, June cleared the table, and I hovered around in the kitchen, somehow feeling even more out of place than I had when she cleaned up my house.

I leaned against one counter while she stacked the dirty dishes in the sink and washed down the table. She was determined to do entirely too much for me, and I'd had no choice but to surrender. Just leaning over to pull fresh clothes out of the dryer seemed to tear my chest apart, and walking up the stairs proved more trouble than it was worth. Still, I couldn't think of a worse scenario than June finding my clothes tossed around on the floor and dirty dishes piled everywhere. She seemed destined to catch me at my lowest.

Not that I'd helped anything. Bossing her around in the barn, shutting her out, pushing her away as hard and fast as I could. I couldn't figure out why she kept coming back.

I cleared my throat, feeling like a grade-A jerk. "You've done an awful lot of work around here."

She draped the wet rag over the kitchen faucet and mirrored my pose, leaning against the counter next to me. "There's nothing wrong with needing a little help sometimes, you know."

"I shouldn't have let it get so bad. After finishing the few chores I'm able to do around the barn, by the time I come in, I'm beat."

She shifted to fully face me, her expression once again lit with stern defiance. "You shouldn't be doing *anything* around the barn. Nothing at all, do you hear me? Can't you hire someone else to help out, just until you're healed?"

"I tried. I haven't been able to find anybody last-minute, and Aaron's already doing more than his usual around here. I can handle it."

"I could—"

I raised a hand between us, cutting her off. "You've done plenty."

Her eager expression fell at the bite in my tone, and she pressed her lips into a pert frown. "The words you're looking for are *thank you*."

"It's not that I don't appreciate you. You've done all I've asked of you, and then some. But I can't just sit around watching soap operas while you do my chores. That's not me."

I expected her to dish out another sassy response about how I was liable to wind up in the hospital, but instead, she looked thoughtful as she gazed up at me.

"No, that's not you. You are an interesting man, Ty Hardy."

"That almost sounded like a compliment."

Her soft smile did me in.

"Almost."

The moment went on too long until I couldn't help myself. I'd spent too much time around her this last week, too much time wanting to touch her and not being able to. Too much time letting myself wonder what it would be like to hold her. To have her to myself. To kiss her.

So Lord help me, I did.

I drew her to me, at once celebrating her closeness, and stunned by how readily she came to my arms. In the moment before our lips met, thoughts of Bret and all the reasons June should be off-limits scrambled around in my brain. But then, my mouth was on hers, and all those excuses shattered in the absolute perfection of our kiss.

Perfection. Bliss. Everything.

Better than all the heated dreams I'd indulged in over the last years, better than my whole lifetime of realities. One kiss could never be enough when I needed her like I needed oxygen to survive. My senses overloaded on her sweet scent, her soft mouth, the warmth of her body against mine.

She opened up to me, and logic and reason escaped my grasp. I couldn't have given my own name if I'd been asked. I only had one thought in my mind—*June.*

june

OH. My.

All the tiny sparks of attraction that had zinged between Ty and me coalesced into a fireball when he kissed me. I'd wondered what it would be like—you don't spend time around a man like that without wondering what it would be like to be kissed by him. But none of those vague daydreams could compare to the vivid reality. I kissed him back without hesitation, ready to get lost in this new side of him.

Who could have known this sometimes cranky rancher would be such a gentle kisser? Ty was all surety and confidence, but with nothing selfish or demanding in his give and take. He teased and explored my mouth, his hands lightly running along my back, until my whole body sparkled with awareness. It felt like we had been made especially to kiss each other, like we knew already what the other wanted, what they needed.

My thoughts swirled out of focus, everything else paling compared to this single perfect moment. I laced my arms behind his neck to pull him closer, to ground myself before I drifted away entirely. Was this really happening? I pressed harder to him to confirm it, and he groaned against my mouth.

I dropped back to earth. My eyes flew open, and I pulled away. For that brief, glorious window, I'd forgotten his injury.

"I'm sorry," I said, a little dazed and out of breath. "Are you okay?"

His eyes had grown dark and heavy-lidded, his lips rough and pink. Just the sight of him like this set me on fire again, and I drifted back into his space, my gaze on his mouth. I leaned forward a touch, ready for another kiss.

"It was my fault."

The edge in his voice made me take half a step back, replacing the distance between us. Once again, the grimace that lined his face made him look like a man torn apart.

"I shouldn't have done that," he added.

All the delight coursing through my body went cold. "Why shouldn't you?"

He gave me a look as if the answer should have been clear in front of us. "You used to be my brother's girl."

Guilt crashed over me as I thought of the early days in my relationship with Bret, when Ty and I had seemed so close, when we had just fit together. All our little stolen moments, shared laughter, and quiet conversations I had simultaneously adored and agonized over. I'd excused it then as a sort of brotherly affection, but I knew now it never had been, for either of us.

Memories of Bret came flooding back, too. The day he sat me down to let me know he'd never seen me as a serious girlfriend, and, oh yes, he'd already started dating someone else. I was long past worrying over what Bret might think of my actions.

"In case it's slipped your notice, he has a new girl."

"We can't do this," Ty said, shutting me out all over again. "You and me."

"Why not?"

He seemed to pick and choose his words. "Someone would get hurt."

"Someone. Are you talking about me, or Bret?"

In his hesitation, I willed him to say his brother's name. I didn't give a flying flip about Bret's hurt feelings, but I did not want Ty to say *my* feelings were on the line. I did not want to be the only one in this with something to lose.

Finally, he said, "You."

The word seemed to suck the air from the room. My pride shattered, and I paused a beat to gather up the shards. We weren't together, we weren't dating, we weren't anything to each other. This rejection should be a little bump compared to Bret's big reveal last year.

But my heart rocked like a boat taking on water.

I held myself together, but only just. "You want to pretend that kiss didn't happen?"

He paused, leaving me one last glimmer of hope before he snuffed it out again. "That's probably for the best."

I wasn't sure I could pretend. That kiss had felt like cracking open a door I wanted to throw wide and run through. But if his interest in me was purely superficial, as Bret's had been, I wouldn't rush headlong into fresh heartache. At least Ty had the decency to be up front about it.

"I guess I should go, then." I steeled myself against the mess of emotions churning and roiling in my stomach. I would take this hit like a champ, even if I already felt down for the count. "You've got things pretty well in hand here."

Ty walked me through the house, a silent storm cloud at my side, and opened the door onto black night. It felt like a lifetime since I'd walked across the threshold tonight, casserole dish in hand.

"Oh." I turned back to him but didn't quite meet his eye.

"When you're ready for the lasagna, heat it up for twenty minutes at three-fifty."

"You can take it with you if you—"

"Don't be a complete ass, Ty." His mouth twitched, but he didn't quite smile. Of course he didn't. "I'll see you around."

His answering nod seemed to pain him, but I refused to read anything into it. I'd done that plenty with Bret, and had gotten everything exactly wrong. This time around, I would take Ty at face value.

No matter how much it hurt.

* * *

Pop lounged in his recliner, watching television with a glass of iced tea in his hand when I walked in. I gave a half-hearted wave, and he muted the sound.

"Ty like the lasagna?"

I bit my lip, not wanting to recap my night. "He'd already ordered pizza, so I left it for tomorrow."

"That's real sweet of you. It's a shame William and Rebecca aren't around. You know his mother's gonna lose her mind when she finds out he got hurt and she wasn't here to baby him."

"I can't imagine Ty would like that any more than he liked me hanging around trying to make sure he's taking care of himself." All my foolish efforts on his behalf paraded through my mind, driving the point home.

"Some men don't like to be tended." Pop squinted up at me, the lines around his eyes showing all the weather and age of decades working outside. "Then again, it probably depends on who's doing the tending."

"Well, he's given me notice. I'm off the clock." I did my best to pretend my heart hadn't been bruised by Ty's rejection.

Pop didn't look surprised. If anything, this news amused him. "I think he'll come around."

"'He'll come around'? We're talking about the same Ty Hardy, right? He's the most bullheaded man I've ever met."

"Is that right?" Pop's eyes twinkled up at me like I'd said something else entirely.

I shook my head at his innocent act. He knew exactly what Ty was like, but I wasn't in a mood to argue over just how infuriating Ty Hardy could be. I moved through the living room into the kitchen, where I found Jed leaning over the sink, eating a slice of pie held in his fingers.

"You have the manners of a cave man. Didn't the Army teach you anything?"

He shrugged, popping the last bite of crust into his mouth. "Where do you think I learned this? No fuss, no muss."

I found the pie dish on the counter and groaned in delight.

"Cherry peach?" I served a slice onto a plate. Pie would be a good step in the right direction to a mended heart. "You didn't make this, did you?"

Jed made a noncommittal sound while he finished chewing, and when he finally swallowed, he called, "Pop, who brought the pie again?"

Pop turned his head, tearing his eyes from the TV. "Neighbor. June, you know Marilyn Wells, don't you?"

Marilyn Wells wasn't what I would have called a neighbor —she lived practically across town. "She owns Fine & Dandy."

"That's the one."

Fine & Dandy was the type of small-town home decor store I went nuts over. Perfect little pieces at perfect little prices. I stopped in now and then when I visited town, but I couldn't recall ever talking with Marilyn about anything more than the latest floral mugs she'd just got in. Certainly, she'd never brought over baked goods before. I had no idea the woman was such a pie artist.

"This is amazing." The tart cherries mixed with the sweetness of the peaches, giving the right amount of zip. "Is this our fruit?"

He hitched a shoulder. "Might be. I took her some last week."

"Well, I'm impressed. She should expand her store."

"I'll tell her you like it."

I finished off my slice of pie in a few bites. Maybe I should have followed Jed's lead and eaten it over the sink. I put the dirty dishes in the washer and poured myself a glass of milk.

Jed leaned one hip against the kitchen counter. "So. Did you have a nice night?"

Ty's kiss flashed through my mind again, warm and perfect, followed by his declaration that getting involved with him would only hurt me. The dull ache in my chest said it was already too late. I made a vague gesture, not ready to open up yet about the mess that had been my night.

"What's wrong?" His gaze hardened. "Do I need to add another Hardy to my punch list?"

"No. We just argued. Kind of."

"What did you argue about?"

I opened my mouth to answer but couldn't find the right explanation.

"Oh, Hardy's on the list now."

Soft laughter rippled through me at this glimpse of his protective streak. "Don't do that. It's fine."

"You give me the signal, I'll take him down, broken ribs or not." He looked me over. "What exactly did you—"

Pop joined us in the kitchen, sparing me from having to make up a weak answer to Jed's question.

"Wade and his clan are coming for dinner day after next. Plan to be here, okay?"

Wade's job as a firefighter/EMT down in Georgetown meant we had to plan family dinners around his one day on/two days off schedule. And Pop thought *my* job was strange.

"Anyone else joining us?" Jed asked. "Family? Friends?"

Pop stared him down. "Everybody's welcome."

Jed seemed disappointed in this nonchalant attitude about doling out invitations, but he shook it off. "Fine. I'm going down to The Broken Hammer for a while before I head home. June, you want to come?"

"I think I had enough on Saturday. Sorry."

His usual mischievousness fell away, replaced by a tender look of concern. "Are you sure? Might do you good to get out a little."

I nodded. "I'm sure."

He watched me another minute but seemed to think better of pushing for a deeper answer.

"That's probably better for me, anyway," he said with a fresh grin. "You'd just be dead weight with the ladies."

Pop smacked him on the arm. "Be a gentleman."

Jed put one hand over his heart. "I wouldn't dream of being anything else."

He gave another grin that probably worked wonders on the women of Magnolia Ridge and disappeared out the front door.

Pop turned to me, shaking his head. "I hope he works through this soon."

"Works through what?"

"That." He nodded toward the door, like Jed's ghost still stood there. "His loneliness."

I snort-laughed at that. "I wouldn't say Jed's very lonely."

He mostly spared me the details, but let's just say Jed's social calendar didn't have many blank spaces.

"He could spend every night with a different woman and still be lonely. Your brother's hurting, he just doesn't want to see it." Pop leveled a more serious look at me. "It can be hard for a man to be alone."

Pretty sure he wasn't talking about Jed anymore. Either way, I wasn't in the mood for a conversation about lonely men right now. I stretched my arms wide and faked a huge yawn. "I think I'd better get to bed."

He seemed to store away whatever he wanted to say. "Get on up there, then."

"Goodnight, Pop." I gave him a quick hug and darted up the stairs.

With the echo of Ty's kiss still burning on my lips and my blood pulsing with stifled hopes, I couldn't bear the idea of talking about Ty with my pop. Whatever he wanted to ask me could wait for another day. Maybe by then, I would have an answer.

june

THE MORNING'S DISMAL, gray light suited my bleak mood just fine. I set up shop at my pop's kitchen table, arranging virtual rooms on my laptop and sending off designs to clients I would never meet, wind whistling against the house. After so many days of mucking around at Ty's ranch, staying home felt like playing hooky from my duties. I reminded myself that the quick designs and simple mock-ups my e-customers requested *were* my duties, but my thoughts kept drifting to the horses on the ranch.

Let's be real. I mostly thought about the rancher, the source of my bleak mood.

The memory of that kiss we'd shared sent a never-ending waterfall of shivers tumbling down my spine. I wasn't sure I'd ever been kissed like that before, like I meant everything in the world to a man. He'd held me like I was precious to him, like the kiss meant something.

Showed how much I knew, since Ty had also said the kiss had been a mistake. I'd already been down that road with one Hardy. I wasn't looking to go through it a second time.

Ty wasn't Bret, I knew that. But if he was so sure he would

wind up hurting me in the long run, I shouldn't let myself get carried away just because we'd shared one amazing kiss. But, oh, the ghost of that kiss haunted me, echoing in the back of my mind until I could hardly think straight.

Nope. That was the way of France. I'd told myself to be a robot, and a robot would absolutely not get caught up in emotions over some surly rancher.

Pop walked into the dining room decked out in his orchard finest: Coveralls and work boots. "How goes the internet work?"

I moused over an image of a plush armchair and dragged it onto a picture of my client's sparse bedroom. "I'm doing a room refresh for a newly-divorced woman in Vermont. She wants the feminine room of her dreams now that her jerk of a husband's no longer around to tell her it's too girly."

His eyebrows lifted. "They usually give you that much information about their personal lives?"

"Not usually." Most of the time, clients kept the information on their request form to facts about their tastes, interests, and vision for the room, but every once in a while, someone took the three-hundred-word limit as a challenge.

"You going over to Ty's after you're done?"

My fingers paused on the keyboard. When I left the ranch last night, we hadn't said anything about me going back again. In the moment, my ego had been too bruised to consider it. He'd never wanted me there in the first place. He didn't care about the bet, and I cared about it more than I should. I needed to do as he asked and leave him be.

"I told you last night, he doesn't want me to keep helping him."

Pop puttered around in the kitchen looking for something like he hadn't heard me.

What would happen out at Ty's if nobody did the work I'd been covering? Aaron could only do so much working two jobs, and Ty shouldn't be doing anything at all. Feeding, watering, mucking—it didn't sound like a whole lot, but a dozen horses out there relied on it getting done every day.

I ran my fingers between the rows of my keyboard, thinking over Ty's comments about sickness and disease breeding in dirty stalls. "If you needed help on a ranch like Ty's, how would you find someone?"

Pop stopped opening and closing cupboards. "You fixing to do some hiring?"

"No, but aren't there all kinds of high school kids who would be willing to help out, just for the chance to be around the horses?" I was sure *someone* in Magnolia Ridge had to be available, and I was just as sure Ty hadn't done much at all to find anybody.

"You could try down at the feed store or Ranch and Home. They've got job boards. Sometimes, kids post their phone numbers if they're desperate for a position."

"I don't know if he could pay anything." I didn't like to ask how much this setback would wind up costing him. He still had the boarders, but losing all his training income until he healed up sure sounded like a lot.

"That changes things. He might get lucky and find somebody if he was willing to do a lot of calling around asking for help. That seem likely to you?"

I released a disgusted laugh. "That's never going to happen. He's too stubborn and pig-headed to ever ask. Even if he did find somebody, he'd probably run the kid off with all his growling, anyway."

Pop's raised eyebrows made me clamp down on the rest of my tirade. I'd seen enough of his suspicious looks the last few days, I didn't need to dig my hole any deeper. He went out the back door, leaving me to work on the frilly-chic bedroom I had going, but my concentration was shot. Would I really let the horses suffer just because I was mad at Ty?

Pop wasn't gone long before he came inside again and grabbed a set of keys off a peg in the kitchen.

"Storm's coming on." He nodded out the kitchen window, and I followed his gaze. The gray clouds of the morning had turned dark and menacing, casting the house in shadow. "I've got to get out there and double-check all the hail netting."

"You need any help?"

"Jed's on his way." He started out the back door again.

"What about Ty's?"

I wasn't even sure what I was asking. Could horses weather the storm if things got bad? They had a couple of shelters out in the pastures, but would they use them? Did Ty have everything covered? Whatever needed to be done out there, he couldn't do it himself.

Pop paused. "Maybe somebody will have mercy on him." He winked at me, but his mood grew serious. "If you're thinking of heading over there, do it now. I don't want you driving in the thick of it. Summer storm like this can be as slick as ice."

With that, he left.

I sighed, closing my laptop. *I'm just doing the Lord's work.*

EIGHTEEN

I SHOULD HAVE KNOWN BETTER than to trust the weather reports.

The day had started overcast, without a trace of blue in the sky. I'd hesitated letting Aaron turn the horses out that morning, but the cloud cover had been predicted to burn off after a few hours, and I'd given the go-ahead. Skies had grown darker as the day wore on, and a stiff wind whipped up from the north. I'd been debating what to do when my phone pinged a weather alert.

Thunderstorms. I would have no choice but to bring the horses in. In theory, they should be used to Texas's summer storms, and able to withstand a few hours out in the wind and rain. In practice, if something could go wrong, it would. Most of the horses out there didn't belong to me, and I couldn't risk harm coming to them. It had always been my practice to stable them when weather got rough. Today was no different, broken rib or not.

I strode across the yard to the barn, huddling against the buffeting wind. I should have listened to my own gut. What was wrong with me that I couldn't recognize a storm brewing up when I saw one? I'd lived out here long enough to know the signs. Either my instincts were off, or I'd been too cowed by my injury to follow them. Wasn't sure which option was worse.

I grabbed a rope halter off the tack wall, dread already weighing me down. A few days ago, I'd tried to halter a horse and had nearly doubled over from pain. But with Aaron out at Belton Grove for the rest of the day, I couldn't very well do nothing.

I walked out of the barn and nearly ran headlong into June. "What are you doing here?"

She was the last person I'd expected to see on my ranch again after last night.

Lord, last night.

I tried to convince myself this was all for the best, that having her mad at me and thinking I didn't want her would be the easiest thing for everybody. By the time I'd fallen asleep in my recliner set up, I'd half-believed I could go on like we hadn't shared a staggering kiss that made me forget every other woman I had ever known. I couldn't even blame such idiot thoughts on the pain pills, since I'd quit taking them.

"Working," she said, the little line already set between her eyebrows—I'd managed to tick her off in five seconds flat. She strode past me, shoved her feet into a pair of rubber boots, and tugged her gloves on like she was about to commit murder. "The real question is, what are you doing here? You're not supposed to be doing anything."

I looked her square in the eye, and that was all it took. Her scowl disappeared; her eyes softened. Stress must have been stamped all over my face for her to recognize it so quickly.

"What do we need to do?"

How did she always *know*? I didn't have time to question her uncanny intuition or my underlying feelings about her reappearance. "Storm's blowing in. I have to stable the horses."

She looked out at the dark clouds looming over the pastures, her worry hardening to determination. "I'll help you."

I stopped looping the lead rope over my arm and stared her down. Normally, rounding up the horses alone was easy enough, but just now, nothing came easily. Even with June's help, the storm might hit before we could get all the horses in. As if my thoughts weren't bad enough, my phone pinged again. Hail reported five miles away.

"You can't do it all yourself," she said, reaching for the halter. "Just tell me what to do."

I wanted to tell her she couldn't do it, that she *shouldn't* do it, but I had no choice. And honestly, she had already proven a dozen times over that she could handle whatever I dished out at her. Why not this, too?

"Come on." I strode out to the back pastures, June at my side, loose strands from her bun whipping in the wind. The temperature had dropped since my walk to the barn, but it hadn't started raining yet. We could do this.

"Have you ever haltered a horse?" I asked.

"I think we did in Girl Scouts."

Great. Girl Scouts. Hopefully, some of the lesson had stuck.

"Horse's muzzle goes through here," I said, pulling the halter over one of my forearms. "Then you bring up the sides, and knot it here on the neck. Got it?"

She glanced over my quick and dirty demonstration. "I think so."

I caught the hesitation she tried to hide. This could go all kinds of wrong, for everybody involved, but doing nothing would be the greater risk. I'd left two messages for Aaron, but when things were busy out at Belton Grove, he wasn't likely to answer, and wouldn't be able to leave anyway. A larger outfit with more horses to tend, that ranch sat directly in the storm's

155

projected path. Aaron might already be up to his neck in hailstones and spooked horses.

"We're going to call in the calmest horses first, and with any luck, a few of the others will come to the gate to wait their turn."

"Okay." She threw her shoulders back and shook out her hands. "I'm ready."

I really hoped she was.

Unlatching the pasture gate, I let her through then whistled, long and high. The most seasoned horses looked our way.

"Go a few yards in and call Miss Kitty to you."

June's shout didn't do much in the worsening wind, but the old mare's ears pricked. She took a few hesitant steps toward June, like she wasn't sure about this stranger or what she wanted.

"Don't approach her head-on. Move to her side so she can see you."

As the horse trundled across the pasture, June walked toward her at an angle. Miss Kitty wasn't used to coming in at this time of day, and probably didn't care about the storm, but she had belonged to my Gram, and did as she was told. When the mare was only a few feet away from her, June held out one hand, offering to stroke her muzzle.

"That's the way," I said as she petted the horse.

Looking like she thought the horse might kick the way Bullet had, June looped the halter over her muzzle and tossed the end over her neck. Miss Kitty had been around long enough, she didn't even notice when June knotted it on the side.

"You got her." I clapped my hands together, immediately regretting the gesture. Until these broken ribs, I'd never realized I could miss a thing like breathing normally or raising my voice. I missed doing a whole lot of things lately, most of them unspeakable around June. Most of them would directly involve June if I had my way.

As always, this wasn't the time.

June walked Miss Kitty toward the gate, and just like I'd hoped, a few of the older horses followed. They jostled each other for position, trying to sneak out with Miss Kitty, but at least we wouldn't have to chase them down across the pasture. I ground my teeth together thinking about what kind of a fuss the colts might dust up for her, but we would have to take one thing at a time.

I helped June through the gate with a few choice commands to the horses that tried to shoulder their way past. "Can you get her into her stall?"

"I think so." She led Miss Kitty into the barn like an old hand. It had been a while, but Gram had taught her well. I tried to imagine what those Girl Scout afternoons had entailed. Probably a lot of practical instruction and just enough gentle encouragement from Gram to keep them interested. She'd always had the patience of a saint. How else had she managed to teach me my way around the ranch?

In another minute, June returned with the halter and lead rope, a huge smile across her face. "She's all tucked away."

"One down, eleven to go."

"Little victories, Ty."

June got the hang of leading the easier horses in to their stalls well enough, but I kept my eyes on the skies. In the time we'd been working, the rain clouds had blown in, great dark smudges that streaked toward the ground. Thunder rolled in the distance, and flashes of lightning lit up the gloom. Any minute now, the sky would open up and dump rain. We had no choice but to move on to the flightier horses.

June had handled the old ones well enough, but her confident air faded a bit as she called to Jake, the first of the more questionable lot. His ears flickered toward her, but the rest of him didn't move.

"You have to let him know you're in charge." If she didn't lose her jitters fast, Jake would walk all over her. Hopefully, not literally.

"Jake," she called again, trying to put more heart into her voice. She inched closer at a broad angle so he could see her coming.

"Storm's coming on faster than you're walking, June."

"Not helping," she called back.

Finally, Jake cottoned on that he was going to the barn and his grain, and let her get the halter on. "Stay close to his head," I instructed. "Don't let him lead you."

One by one, June called out each horse's name as she edged into the pasture, her hand out to soothe and pet them. A couple toyed with her a little, but they didn't fight her much on the change of scenery. Horses could hold their own in a thunderstorm, but most of them seemed to recognize they would be more comfortable in their stalls.

As she brought horse after horse into the barn, I kept watch over Bullet, who pranced circles in the far corner of the pasture. The sly beast knew exactly what June was doing, but made no move to be a part of it.

Finally, she'd narrowed them down to three: Spirit, Opie, and Bullet. The horses I'd made the least progress with before my injury. I could leave them to pasture to ride out the storm, but both choices held their own dangers. On one hand was the risk of injury June faced from the animals. I wouldn't forgive myself if she got hurt handling green colts at my request. On the other hand, I'd never left a horse out in a storm since I'd taken on my business. Even the orneriest one could get in a bad way from flying debris, broken tree branches, or a bad bout of hail.

I didn't like calling to let my clients know I'd have to delay their horse's training, but I'd like calling to let them know their horse had been injured or killed even less.

Spirit must have had enough of the rumbling thunder pressing in on us. He defied his name and went right to June when she called. He pranced a little outside the gate, leaving half a minute where I feared he might bolt, but June never let go of the lead rope.

Rain fell in fat drops now, picking up intensity like a snowball starting downhill to become an avalanche. Even soaked to the bone, June never gave up. My heart pounded in my chest, my hands clenched tight around the metal gate as I watched her creep across the pasture toward the last two horses. They were young and didn't yet know how to interact well with people. I told myself they weren't dangerous, but my heart wouldn't listen.

Just as she made to secure the halter over Opie's neck, lightning cracked right over us. The horse reared, his forelegs waving high over her head.

For one horrible second, I thought he'd struck her. Watching helplessly from the fence, my whole body seized up. She stumbled backward out of the horse's way, and fell hard in the grass.

I shot through the gate in a heartbeat, ignoring the pain exploding in my chest.

"June!" I called uselessly while running toward her, each step a tornado rippling across my battered ribs. Opie shuffled away from her, still close enough to be a trample threat if he completely lost his head.

She rolled onto her side and pushed into a sitting position. Soaked through and covered in mud, her glare lit fire. "What are you doing? You shouldn't be out here."

"*I* shouldn't be out here? I never should have sent *you* out here. Are you hurt?"

She stood and swept the worst of the mud off her rear. "Just knocked the wind out of me. I'm fine."

Rain streaked down her face and into her eyes. I pulled off my Stetson and sat it low on her head. "Go back to the gate. I'll get the last of these."

Her fake laugh cut into the air. "*You* go back to the gate. I can handle this."

"I'm not going to let you risk your neck again."

"Are you telling me you've never fallen down before?"

My past injuries weren't the point. I'd never had to watch someone I cared about risk her neck over a wild animal for me before—*that* was the point.

"That could have been a whole lot worse. I never should have let you try to lead these young ones." I held out my hand for the halter.

She spun on her heel and called to Opie.

My blood boiled, overtaking the fear that had filled me just moments before. "Impossible woman. Why won't you listen?"

She glanced at me over her shoulder. "Because you look almost as bad as you did the day you were first kicked. Go back to the gate."

My ribs ached pure misery, but I never should have asked this much of her. I knew what to watch for when working with my horses, but June had no idea what they might do or the signs they were about to do it. With thunder breaking all around us and lightning flashing across the sky, the horses were unpredictable at best. Dangerous at worst.

"We'll figure something else out." I knew already it was this, or leave the horses in nature's hands.

June called to Opie again, and the horse took a few solemn steps closer. He seemed ashamed of himself for his bad behavior, and after a few tries, let June halter him. I walked with them back to the gate and led them through, numb now to the tumult raging across my ribs.

She put Opie in his stall, but when she tried to get back in the pasture, I blocked her way. Standing toe to toe with me in the pounding rain, she glared up into my face. She quirked one little eyebrow beneath my Stetson as if challenging me to defy her, and my heartbeat quickened even as the moment seemed to slow.

Now is not the time, you fool.

"I'll get Bullet." I held out my hand for the halter.

"Ty, you can't do this. You've gone pale from running out there to check on me."

"Try to imagine how I'd look if he'd kicked you." I couldn't think about anything else, my mind filled with heartbreaking possibilities. That sickening moment when I thought Opie had struck her had nearly sent me to my knees.

"It's going to be fine."

"I know," I said, holding out my hand. "Because I'm going to get him."

"Ty—"

I took her by the shoulders, my hands gentle but firm. "June, you can challenge me on everything else you want, I promise. But this is the horse that tried to kick a hole through my ribcage."

She glanced down at my chest as though she could see through my shirt to the black and purple bruise that blossomed there, and a touch of color washed over her cheeks.

I let go of her before I could do something stupid in an already charged situation. "I won't let that happen to you."

As if on cue, tiny ice pellets mixed with the heavy rain. She only had on a wet T-shirt and jeans, and I at least wore long sleeves.

161

"That decides it." I had to raise my voice over the noise of the hail striking through the yard and pinging off the barn roof.

She brushed her hands down her arms to try to protect them from the onslaught.

"Okay. You win." She pulled off my hat and leaned up on tip-toes to set it on my head. "You need this more than I do."

Placing the rope halter in my hand, she wrapped her fingers around mine, her warmth drowning out the chill around us. "Be careful."

I squeezed her fingers back, but had no time for more reassurances. "Take cover."

She nodded and darted into the barn. I whistled for Bullet as I crossed the pasture's expanse, hoping the horse could hear me over the noise of hail and rain. Hailstones stung the bare skin on my neck and hands, urging me to hurry up and get myself and this fool horse under shelter.

"Bullet!"

I took slow and measured steps toward him. I'd never been afraid of a horse and wasn't about to start with this one, but I wouldn't have the same control I usually had with him. If he reared or tried to bolt, I wouldn't be able to do much more than watch him go.

Whether the horse could hear me or not, I spoke to him as I drew closer. Bullet took a few steps toward me before he darted back to where he'd started. My chest ached, every inch of my exposed skin stung from the barrage of hail pellets, and I wanted nothing more than the rest everyone had been demanding I take, but I couldn't leave the pasture without this horse.

When I finally reached Bullet, I slid a hand along his neck, trying to soothe some of the fright out of him. I slipped the rope halter over his muzzle, slow enough not to startle him, but steady enough to show him I would get my way in the end. As I tied the halter on, he jerked his head away, wrenching my hands along with him. I held tight on instinct, the muscles in my chest screaming out as my arms strained, but I kept my cool and finally secured the halter.

I talked low to him the whole brisk walk to the pasture gate, thanking him for not putting up much of a fight. I had to hold on tight to the lead rope just once, when lightning flashed directly ahead of us. Bullet shied but didn't bolt, thank God. June let us through the gate, and we all sought shelter in the barn. The horse rushed to his feed bucket, and I secured the stall behind him.

June stood in the barn aisle drenched from head to toe, staring at me, eyes wide. For a moment, I thought she might be in shock—then a massive grin spread across her face. She radiated so much pride, I couldn't help but return her smile. Relief and joy all tumbled together, the best reward for my efforts. My chest blazed, my arms and legs had gone numb from the rain and hail, and my head swam, but we'd brought in the horses.

"Wow," she breathed, that elation turning into something else. "You should do that more often."

"What?"

"Smile. Your smile is..." That tinge of pink came back into her cheeks, washing her skin with my favorite color. "It's devastating."

Not as devastating as her. She had brought in my horses and even got knocked down without missing a beat. Her willingness to run around in the rain and hail, doing whatever it took to help me out, ignited a fierce admiration in me. She was a lot stronger than I had given her credit for, that was for sure.

Stronger, sexier, sweeter. She was everything to me.

Everything I knew I couldn't have.

"You were great out there." My voice held decidedly less enthusiasm than I felt.

Her huge grin faltered. "Thanks."

And just like that, her spark winked out. I'd killed the moment. What was wrong with me?

A shiver rippled through her, and she wrapped her arms around herself. The barn was dry and a touch warmer than the chill outside, but that didn't mean much when her thin T-shirt and heavy jeans were wet through.

"Let's get you inside."

She didn't argue, but followed me to the open barn door. Hail skipped and bounced through the yard, pinging off the fences and gates. The pellets weren't big, but it wouldn't make for a fun walk back to the house, either.

Stepping closer, she adjusted the Stetson on my head as though reassuring herself I had a sliver of protection from the hail. Then she shifted away, her eyes lingering on my mouth, and her own lips parted. Despite the chill, heat bloomed inside me at the memory of our kiss, and my unrelenting ache for another.

Before I could think too hard about it, her eyes snapped back to mine. "I'm going to run for it."

With a last glance at me, she ran through the doorway toward the house, shielding her eyes from the hail.

I pushed all my desires down, reminding myself I had no right to be disappointed. This was what I wanted. Or rather, this was what would be best for June. What I wanted... Now that was something else entirely.

NINETEEN

BY THE TIME I reached the cover of my front porch, my chest was nothing but anguish, and the back of my neck stung from hundreds of tiny hail strikes. I hadn't had the heart to run for it like June had, so I'd walked the distance, the pain endured my due penance. Whether that punishment was for wanting her, or not doing anything about it, I didn't know anymore.

The rubber work boots she had worn stood next to the door. Something comforting and warm flashed inside me at the idea of her waiting for me inside my house. I'd never come home to anybody before, but I liked the idea of coming home to June.

I shook my head at the romantic notion. Here I was thinking like a fool again. I wasn't coming home to her—we had just outrun a storm together, that was all. I ran my work boots through the mud scraper and followed her lead, tugging them off to leave on the porch. I let myself inside, but the living room and dining room stood empty. The dark clouds overhead made the house gloomy, a stark contrast to the cheer I'd thought to find waiting for me.

"June?" I called, letting the searing in my lungs shake the crazy thoughts from my head. Something needed to.

"I'm up here." Her muffled voice drifted down the stairwell. "I'm ransacking your closet."

My closet?

"And your bathroom." She grinned as she walked downstairs toweling off her wet hair, her bundle of muddy clothes tucked under one arm.

I froze, taking her in. Lord Almighty. Seeing her in my old Johnny Cash T-shirt and worn sweatpants did something dangerous to me, lighting me up with longing and need. Minutes ago, I'd been cold through, but now, a crackling fire surged to life inside me. Maybe it wasn't the best idea to be alone with her in a darkened house, after all. I felt suddenly predatory, possessive. My mouth went dry by the time she reached the main floor.

A line crinkled the center of her forehead.

"I didn't think you'd mind." She looked down at the oversized shirt she wore and my old gray sweatpants cinched around her hips, way too long for her. "I didn't want to get everything wet. Maybe I shouldn't have—"

"No," I interrupted, finally finding my voice. "It's good. You look good."

Good did not begin to describe how she looked right now. *Edible* was more accurate.

"Okay." A hesitant smile crept back on her face. "Do you have a plastic bag I can put these wet clothes in?"

It took me a minute to spin my brain in that direction, stuck on the sight of her wearing my clothes. "Under the kitchen sink."

She went into the kitchen and rummaged around, leaving me dripping in the doorway like an uninvited dog. I'd been gawping at her yet again. I hung my wet hat on the rack by the door, trying to shut up every voice inside me that said this was the perfect time to go for broke and lay it all out on the line with her, tell her the whole truth.

Those voices were idiots.

She came back into the living room, her muddy clothes safe in a plastic bag she set by the front door.

"Here," she said, holding out the towel she'd been using on her hair. "You should dry off."

Dry off, kiss her senseless, one or the other.

I took the towel and passed it over my face, but that was a mistake. It carried a whiff of her floral shampoo now, and I had to stop myself from pressing it to my nose to breathe it in.

"I'll get you some dry clothes." She darted back upstairs.

"You don't have to," I sighed out, knowing she would anyway.

I ran the towel over my head, scraping my fingers through my hair, trying to get a hold on this overpowering want. Before I could, June reappeared beside me with a stack of fresh clothes. Although she'd chosen a T-shirt for herself, she'd brought me a button-down. She noticed everything—she had to know I couldn't pull shirts over my head. Something about that small sign of her care and concern threatened to break me apart.

"Here's a shirt, jeans, and um…" She bit her bottom lip, thrusting the clothes out at me. "Briefs."

Great. Just great. She had rifled through my underwear drawer. That was one way to shut down all my heated thoughts.

I took the clothes without a word and shut myself up in the downstairs bathroom. Biting back groans as I peeled off wet clothes, I couldn't ignore the ache and pull in my chest. After all that running around out in the pastures, I took my time with the painful production so I wouldn't aggravate my injury any worse than I already had. Maneuvering around in the half bath

167

made me feel huge and ungainly, like a bear in a tea shop. Lately, the stairs to my bedroom were too much to manage, and I did all this right out in the living room, but there were only so many indignities June needed to witness.

I pulled my shirt off and paused to look at the bruise that bloomed across the center of my chest. It had gone green at the edges of the black and purple whorl, like the sickly iris of a zombie eye. I lightly ran fingers over the broken parts of me: muscles, bones, heart. Two would mend up pretty well in time. The third...I just didn't know anymore.

I finished getting dressed but lingered in the bathroom. Yes, I was hiding out, but June was everywhere now: her scent in the air, her body in my clothes, her hands in my *briefs drawer*. I just needed a minute to think. That I was thinking about *her* didn't help anything.

When I finally left the bathroom, all the lights were on and the house smelled of tomatoes and garlic. Two plates and water glasses sat on the table in anticipation of dinner. June busied herself in the kitchen, putting clean dishes away.

"How long was I in there?" I asked, taking it all in.

"I don't know about you, but after that, I'm starved." She grabbed something off the counter and brought it to me. "Here. For your chest."

An ice pack. Lord, but she was a good woman. "I don't pay you enough."

I pressed the pack against the fire in my ribs while easing onto a dining chair.

She shot me a grin. "You can't afford me."

Wasn't that the truth.

"How *is* work going? You're still with that online outfit." That I thought she would have been out of there by now could go unsaid. Nobody liked to hear they weren't doing as well as someone else expected, I knew better than anyone.

She nodded, checking on the lasagna in the oven. "It's steady."

I caught her flat tone, the way she barely acknowledged the question. "How is it really?"

She hesitated. "It's...solitary. Everything's done through emails, so I never interact with clients face to face. I've never even met my boss in person. I just log in, do the work, log out. It's a good job, but..."

"It could be better," I finished. "I thought you were going to start a company with your friend. Kim?"

She had talked about it enough last year, I'd expected it to have happened before now.

Light danced in her eyes as she looked over at me. "I'm surprised you remember that."

I remembered every conversation we'd ever had. I'd tucked them all away to treasure long after she moved on. Her voice, her smile, her soft words. All of it.

"I listen," was all I told her.

"I guess you do. Kim got a job offer in Houston not long after things ended with Bret." She winced at that pair of bad memories. Her year had been a lot rougher than she let on. "It was more secure than starting a new partnership would be, so she went for it."

She looked out at the storm clouds beyond the kitchen window. Thunder still broke in the distance, and rain came down in sheets, but it sounded like the hail had let up.

"So where does that leave you?"

"I still want to start a company. It's just a lot more daunting doing it on my own."

"You'll get there."

She turned to me, doubt written in her eyes and tugging at her mouth. "You think?"

"Sure. I believe in you, June. You can do anything you put your mind to, no question."

Her eyes brightened, the gloom gone. What I wouldn't give to make her shine like that every day.

One of her shoulders shifted as she pulled the warmed lasagna and bread from the oven. "Anyway, my job is flexible enough that I can still decorate my cousin's wedding, tend to a cantankerous rancher's horses, *and* tend the cantankerous rancher. I think I'm in a pretty good place."

"Cantankerous?"

She grinned. "Doesn't it fit?"

I frowned at her, but my scowl disappeared in the face of her teasing. I was no match for that. Never had been. Add it to the list of June's unwitting weapons I had no defense for. Her open heart, her fiery determination, her stubborn streak as wide as the day is long—I might as well lay down my arms now.

"So," she said as we started in on the lasagna. "Are you ever going to tell me who you hired to help remodel this place?"

"You have a real knack for not letting things go."

"I'm just curious. This is what I do, you know. And I'm not criticizing, I'm complimenting. It's really good."

"You like it?" I couldn't keep the interest out of my voice. I wanted to know.

"I love it. It's exactly my style. Remember that time you asked me about how I'd decorate my dream house? I'm pretty sure I described exactly this. I told you all about the oak floors, the Craftsman trim, the—"

She stopped like she'd been distracted by something. Or realized something. I scowled down at my plate, but her eyes weighed heavy on me, daring me to look up. So of course I did.

Just like that, she figured me out. I wasn't sure how much I should be around her now that I couldn't hide a thing from her big blue eyes. I didn't have many secrets, but she would know them all in another day or two. And then where would that leave us?

"Oh." Her soft little exhale killed me.

That day when I'd asked her about her dream house, I hadn't been fishing for information—I'd just been interested. Like all our other conversations, I had filed it away, another memory of June to look back on.

Then last fall, I'd finally had enough of living with Gram's old pastel walls and puke-green cabinets, and I remembered the vision she'd described. June's dream house plans hadn't been grandiose or even that elaborate, they had just taken a little time and effort. I never thought she would recognize her fingerprints all over my house, but then, I had never really thought she would be *in* my house on the regular to see the results.

Even if, somewhere deep down, I'd hoped.

She still stared at me, surprise and wonder flitting across her face.

"Just tell me what I owe you." The words came out too rough, as if I could shake her look of recognition, like she had seen into the deepest part of my heart.

That furrow I knew so well appeared between her eyebrows. "What you—what?"

I turned back to my plate. "Your consultation fee. It's not right for me to pick your brain and use your ideas for free."

"You don't have to—"

"I'd feel better if I did." I risked a glance at her and wished I hadn't. Her confusion had hardened into disbelief.

"Really?" Her voice went flat as she stared at me. "You'd feel better if you paid me for a conversation we had a year ago?"

GENNY CARRICK

I cleared my throat, hoping the fire in my lungs would clear my head. "It's only fair."

"You are an ass, Ty Hardy." Her glare held a trace of affection, as if I amused her against her will. "You're really bad at asking for help, you know that, right?"

Lord, did I ever.

TWENTY

june

POP FROZE when I walked in the front door, his pen stuck hovering over a crossword. Standing there with wet hair in Ty's too-big clothes, I could imagine what conclusions he was drawing about how we'd spent our afternoon.

"We got caught in the hailstorm," I said quickly. Probably too quickly, from the way his eyebrows twitched up. *Not guilty at all, June.* Nothing had happened today, though.

Nothing except Ty had endured all kinds of pain to corral a horse he thought might hurt me, told me he believed in me so that my heart swelled, and admitted he'd remodeled his house based on a long-ago conversation we'd had.

Nothing sure felt like a whole lot of something.

"We had to bring the horses in," I went on. "And I got all muddy. So I borrowed fresh clothes." I lifted the bag of wet clothes as proof before setting it by the door. I'd tackle the laundry later. Spending time on Ty's ranch was putting a real hurt on my wardrobe.

"Uh-huh. You get them all taken care of?"

"A couple got wet is all, and one got hit with some hail, but

Ty said he'd be okay. The horse, I mean. Is everything okay out here?"

Words still spilled out of my mouth too fast, but Pop wasn't giving me the skeptical eye anymore, so I took that as a good sign.

"Not much damage. I wasn't sure when I first set it up, but that hail netting was the best investment I ever made on this farm."

"That's a relief." A bad hailstorm could wipe out our whole crop of stone fruit in one devastating afternoon.

Pop absently rubbed at his ring finger that no longer straightened all the way. "I take it Ty rethought his decision to shun your help."

I hesitated, my emotions in a tangle. Despite Ty's repeated words of thanks, I wasn't sure just how much he appreciated my continued presence on his ranch. "I guess so."

Pop's eyes were too keen on me, like he could see everything I hadn't said. "Ty's a good man. I don't have much to say on his brother, but Ty...I can respect a man like that."

"He's built a good reputation as a trainer." I knew that wasn't what Pop was getting at. *He's a good man.* He liked and respected Ty—that meant worlds to me. It wasn't true for everyone we knew, and certainly hadn't been true for Bret.

"That he has. June, sit down a minute with me, will you?" He gestured at the empty chair across from him.

I drew in a deep breath, shoring myself up. I did not want to have this conversation. He would finally come right out and ask what was going on between me and Ty, and what could I even say? If I didn't know what I felt or where I stood with Ty, I couldn't very well explain it all to my father. Even so, I sat down at the table as asked, nerves flaring up in my stomach like a teenager about to get the third degree about a high school crush.

"I, uh, I've got something to talk to you about." He fumbled over his words as if talking with me was new to him. He kept toying with his fingers, squeezing the tips and knuckles as though they were cold.

It took my muddied brain a minute to realize he was nervous.

Oh, no. He wouldn't try to talk to me about the birds and the bees, would he? I was twenty-nine years old, for goodness' sake. Of course, I'd just come home wearing Ty's clothes—maybe he thought a refresher conversation was in order.

"We don't really have to talk about this," I said in a rush. "Ty and I are just friends. I'm just helping him out while he recovers, that's all. There's nothing more going on between us. Just friends."

Pop looked at me like I'd tried to feed him the world's biggest lie. "I'll remember you said that, but that's not what I wanted to talk to you about."

"Oh." My father wasn't an idiot. We both knew what an unforced denial meant. At least he didn't want to talk about it.

Yet.

He cleared his throat and scraped a hand across the shiny scruff on his chin a few times, the sound like scratching sandpaper. He pulled his palm over his silver hair, smoothing it down.

"June, I've invited someone to join us for our family dinner tomorrow night."

"Oh." That information seemed...random.

"Marilyn Wells." He paused, waiting for some acknowledgement.

"Sure, Marilyn from Fine & Dandy. She brought you the pie."

"Yes," he said slowly. "That's the one."

He glanced up at me, and in that hesitation, the pieces clicked together.

"Oh. *Oh.*" If only I could manage to say something more useful in this conversation than *oh.*

"We've been seeing each other," he said, watching for my reaction. "Romantically."

"I gathered that."

His mouth pulled into something between a smile and a grimace. "I haven't been quite sure how to tell you."

My father was dating. This news swept through my mind, searching for something to hold onto. I couldn't rightly say it didn't make sense—a kind, decent man, whose good looks defied his sixty-five years, Pop would be a catch. And yet, he was my pop. Imagining him squiring anyone other than my mother around Magnolia Ridge just didn't seem right.

"How long have you two been...seeing each other?" The question felt all wrong in my mouth, like reading words from a language I didn't understand.

"A couple of months now."

I sucked in a breath, my thoughts slamming against a wall. "A couple of *months*? Do Wade and Jed know?"

"Yes." For a moment, he looked almost guilty, but his eyes sparked. "I didn't want to say anything to get you worried if it wasn't serious."

I guess I could understand that, but his confession only brought up a whole new set of questions. "So it *is* serious?"

He hesitated. I marveled at how much could be said in those little gaps of silence.

"I care about her. Very much."

A tiny, terrible part of me wanted to rail against him for forgetting my mother so easily. How could he move on after only two years? I knew how much he loved my mother, had seen that love play out in their everyday interactions my whole life through. And I had seen how losing her had gutted him.

176

Now, he was suddenly over that, ready to move on with Marilyn Wells, the pie-making home decor queen?

"I'm not asking for your okay, June. But I sure would like to have it."

I paused, torn. I couldn't give away my approval just like that, as if this wasn't a monumental adjustment, but I wouldn't rage like a little girl who hadn't gotten her way, either.

"I just want you to be happy."

His face lit up, and I knew he had feared the sort of sullen resentment that had crossed my mind. The sort of resentment that still felt like a very real possibility, even though I'd meant every one of those words.

"I *am* happy."

"Good." I forced a smile and reached across the table to hold his hand.

He squeezed my hand right back. "So. About Ty—"

I stood from the table. "I'm going to go take a shower. Running through the rainstorm doesn't count."

He didn't try to talk me out of my quick departure, but I saw the gleam in his eyes.

He knew he wasn't the only one keeping secrets.

june

AFTER FOUR MONTHS OF WAITING, the time had finally come to go full Maid of Honor.

I'd met my cousin and Aunt Darlene at Brides Galore, Magnolia Ridge's fancy bridal boutique, where Eden had reached a state of near-panic, one worry after another streaming from her mouth. With only a few days until the wedding, the calm façade she'd clung to was unraveling faster than I could stitch it back together.

"If there's anything wrong with the alterations, there won't be time to fix it. Five days isn't enough. What if it doesn't fit right? What am I supposed to do?"

"Here, drink this." I passed over a mug of chamomile tea I'd prepared in the boutique's lobby. I'd swiped my Pop's smallest bottle of bourbon before leaving the house and had administered a little to Eden's tea to take the edge off her nerves. She sniffed it and gave me the stink eye. Still sipped it, though.

"Of course there's time, that's why there's a final fitting. They wouldn't schedule it now if they couldn't handle it. Everything is going to be fine."

She ran her hand down one of the veils on display as though she hadn't heard me.

"She sounded strange when I gave my name." She nodded toward the receptionist who stood behind a small counter. "Maybe she knows something's wrong with the dress."

"What could possibly be wrong with the dress?" Aunt Darlene whispered like we were gossiping in the middle of church.

"I don't know," Eden whispered right back. "Maybe the seamstress never got around to the alterations. Maybe someone accidentally spilled something on it. Maybe a raccoon got in the storage room, how should I know?"

A raccoon? I fought the impulse to laugh at my sweet, pragmatic cousin as she crashed full speed into crazy town. Taking her free hand, I gave it a squeeze.

"Hey," I said, drawing her attention away from the organza and lace in front of her. "Everything's going to be perfect. Try to relax. Breathe."

She made a show of taking a deep breath, but the worry lines didn't leave her forehead.

"Would you still marry Booker even if your dress was a little too long or a little too tight? Even if a few flowers were out of place or the books were all mildewy?"

She looked startled at that terrible image, but a weak smile crossed her face. "Of course I would."

"There you go. Try to focus on that."

She nodded and seemed to take courage from the idea. "You're right, you're right. I'd marry him no matter what. I'm freaking out, aren't I?"

I exchanged a look with Aunt Darlene. "A bit."

"I can't help it." She ran a shaky hand across her forehead. "It's all happening so soon, you know?"

"We know," Aunt Darlene said.

179

From all I'd heard, my aunt and uncle had balked at the quick timeline of events, but Eden and Booker had held firm. They wanted their forever to start as soon as possible, and I couldn't blame them for that. But throwing a wedding together in just a few months wasn't for the faint of heart.

"Distract me." Eden sipped at her mug and winced. Maybe I'd poured a little more bourbon than I thought. "With more than just spiked tea, I mean. Are you still working over at Ty's? How's that going?"

I held up my palms. "No more blisters, so that's an improvement. I'm getting so good at mucking stalls, I think I'll add it to my resume."

"You can add *Before* and *After* pictures to your gallery wall."

I squeezed her hand again. "Genius."

"Has he let you ride a horse yet?"

"No, but I think I'm wearing him down."

She laughed, apparently amused at the idea of Ty Hardy being worn down by anybody. If only she knew. What was it about his stubborn refusal to ask for help that made me so determined to force-feed him that help?

His hardheaded attitude didn't intimidate me—it only brought out my own willfulness. At this point, I wasn't sure we were any closer to the truce that had first driven me out to his property.

Truth be told, that truce didn't have quite the same appeal it once had. I would far rather have our fiery disagreements than any bland *making nice* I'd once sought out.

"Eden Webb?" A young woman with long black braids came forward to greet us. "My name is Tara, I'll take you back now."

My skills with a pitchfork forgotten, Eden's face crumpled with worry again. The three of us followed Tara into a small room lined with plush chairs in muted colors, a massive mirror on one wall. The wall opposite had a changing screen in the corner, and a large silver garment bag hung on a hook. Aunt Darlene and I took our seats, but Eden hovered by the garment bag, wringing her hands. Her eyes followed every movement Tara made as she unzipped the bag and drew out the wedding dress.

Aunt Darlene and I gasped in wonder right on cue. Eden touched the silk with shaky fingers, looking on the verge of tears—happy ones, this time.

"Ready to try it on?" Tara asked.

She nodded and ducked behind the changing screen with the dress. Tara stood at the ready, waiting to help her into it as needed.

"You deserve all the Maid of Honor awards," Aunt Darlene whispered at my side. "I love her, but my girl's a wreck."

"It hasn't been so bad."

She gave me a shrewd look. My pop's younger sister, they shared the same perceptive gaze and skeptical mouth. "I know what she's like. It can't have been easy to pull this together for her in only a few months. I thought she would have been more comfortable planning it for next year, but they didn't want to wait."

I might have expected a longer courtship and engagement from my ever-practical cousin, but I didn't question their timing. "I guess when you know, you know."

Was it insane that my thoughts immediately went to Ty? Yes. Yes, it was insane. I tucked away that evidence of my own trip to crazy town.

"Oh, yes indeed. Madly in love, those two. Still would have been nice to have a little more time to throw this wedding together. She didn't have many declines on the RSVP list, so I guess I shouldn't complain about short notice."

The RSVP list sent my thoughts in a whole new direction. Had Pop invited Marilyn to the wedding? The question set an uncomfortable tension inside me, like a spring pulled taut, but I couldn't bring myself to ask my aunt if my own father had a plus-one. It seemed like something I should hear from him. Not that he'd been all that forthcoming with me so far.

I wondered how much his hesitation in telling me had to do with waiting to be sure he and Marilyn were serious, and how much had to do with his own guilt about moving on. Or did he feel any guilt at all? Was he really over my mother, just like that?

Eden stepped out from behind the privacy screen, and I sucked in a breath. Her A-line dress had a tulle overlay with delicate appliqué at the waist that made her look like a Greek goddess. She moved forward, stepping onto the small platform set in front of the huge mirror, her eyes glistening with tears.

"Oh, honey." Aunt Darlene stood to help smooth out her veil as she looked her over. "You're gorgeous."

"The dress is absolutely perfect," I said.

Tara pulled lightly along the dress's hem and traced fingers along Eden's sides, indicating the alterations, but Eden was too far gone to pay much attention.

"I'll give you a moment." Tara slipped from the room.

"It's really happening," Eden whispered to her reflection in the mirror. "I really get to marry Booker."

"In a few short days," Aunt Darlene confirmed. She moved so they appeared side by side in the mirror and rested her head on Eden's shoulder. "I want you to know how proud I am of the woman you've become. Your father and I are thrilled beyond words to see you so in love with Booker, and ready to build your lives together. We couldn't have raised a better woman, or asked for her to find a better man."

My aunt's sweet words needled at me until I couldn't breathe, my lungs stopped up tight.

"Thank you for everything you do for me, Mom." Eden

swiped at her tears to keep them from falling on the dress. "I love you."

"I love you, too, honey."

I tried to swallow down the lump in my throat, but it refused to budge.

"I think I forgot something in my car." I bolted across the room and slipped out the door, didn't stop walking until I reached the parking lot, taking deep gulps of air to fight the sudden sense of suffocation.

My vision swam with waiting tears, my heart pinching and squeezing in my chest. I longed to hear those words from my own mother, to see the pride and love in her eyes as I prepared for my wedding day. But that was gone forever. Unfair to have lost her so soon, so suddenly. Childish to think it, but that was the only thought stuck in my head. *Unfair.*

I fought the tide of tears, willing myself to keep it together. I couldn't let Eden find me bawling by my car, wishing for my mother.

But I couldn't help wishing for her. I still missed her with a fierce longing that left me aching inside, hollowed out by grief. Her memory was so fresh in my mind and heart, it burned. How had my father moved on so easily? And how was I supposed to pretend I was okay with it?

After a few minutes, Aunt Darlene walked out of the bridal shop and across the parking lot. I was readying an excuse, but she didn't give me a chance to use it. She held her arms out wide.

"Come here, baby girl."

I let myself sag into my aunt's embrace. The threat of tears eased away, but I couldn't shake my sorrow for all I'd lost.

"Your Mama loved you so much." She pulled back to hold my face in her hands. Steel blue eyes exactly like my father's stared into mine. "It's a crime she's gone. I know you miss her something awful. But you still have folks who love you, family who would do anything for you. Don't ever forget that."

I nodded, searching for the strength to speak. "I won't."

"We're here for you no matter what. Always."

My aunt's reassurances couldn't erase my mother's loss, but they reminded me I wasn't alone. For now, that was enough.

* * *

By the time I pulled onto Victory Ranch that afternoon, the horses were already out to pasture, enjoying a cooling breeze. The previous day's summer storm had blown away, leaving only patches of drying mud behind. Aaron worked one of the younger colts in the round pen, but the rest of the horses stretched their legs in freedom.

I went straight to the barn, where Ty sat on a low bench watching Aaron's progress. Finally, he was taking a break for a change, instead of stalking around the ranch like a wounded animal on a mission to make his injury worse. As if sensing my approval, he stood as soon as he noticed me.

"June." He sounded as though I'd caught him doing something shameful instead of just sitting down. "Good to see you."

He wore an indigo button-down rolled at the sleeves, his ever-present Stetson shading his eyes. Why did just being around Ty have to make my legs go all wobbly and my mind come screeching to a halt? All I could think about was how his rolled shirt sleeves showed off his forearms and the sinewy muscles exposed there. His dark gaze was all kinds of wonderful. I had the crazy impulse to kiss the man hello.

He looked me over a little more pointedly. "Are you okay?"

"Sure." I shook off my ogling and tried to pull my senses together. "Why?"

"You seem out of sorts."

My emotions were a spaghetti mess over that kiss I obviously hadn't managed to forget, and the growing tenderness I felt for this man who as good as said he didn't/wouldn't/couldn't feel the same. I supposed that probably qualified as out of sorts. Throw in the waves of grief that had tried to drown me at Eden's dress fitting, and I could use a little bourbon-spiked tea myself.

"I guess I'm just thinking about a conversation I had with Pop," I said, tugging on a pair of rubber boots. The truth, even if it wasn't the only source of my distress. Thoughts of Pop and Marilyn elbowed in between thoughts of Ty, giving me even more reasons to fret. I grabbed the wheelbarrow and pitchfork and started mucking the first stall while Ty looked on. "He's dating someone, if you can believe it."

I couldn't believe it yet. Dating didn't seem the right word for people in their sixties. The idea conjured images of my father and Marilyn Wells sharing polite but formal meetings over coffee, neither quite knowing what to say. Long walks where she lightly held his arm and they talked about retirement plans. Pop on Marilyn's doorstep with a corsage. Adorable and disconcerting both at once.

Ty nodded. "Yeah, I suppose he is."

I stopped mid-scoop. "Wait. Did you know he's seeing Marilyn Wells? Did he tell you?"

Guilt twitched across his face and he seemed to rethink his original answer. "I've seen them together around town and put two and two together."

"You saw them a lot?"

Now he looked like he didn't want to answer at all. "A few times."

Ty wasn't a gossipy man. If he had come to the conclusion my father and Marilyn were an item, they were doing more than talking shyly over coffee or taking chaste walks in the park. Had he seen them holding hands? Snuggling? Kissing?

My stomach rolled at the image. I wasn't a child. As much as I missed my mother, I could handle my father having a *lady friend*. Probably. Maybe? I'd never had to deal with it before—how could I know?

"Why don't people tell me things?" I said half to myself, going back to mucking out the stall. "Wade and Jed knew for months, and they never said a word."

Jed's knowing glances and odd requests for dinner guests made sense now in light of Pop's revelation. He'd been trying to nudge our father into confessing about his love life, but he hadn't bothered to tell me directly. It was Pop's secret, I supposed, but still. Jed might have told me.

"I was in college when my old dog Buster died, and Mom and Pop didn't call me for almost a week." I put my frustrations into every movement of the pitchfork, mucking the first stall in record time. "When Mom got her diagnosis, they didn't tell me for three days. When Bret—" I paused, letting a scoop of manure hit the wheelbarrow with a significant thump. "Well, you can guess what *he* didn't tell me. Why don't people just tell me things?"

When Ty didn't answer, I moved out of the stall to look at him. I thought maybe I'd rambled on too long until he lost interest, but instead of finding irritation in his eyes, his expression reflected pure tenderness.

"Maybe they just don't want to hurt you," he finally said.

"Still not a great reason to keep secrets."

"You've got a big heart. Who would want to trample that?"

Maybe that was what it boiled down to. I did have a habit of seeing the emotional side of things, as my father and brothers had pointed out a million times. I'd practically hyperventilated in Brides Galore's parking lot earlier just from seeing Eden and

Aunt Darlene share a sweet moment. That might have proved Ty's point, but it didn't make being left in the dark any easier to take.

"Are they protecting me, or protecting themselves?"

Ty flinched like I'd brandished the pitchfork at him. He slipped out of the barn, and I went back to mucking. He wasn't a gossipy man, I reminded myself. He probably didn't have much interest in listening to me vent my frustrations over family secrets. Still. He didn't have to bolt at the first sign of serious talk.

That was Bret all over again. A pro at meaningless conversation disguised as heart-to-hearts. Did it really matter what someone's favorite movie or color was if you didn't care about their actual *life*? Ty wasn't chatty with small talk like Bret, at least, but he didn't often invite deeper discussions, either.

Those times he did, though—*oof*. I could get used to him opening up a little, like when we talked about him growing up on the ranch, or our conversation about my mom. But expecting confidences from a man like Ty would be a recipe for heartache.

Pretty sure I was already mid-recipe.

The time it took me to muck stalls had improved since that first miserable day, and I managed the whole dozen in just under two hours. Each one was cleaned, sifted, and laid with fresh bedding by the time Ty returned to check my progress.

"Not bad," he said with a nod as he passed the first few open stall doors. "You've really taken a shine to this."

"You don't have to sound so surprised." Frankly, it surprised me, too, but the lilt of amazement in his voice when he offered such praise made it feel like my every achievement amounted to an unexpected event.

"I wasn't kidding when I said I thought you'd be long gone by now. Most would."

"I guess I'm not like most."

His mouth curled into a slight smile. "No, you are not."

I would take that as a compliment. Our silence stretched on, each apparently waiting for the other to say something more. When we didn't, I was left gazing into his eyes, basking in their golden glow.

"Should I get the feed started?" I blurted. Talking about the horses was much easier than talking about anything else running through my mind.

"They'll take their meals out in the pasture. No need to feed and water tonight."

"Is that it, then?" I stretched my arms to work the kinks out of my shoulders. I might not mind doing the work, but I'd discovered all sorts of new aches in places I was sure had never hurt a day in my life. Not to mention all the fun new smells. I didn't mind the definition in my arms, though.

"It's a different schedule when they're out all night."

We walked to the pasture fence and looked out across the fields. The horses wandered, grazing lazily in the fading heat. It would have been a more pleasant sight if I weren't already tired to the bone.

"I guess it's lucky we're done early," I said. "I should leave soon to get ready for my family dinner, anyway."

Ty glanced from the pastures to me, the arch of his eyebrows silently asking for more information.

"Wade and his crazies are coming over," I explained. "My nephews, I mean. *Marilyn* will be there. It's going to be so many levels of awkward, you have no idea."

"Yeah. About that." He tried to clear his throat, but the sound got strangled somewhere in his chest. "I think I should tell you, your dad called and invited me to your family dinner tonight."

Of course he did.

TWENTY-TWO

june

I HAD JUST enough time to speed-shower and change clothes before the squealing started. The boys' shrieks echoed up the stairs and straight into my eardrums. Before I made it halfway down the stairs, Dylan and Beau attacked me in an energetic cuddle of little hands and arms that threatened to pull us all down in a heap.

"Auntie June!" Dylan shrieked up at me. "Do you want to play chase? You can be it!"

"We're gonna chase you!" Beau gave me a slobbery, sticky hug.

Five and three years old, Wade's little boys didn't have a slow speed that I had ever seen, and they always tried to suck me into a game of their own invention. These tended to include a combination of tag, hide and seek, and someone getting thumped on the head for mysterious reasons. Usually, the thumped head was mine.

I hugged them back hard. They were a handful, but I never quite got enough of them during my short visits. "How about after dinner?"

They took my answer as a promise and tore back down the

stairs and into the yard. Hopefully, I could hold off whatever destruction they had in mind until after the Queen Mother of all awkward family dinners.

I leaned against the stair rail, wishing I could pause time. I wanted to believe my pop's intentions had been pure when he invited Ty to join us for dinner, but I suspected he was trying to throw some of the attention off his lady friend.

Marilyn.

Anxiety and a newfound spite curled through me but dissolved again when Wade's wife, Annie, walked through the front door.

"Annie, you are absolutely—"

She raised a hand. "Don't say it, I know. I'm massive. I'm about to pop. I look like I swallowed a watermelon. I've heard it all."

I gave my sister-in-law a hug from the side. Annie's pregnant belly stood out front and center these days, but that's not what I noticed first. "I was going to say you're glowing."

Her mouth twisted like I was trying to sell her something.

"It's true. When I saw you a couple of months ago, you were still a little green."

"I'm glad that's over, I guess. Now everybody thinks they can tell me how big I am, like the pregnant woman doesn't know she's monstrous."

"You're not monstrous." My oldest brother, Wade, walked in the house carrying two bags I assumed were filled with a combination of diapers, extra clothes, and toys. "You are a glorious vision. Anybody who says different can come see me, and I'll set them straight."

He set the bags down, wrapped his arms around his wife, and gave her a luxurious kiss.

"You've never looked better to me," he murmured. She smiled up at him, thoroughly consoled.

I found their loving display equal parts adorable and sickening. Nine years married and they still looked at each other like infatuated newlyweds. Their relationship set a little ache of longing in my heart, even if I'd never admit it to my brother.

Wade turned to me and gave me a quick hug, patting my back too hard. "How have you been, Junebug? I heard you took a job as a hand on Hardy's ranch."

I rolled my eyes. Jed would go blabbing around to Wade. Apparently, I was the only one left out of the family loop. Of course, I was the only one living forty miles away in Austin. "Not quite."

"But you have been doing work for him, have I got that right?"

I hesitated, knowing how this would go. My brothers weren't overly protective of me, but they always had their radar up for anything that might prove embarrassing. The more embarrassment they could heap on, the better. "It's a long story."

Jed wandered into the living room like he'd been waiting around for his cue. "Ty got kicked by one of his horses, and June's been trying to stop him from working himself into the grave ever since."

I would sprain my eyeballs from rolling them so much tonight. "I guess it's a short story."

"You already dated one of the Hardys," Wade said. "After how that ended, I'm surprised you'd want to date the other one."

I laughed off his little joke, even though it stung for all the poor judgment it implied.

Annie smacked him on the shoulder, but he didn't seem to understand why.

"What? Someone had to say it."

This whole dinner would be one long exercise in trying to

shut my brothers up. "Ty and I aren't dating. We're just friends."

Wade gave me his Oldest Brother Knows Best smile, all smug condescension. "Yeah, so were Annie and I." He rubbed her big belly to hammer his point home.

"It's not like that." Frankly, I didn't know what it was like, but denial seemed the best course of action if he was going to go around throwing baby bellies in my face.

"But Ty *is* coming to dinner tonight," Jed said with a grin.

Wade gave me another smug look. Christmas had come early for my brothers.

"Pop invited him."

"I wonder why Pop would go and do that." Wade put a finger on his chin, miming deep thought.

"Maybe to take some of the heat off his lady friend y'all never told me about?"

"Sure, that tracks. So Ty's just an ordinary neighbor, and this dinner isn't significant for you personally in any way?"

I sputtered and stammered over a smart-alec response that wouldn't come while Wade grinned like I'd handed him a written confession complete with sordid details.

"I'm going to check on dinner."

"I'll help you." Annie gave Wade a parting glare, but his knowing grin never wavered.

There wasn't much for me to do in the kitchen besides escape. Jed and Pop had the barbecue out back going with ribs and chicken breasts on, and I'd made up a potato salad and coleslaw earlier in the day. A pot of water boiled away on the stove, ready for the pyramid of fresh corn waiting in the wings. I plucked stray silks off the cobs to keep up the pretense of checking on dinner. Not that it mattered. My brothers knew how to get my goat whichever room I was in.

Annie lowered herself onto a dining chair and glanced me over. "Are you ready for tonight?"

"As ready as I'm going to be. I might empty Dad's liquor cabinet after everything's over, though. I can't believe he invited Ty."

Her eyebrows twitched. "I was talking about having Marilyn over."

"Oh. Right." Another unforced error. I was getting good at them. "That's going to be weird, too."

"Your dad's seemed happier these last few months. That's got to count for something."

It did count. I was just having a hard time reconciling that with my own happiness on the subject.

"It is *interesting* your dad invited Ty," Annie said, a tiny smirk on her mouth.

"He probably feels bad about Ty being injured." Awfully late to try for nonchalance, but I gave it a go anyway.

"Hmm," Annie mused aloud. "That's not what your blush in the living room said."

"When did I blush?"

"As soon as Wade mentioned Ty."

My cheeks heated all over again. I couldn't find the right words to try to explain away something I wasn't sure I *wanted* to explain away. Easy enough to keep up a flimsy façade with my brothers—I'd had enough practice growing up—but I trusted Annie not to crow about my would-be love life. If I could even call it that.

"Things are...awkward between us."

Her smirk turned sly. "How awkward?"

The half-shrug I gave must have said more than I intended. Her mouth dropped open, and she leaned both elbows on the table. "Are we talking kissing? More? He can't be doing much

193

more with broken ribs. I mean, maybe, if he kept perfectly still, but how much fun would that be?"

I waved at the air in front of me with a frantic glance toward the living room. "Keep it down. Wade and Jed can't know a thing."

That they suspected was bad enough. If they had any actual facts, it'd all be over for me.

She flicked her eyes toward the living room but didn't abandon the conversation. "So, which is it? Kissing? Or more?"

"Kissing. One kiss," I clarified. "But it was…"

Just thinking about that kiss made my lips ache for him to do it all over again.

"Oh, wow," Annie sighed. "This *is* going to be an interesting night."

The doorbell rang. A spark of excitement flashed to life in my chest, and my neck went strangely hot. My pop and Marilyn wouldn't ring the bell. It could only be Ty.

Annie waved me toward the living room. "I'll finish up. You'll want to get to the door before your brothers do."

I mouthed *thank you* and darted out of the kitchen, but too late. Jed had the door thrown open wide for Ty, welcoming him inside.

"Good to see you, Ty," Jed said as he offered his hand.

Ty shook it. "Thanks for inviting me."

His gaze darted to me, and a thrill burned through my chest. Had eye contact always made me this…flammable?

Or was that just now? He gave me a nod and turned his attention back to Jed. "Your father knows I haven't been up for much by way of cooking lately."

Jed scratched his stubbly chin. "Really? I thought some pious lady over at the church was bringing you meals."

Holy crap, I would have to murder my brother when this was over.

Ty held Jed's gaze. I could have kissed him for not giving me away. Also, I could have just kissed him.

"I haven't been contacted, no," he said.

"Well, we've got plenty to go around." A slow smile played across Jed's face, and I dreaded whatever he was about to say. Maybe he would be generous and get this all out of his system in one go, but no telling with him. "I have to ask—is June really mucking out horse stalls for you?"

"She is."

I could almost believe a glimmer of pride had shone in Ty's eyes, but it might have been a trick of the light. I hadn't expected a fountain of praise, but a two-word answer knocked my ego down a peg. I'd worked my butt off out there, and all he had to say was, *She is?*

"Any chance I could stop by and take a few pictures of her mid-shovel? For posterity's sake?"

"You take pictures, and you won't have any posterity to worry about," I warned.

Jed grinned at me. "I'm just saying it would be a sight to see. I'd pay good money for a picture of my baby sister knee-deep in manure."

"Probably best if you don't," Ty said.

Thank the Lord. At least I had Ty on my side.

"It might startle the horses." He cut a look to me. "We wouldn't want that now, would we, June?"

I narrowed my gaze at him. Great. I had three of them to deal with tonight.

Dylan and Beau ran through the front door, granting me a brief reprieve from this first round of embarrassments. The two boys barely paid attention to the adults as they tore into the front bathroom and turned the sink on full blast. Wade trailed inside after them, having apparently fallen behind in their game of chase.

"Ty," he said, straightening up. "I hear you're desperate for ranch hands these days."

Lord, this night was shaping up to be the worst.

Thankfully, our pop arrived, cutting off the second round of "Let's Embarrass June." He had one hand on Marilyn's waist as he ushered her through the door, protecting her from his children while propelling her toward us.

Anxiety burst to life again in my stomach, quenching whatever appetite I'd had. I'd known Marilyn my whole life, had had dozens of perfectly normal conversations with her at Fine & Dandy, but this evening sat somewhere just shy of perfectly normal.

Ty gave me the tiniest smile, and warmth threaded through me. Strange how the barest twitching of his mouth could bolster my mood as I faced a fear I'd never thought to imagine before.

Wade, Jed, and I lined up in front of Marilyn Wells like the Von Trapp children ready for inspection. Her eyes shone with friendly enthusiasm as she went through her round of hellos, accompanied by my pop's eager introductions. She had only a shimmer of grays in her long, dark hair compared to Pop, who had more salt in his pepper these days. They both looked happy enough, and I tried to remind myself that was the main thing.

"June," Marilyn said when she turned to me. "It's so good to see you again."

"It's good to see you, too." I heard the stiffness in my voice but couldn't manage to sound more casual when meeting her as my pop's lady friend for the first time. Easy conversation about home decor trends in central Texas was nothing compared to this.

After saying hello to Annie, Marilyn looked to Ty. She didn't seem surprised he'd been included in the big family dinner. I guessed Pop had filled her in on everything before they turned up. At least somebody got a little advance warning around here.

Ty stepped forward with an outstretched hand. "Nice to see you, Mrs. Wells."

"I'm glad you could join us tonight," she said. "Clint told me about your injury. Such a shame, what with your record and all."

"It was bound to happen one day." He kept his tone light, but his jaw tensed. He viewed people's ongoing concern as one more reminder that he wasn't what he should be, and that ate at him.

"Nobody's invincible," I said.

Ty met my eyes, and I bobbed my eyebrows, an unspoken *Not even you*. He subdued a smile in return. Happiness circled through me and threatened to splash itself across my face in a moony grin.

Nope. No sense doing that in front of my family. Tonight would be full of enough awkward displays.

"Should we round up the boys?" Pop asked, pushing through our little group. "Jed, why don't you plate up the meat?"

In the hustle and bustle of getting all the food on the table and the chairs situated around it, the tight knot of nerves in my stomach uncurled. This was just a normal family dinner. A normal family dinner with my father's new girlfriend, and my new...*something*. No label I tried on Ty fit quite right.

"I hope we don't have any disasters of the Dylan or Beau nature like we did last time." Pop aimed a steely gaze at each of his grandsons. His attempt to intimidate them completely fell apart when he tousled their hair as he walked past.

"Do you happen to have a tarp I could lay down under their chairs?" Wade asked.

"Anything they throw, you'll be picking up."

197

"You heard Grandpop, boys," Wade said to his sons. "Be on your best behavior."

The messy, mischievous grins the boys beamed up at him didn't have anyone convinced they would.

We took our seats, and Pop said a brief word of grace. Then it was a free for all, as platters were passed and food dished up. The spicy scent of the barbecue had my mouth watering before the plate ever reached me, and I tucked in with the appetite I'd stored up all week with every shovel and scoop on Ty's ranch.

The table buzzed with light conversation mostly related to the delicious food, praise for those who'd prepared it, and gentle reminders that Dylan had a fork he should use. Strange that a gathering topped with an ample helping of awkward tension could feel so like home. My sad little dinners for one in Austin couldn't compare.

For a while, nobody said anything more pressing than "pass the corn", but from the way my brothers and I snuck glances at each other, we were all searching for something nice and neutral to say. They'd forgotten their delight in my awkward situation, and we were all on the same team again, rallying to support each other in this unknown territory.

Strike that. Jed hadn't forgotten about my awkward situation. His sly looks across the table at Ty and me didn't give me much hope he wouldn't embarrass me tonight. Before he could grill Ty over who knew what, I took matters into my own hands.

"How is your store doing, Marilyn?" I phrased the question as though asking after a sick pet, but at least it was something.

"We're doing very well, thank you, June. You should drop by, I'll show you the latest inventory."

She shared a quick glance with Pop. He winked at her, and I had the feeling they were in on something.

Well, obviously they were.

"I'll do that." I usually stopped by when in town, but it would be hard to browse throw pillows and wood-burned cutting boards now, with my pop and Marilyn on my mind.

"What was that award the store won?" Pop asked between bites. "Best Home Doodads, or something like that?"

"It isn't really an award," Marilyn said with a modest laugh. "We were voted Favorite Stop for Home Decor by the local paper. There wasn't much competition."

"Paper doesn't lie. Magnolia Ridge loves Fine & Dandy."

The words *Magnolia Ridge loves Fine & Dandy* sounded so bizarre coming from my father's mouth, I almost laughed. Apparently, he had become something of an expert on home decor stores in the last few months. The affectionate look Marilyn gave him said his praise, however strange for me to hear, was well-received.

Watching my father make eyes with a woman who wasn't my mother turned my stomach a little. As much as I wanted to be happy for him, a furious ache overtook me. Mom had only been gone a little over two years. Wasn't it too early for this... whatever this was? Dating?

I wasn't in charge of his life, but he had never even hinted at being ready to date again, let alone that he had a woman in mind. The fact that he hadn't told me because he thought I couldn't handle it only intensified the twist in my gut. I fixed my eyes on my plate, forking the same clump of coleslaw again and again on the tines.

Ty nudged me with his elbow. I shifted away and shot a sideways glare at him, but it faded in the utter tenderness of his look. It was like he read all the turmoil raging in my heart, and wanted to pull me out of that funk. Once again, knowing I had him in my corner shored me up against the waves of longing I'd let drag me down. Maybe I didn't feel any better about my father dating, but I wouldn't mope about it in front of everyone, either.

"Wade," Marilyn said slowly, as if testing the waters. "You must be excited to add to your little family shortly."

"We are." Wade looked at Annie with enough affection in his eyes to get her pregnant all over again.

"Show off," I said under my breath. He shot me a wicked grin, the bliss of the happily entangled.

"Do you know if it's a boy or a girl?" Marilyn asked.

"We want to be surprised," Annie said. "I'm hoping for a girl, but I'll be happy either way."

The last part was just talk. Annie wanted a girl in the worst way—not a thing most mothers-to-be were willing to admit.

"She wants a little more femininity," he said. "Our house is mostly football games and armpit noises." Dylan put one hand up his shirt to demonstrate, but Wade stopped him. "Not at the dinner table, little buddy."

"I've only got granddaughters," Marilyn said. "And they have their share of that, too. It's always what you least want them to do that's the most interesting, isn't it?"

"What's the point if it isn't forbidden?" Pop asked.

Every time I visited, Dylan and Beau entertained me with an alarming assortment of rude noises that resulted in squeals of delight from each other and a faint queasiness in me. A wonder Annie didn't mainline Tylenol against the headache of nonstop raspberry sounds.

"Jed," Marilyn said after a few minutes. "How are you adjusting to life back home?"

A standard question for a somewhat recently returned vet, but something in either her sincerity or the situation must have affected him. He didn't spout off a cheeky response like he usually did, anyway. "I'm getting there."

His answer was more than he normally allowed himself to

admit. After twelve years in and out of a war zone, he had seen and done things I would never dare ask him about, and he'd never offered to tell me. I knew he was happy to be home, but he had such a fun-loving attitude most days, I was ashamed to admit I didn't often think about what he was home *from*.

"Now, all you need is to find a good woman and settle down," Pop said.

Jed's smile lit up his whole face. "And ruin my streak of bad women?"

Pop shook his head, glancing significantly from him to Marilyn. She laughed, though, spoiling the reprimand.

"You'll find her when you least expect to," she told Jed. "They always do."

"Then I guess she should show up any minute now." He looked over his shoulder like the devil himself was about to walk through the door, bride in tow.

"So, June," Marilyn said as if contractually required to speak to each of us in turn. "I understand you've been helping Ty out around his ranch."

I looked sideways at Ty. Was he as tired of the same line of conversation as I was? Whatever he thought about the question didn't show in his face. He chewed his dinner like he was just trying to make it through the night.

"I've been doing what little I can. I don't know much about horses."

"I'm sure it's appreciated."

Ty recognized his cue to speak up. "She's been a big help. She might not have the experience, but she's got plenty of enthusiasm."

Jed stifled a laugh. If I'd been nearer to him, I would have aimed a sharp kick to his shin. I made a mental note to deliver the kick later.

"You never had horses out here, then?" Marilyn asked Pop.

"Never saw the need. Although that didn't stop this one from begging for one every day from when she was seven until seventeen." He hooked a thumb at me. "'We can use them in the orchards', she said. 'They'll pay for themselves,' she said."

"My methods would have worked," I told him.

Ty turned to me. "What methods?"

"I had grand schemes of riding my horse through the peach trees, picking fruit as I went."

His mouth curled into a smile. "Innovative."

"It would have saved us *hundreds* on ladders."

"This must be living your dream, then," Marilyn said to me. "Being out there on a horse ranch every day."

I wasn't sure I would call shoveling manure *living the dream*, but I couldn't quite argue the point. My days were long and hard, but satisfying in a way I couldn't explain, and didn't really want to discuss in front of present company. "Doesn't every little girl dream about riding horses?"

"Oh, I know my oldest granddaughter does. Marnie is six, and she tells me every chance she gets that she'll just be absolutely distraught if her Daddy doesn't put in a horse pen for her. They've barely got room for a dog house let alone a horse and barn, but you know how kids are."

"See, we *did* have room," I said to Pop. "But you still never got me that horse."

"Guess you'll just have to get your own."

His eyes twinkled at me in a silent dare. I'd expected teasing from Jed and Wade, but not from him. I couldn't bear to look at Ty after an opening like that. Jed would wind up with a hernia from all his stifled laughter.

"Marnie's had salt poured in her wounds," Marilyn went on. "Her Daisies Girl Scout troop was supposed to earn their Horse Fun badge last weekend, but the whole event was canceled. I guess they had a bad bout of food poisoning over at Sunshine

Ranch, and half the employees fell sick. They're booked out the rest of the summer, and had to refund the girls' entrance fees, fifty dollars each. Marnie's whole troop is just devastated."

A glimmer of a thought formed in my mind. I turned to Ty, who met my gaze with a wary expression.

"We could host it," I said to him. "We could help Marnie's Girl Scout troop earn their Horse Fun badges."

TWENTY-THREE

I HOPED my hearing had broken right along with my ribs. "What's this *we*?"

"We could." June buzzed like a current of electricity ran through her. "It's just a couple of hours teaching them the basics of horses, saddles, mucking, you know."

I did know. I'd had the whole thing described to me in detail when a neighbor down the lane asked me to consider hosting *her* Girl Scout troop last year. I'd politely but firmly declined. Plenty of other ranches around Magnolia Ridge dedicated their summers to that sort of thing, and I hadn't felt a lick of guilt about turning my neighbor down. Getting ambushed over dinner was a whole different story.

"Don't forget a ride at the end," Marilyn said.

"That's right." Delight practically streamed from June's eyeballs. "That's the best part."

I hated to crush that delight, but I had no intention of getting roped into this scheme. "It's not a good idea."

"Why not? Miss Kitty or Bonanza would make great models for the girls to practice brushing and riding. They'd love it."

I wasn't sure if she meant the girls or the horses. She was

probably right either way, but that wasn't remotely the point. "June, no."

"You're not doing anything else out there right now. What's the big deal?"

Like I needed the reminder I was completely useless. My gaze hardened on her, but I kept my cool, well aware of our audience's rapt attention on this asinine conversation. "The big deal is, I'm not running a riding ranch, June. I'm not equipped to handle ten little girls out there."

"Fifteen," Marilyn said.

"Fifteen," I repeated as though that should settle just how wrong this idea was. I could just imagine the barn overrun with girls in pigtails touching every sharp thing they could find and getting themselves into all sorts of inventive calamities. Not going to happen.

"It's only a two-hour visit for the Daisies, they're so young," Marilyn said. "But they'd be thrilled at the chance to see your horses up close."

"I'm sorry, Marilyn, but it's just not—"

"We'll do it," June said. "Have your daughter call me, and we'll work out a time."

Marilyn's mouth dropped open into an 'o' of delight, but when she looked at me, it closed again. "Oh—why don't I let you two discuss it a bit more before we make any decisions?"

June finally turned to me, and I must have looked as furious as I felt. Her smile fell, the buzz radiating from her extinguished. I set my napkin next to my plate, every sound in the room amplified by the awkward silence that had eaten up the table. The other men avoided my eye, unable to look at me after that public castration.

"Can I have a word? Outside?"

She gave a curt nod and flashed a weak smile. I followed her through the kitchen and out onto the back porch. Clint said, "Shall we clear away the table?" as I closed the door behind us.

We stood a moment on the porch, fireflies buzzing in the deepening twilight. I stared down at her, burning with the frustration I had just managed to keep in check while she walked all over me at the dinner table. "Are you out of your mind?"

She lifted her chin higher. "I think it's a good idea."

"You don't much care that I think it's a bad one. It's my ranch, June. You don't get a say."

"I know it's your ranch," she said like it should have been obvious. "This could be really good for you. You just don't want to see it."

"How could it be good for me? I'm all ears."

"It might make up for some of the losses you've had this week, for one."

How desperate did she think I was? "I don't need the cash."

"You're richer than I am, then." She crossed her arms over her chest, and she might as well have dug her heels in the dirt. "I'd like to make seven hundred fifty dollars for two hours of work. And I was never talking about your monetary losses."

"Then what?"

"Your training clients, of course."

For the life of me, I couldn't follow her logic. "You think showing a bunch of kids their way around an old mare is going to get me new business?"

"You said your job is all about word of mouth. You would realize this is good PR if you would just stop to think."

She raised a hand like she was about to poke me in the chest. I tensed, waiting for the pain to shear through me, but she dropped her hand at the last second.

"I've thought of your grandmother fondly my whole life after being out there with her a few Saturdays. You think those kids won't do the same? Word will get around. It's advertising they're paying you for, Ty."

I raked my fingers through my hair, ignoring the tug of pain the movement caused. She had a point, dammit, but that didn't change my feelings. "That's not the kind of reputation I'm trying to build, June."

Her expression brightened at the slight concession. "I know. Your reputation is all about being the Unbreakable Ty Hardy, the man who can tame any horse. You don't have to be steel all the time. Maybe people need to know you're approachable, too."

Great. After all this, she thought I needed personality lessons, too. "I'm approachable. Who thinks I'm not approachable?"

She waved a hand in the air. "Everybody."

I stared harder at her.

"*I* thought you were unapproachable. You're not the easiest man to talk to, you know." Her confidence faltered, giving way to something like shyness. Maybe even tenderness. I really did that to her? In the next minute, she shook it all off. "The point is, this would get your name out there."

"As a Girl Scout host, which I have no intention of ever being."

"Oh," she said, her tone oddly clipped. "I get it now. This is beneath you."

"I didn't say that." I'd sure been thinking it, though.

"Is it because they're kids, or because they're girls?"

Frustration flashed through me all over again. "You really think I'm that old-fashioned that I care they're girls? This is beneath me because this isn't what I do, and never was. I train horses to work, that's it. I don't give pony rides."

"That still sounds like it has something to do with them being children."

I exhaled a ragged sigh. Arguing with her drove me nuts, not least because of all the ways she found to ding me. "It is a little, okay? I'm no good with kids."

I regretted it as soon as I'd said it. A slight smile touched her lips—because of course, she would find that amusing. "I'm sure that's not true."

"You're sure of a lot of things lately."

"Why do you think you're not good with kids?"

Lord, I hated how soft her voice had gone, how sweet and understanding, like she could solve all my problems if I would just give her half a chance.

"I don't have the kind of patience that would make a person good with kids."

"You do realize you train horses for a living, right? I'm pretty sure that takes patience."

"From what I've been told, horses and kids are very different creatures."

I could see her thoughts shifting gears.

"So you don't want kids of your own?"

If I were completely honest, I didn't rightly know. I liked kids in a general sense, but specifics? I'd never been close enough with a woman to consider the question of wanting kids of my own as anything other than a hypothetical. If I had one, specific woman to map out a future with, maybe then. With the right woman, a kid or two might not be a bad idea.

The picture of June and me with two little babies in our arms flashed in my mind.

I blinked down at her. Now see, this was the problem in talking with June. She got me thinking all kinds of insanity that ordinarily would never enter my head.

"I think we're getting off track here."

She straightened, seeming to put away all the questions that had been swirling just behind her eyes. "Okay, then, so you don't want free advertising because your *reputation* and your website are bringing in all the work you need."

I shifted, tensing my jaw. She looked to the heavens.

"Good Lord, Ty, you don't even have a website? Here you are, completely relying on word of mouth to get you business, and you're turning away an opportunity to spread that word? You think those Girl Scouts don't have parents and grandparents with ranches that need work horses? Because I guarantee you some of them do."

I opened my mouth to argue but had to shut it again.

"Right. Well, I think I've made a very convincing argument that we should do the Girl Scouts thing."

"There is no *we*. After the wedding, you're gone."

That little reminder seemed to still the air around us. A few more days, and June would be out of Magnolia Ridge, back to Austin, where her real life waited. A sick feeling grew in the pit of my stomach, and I hated myself for it. I'd known from the beginning her life wasn't here, that she wasn't staying. I was never supposed to let myself fall this hard.

"There might be time to do it before I leave," she said softly. "And if the troop can only do it on a weekend, well, I'll just have to come back then. It's only a forty-minute drive. That's a normal commute for some people."

No part of that reassured me, for reasons I didn't want to deal with just now.

"Come on."

She stepped closer, placing one hand on my forearm. Her soft touch pulsed through me, and I had to slow my breathing before my body got ideas of its own. Her eyes seemed huge in the evening light, sparkling with an earnestness that spoke to every tender part of me I wanted to ignore.

"It's going to be fun, it's going to make fifteen little girls happy, and it will all be over in two hours."

I laughed until my breath burned. "You just want to relive those glory days with Gram."

"I really, really do." She squeezed my arm, a silent plea.

I sighed as much as I could when every breath cut short. "You're going to be doing all of the work."

"I'd guessed."

"The instruction, the demos, the pony rides—this is your show, not mine."

She held her head higher. "I can handle it."

I glared down at her, but she must have recognized she had won the war. She twisted her lips, holding back a smile. I'd be a fool if I did this, an absolute fool.

"Fine," I said, and the grin she'd been keeping at bay spread across her face.

My heart seemed to swell up inside my chest, knowing I was the cause of her joy. It made me want to let her call the shots for me every day.

TWENTY-FOUR

THOSE GIRL SCOUTS move fast when they really want something.

I'd been half-inclined to think June's grand scheme of hosting them would fall apart when it came down to the nitty-gritty. I'd been both disappointed and reluctantly impressed when she and Marilyn's daughter had the event planned out within a day. Apparently, Crystal, Marilyn's oldest, had already scheduled an afternoon of picking up trash and learning about recycling for the troop, but she'd rearranged so the girls could pet some horses.

My horses. I couldn't stop telling myself what a fool this made me. I wasn't doing this for the money, or for the kids, or to try to make myself seem more *approachable*—I was doing it for June, plain and simple. Knowing it probably made me an even bigger fool.

She had a hold on me, and that hold was dragging me to the very edge of my self-control. If I had any sense left, I would go back to pretending I didn't care a thing about her, but I wasn't that good of an actor. Didn't matter anyway, since I'd never been able to fool myself.

June came into the barn lit up like a thousand watts. Her hair was up in a ponytail that trailed dark tendrils, her eyes shining with excitement. I glanced her over, trying not to linger too long on any one area, but in a tight T-shirt and jeans that hugged her just right, it proved an impossible task.

"Now where did you get that?" I gestured to her shirt.

"This?" She tugged at the hem. The dark purple shirt read *Magnolia Ridge Girl Scouts Troop 106* across the front. "Crystal brought it over for me this morning. She thought it would be a nice touch."

"Nothing for me?"

"This is my show, remember?" She grinned as she bounced on the balls of her feet, her running shoes raring to go. "Is Miss Kitty ready?"

She looked past me at the old horse, nodding her approval. I'd had Aaron tie her in the barn aisle so the girls could get a good look without crowding her. She faced the door, the better to see her gawkers as they approached, and I'd left a bucket of grain on her stall gate to keep her occupied. The horse chewed away, and if I had to wager, Troop 106 would get up close and personal with fresh manure during their demonstration.

"So," June said, dragging out the word. "Are you planning on staying out here?" She feigned casual interest as she ran her fingers over the top of Miss Kitty's stall gate.

"I think it'd be a liability if I wasn't."

"I'm sure with Crystal and me and the other moms, it will be fine. You don't have to stay if you don't want to."

"Why, June, are you trying to get rid of me?"

"No, not at all," she said, her voice gone high-pitched. "I just thought, what with the girls and all, this might not be your thing."

"Pretty sure I told you this was one hundred percent not my thing."

"I thought you might rather wait it out in the house, that's all. Have a cup of tea or something."

"I've never had a cup of tea in my life."

She put one hand on my elbow to steer me out of the barn. "It might be a good time to try it. Chamomile would make a nice introduction."

I held my ground despite her pushiness. "No, thanks."

"I've got some bourbon in my purse. That might make the tea more tempting for you."

That stopped me short. "You've got bourbon in your purse?"

"Maid of Honor duties, I'll tell you later." She held tighter onto my elbow, nudging me toward the door. "You should go relax. Tea and bourbon, how does that sound?"

I planted my feet, unmoved by her gentle shoves. "Why are you so set on getting me out of here?"

She stopped her pushing and huffed out a breath, blowing a lock of hair away from her face. "You make me nervous, all right?"

I liked the idea but couldn't quite believe it. "Since when do I make you nervous? I think I missed that when you were challenging me to a bet, doing my laundry without my permission, and trying to take over my ranch."

She looked taken aback. "What? I'm not—"

"Nervous?"

Glaring at my interruption, that tiny, cute furrow appeared between her eyebrows.

"You're the horse expert, all right? Everything I know about horses, I've learned from memorizing the Girl Scouts' suggested lesson plan for the last twenty-four hours. This could be embarrassing."

"You're just now catching on to that?"

That tiny furrow deepened, and her eyes shone with real worry. "There are a *lot* of terms to remember. Gaskin, pastern, withers. I've already forgotten the difference between the cannon and the coronet. What if I call a fetlock a flank?"

"I will laugh."

"Seriously, just go inside for the next two hours, okay?"

As much as I enjoyed her pleading face, this was the sort of request I'd enjoy more for denying.

"I don't think so." I rested one hand on the barn door behind her and leaned closer until the ache in my chest kicked in. Surprise shimmered in her eyes, but she didn't move out of our shared space. "I think I'd better stick close by. What if you can't remember which part is the standing whittle and which is the posterior baffle?"

Her eyebrows drew together in a look of sheer panic. "I don't remember those."

I let one side of my mouth tug back into a smirk. Realizing she'd been had, she pulled away from me. "Just go inside."

"I'm a stubborn man, remember?"

She tried to subdue a smile. "How could I forget?" The smile disappeared again. "These girls have been looking forward to this forever. What if I totally blow it?"

I took her gently by the arm, her skin soft and warm beneath my fingers. "You aren't going to blow it. And if you do, so what? Do you remember all the technical names from when Gram taught you?"

"No."

"What do you remember?"

Her slow smile lit me up inside.

"How much I loved seeing horses up close."

"So give them that. Everything else is gravy."

A car pulled up out front, and I guessed that was the signal the show was about to begin. I started to move away, but June grabbed both my hands. Her panic had faded, and her eyes glowed with tenderness. I had a crazy impulse to forget the kids and pull her into an empty stall.

"Thank you for letting me do this, Ty."

I swallowed hard, the sweetness of the moment urging me to do something I'd regret.

"Don't thank me yet. Your fun's just starting."

She squeezed my hands once before running around the corner to greet her guests. More cars pulled in and drove away as parents dropped off seemingly endless Girl Scouts. Their laughing and squealing got louder with each addition to the fray.

I stepped closer to Miss Kitty.

"You ready to be loved on by a bunch of eager little girls?" Her ears pricked forward, her big brown eyes watching me as I stroked her neck. "Don't do anything to make me regret this, okay?"

Finally, June came back into the barn, followed by three women and what felt like a hundred girls, every one decked out in the same purple shirt. I moved farther down the barn aisle to be less obtrusive, both to June and the girls, but I wouldn't miss this for anything.

June stood in front of Miss Kitty, the girls crowding around her to see. They *oohed* and *aahed* over the old mare like she was juggling chainsaws while standing on one leg. I wasn't sure what June had to be worried about—this would be a cake walk.

She welcomed the girls to the ranch and started in on her spiel about the basics of horse safety. I only halfway listened. Mostly, I just watched her, admiring how at ease she was with those girls. She asked them questions and engaged with them in a way I never could have matched. If ever a girl started to look bored or like she was thinking about wandering off—say, toward the tack wall—June chose that girl to help with her demonstration. She knew what she was doing, I had to give her that.

Then again, maybe she didn't *entirely* know what she was doing. When she started pointing out all the different parts of a horse, she faltered pretty quick after *muzzle*. She glanced to me, and I gave a small nod. Those girls didn't care what the proper names of a horse's body parts were—they were just thrilled to see the horse. She got back on track, hitting the basic terms out of the park and skipping the more obscure ones as the girls repeated after her.

Standing there, watching June show off my horse for fifteen little girls, eager to get them interested in riding and safety, I couldn't help but be impressed. She found what needed to be done and stepped right in to do it. Her headstrong ways could drive me a little crazy, but she was never wrong. She always had good intentions at heart. That heart was quickly becoming the most precious thing in my life. I wasn't sure I would ever get over these last few weeks with her.

"Is this your horse, Miss June?" a little girl in blond pigtails asked.

"No, this one belongs to Mr. Ty." June nodded my direction. Fifteen little faces turned my way before they got bored and snapped their attention back to the horse.

"Which one's yours?" another girl asked.

"None of them are mine," June answered matter-of-factly. "They belong to Ty and his friends."

"That's not fair," Blond Pigtails said, her little chin raised as she looked from June to me. She must have decided I was the villain of the piece, and her eyes flashed fire. I raised my hands in innocence. She turned back to June. "You should have your own horse."

That sounded like June's chance to explain she didn't live in town, that in fact, she had spent less than three weeks on a ranch in her life, and didn't want a horse. Instead, her mouth curled at the edges and she said, "Maybe I should have my own horse."

The woman knew how to get me right in the gut.

june

I WAS FAIRLY certain the afternoon was going well. The girls were interested, Miss Kitty stayed calm, and Ty hadn't laughed at me once.

I'd been more than a little afraid he might. The last thing I wanted to do was remind him yet again I didn't have a clue what I was doing on his ranch. After flubbing the parts of a horse almost immediately, I'd started to sweat, but Ty's reassuring nod had settled me down again. He didn't crack so much as a smile when my mind blanked out over fetlocks and withers. In fact, he'd looked downright proud.

I moved on to demonstrate proper grooming technique, which I'd learned by bingeing YouTube videos the night before. The girls each took turns brushing Miss Kitty in long, slow strokes, touching her about as often with the brush as with their own little hands. I made sure none of them got too close to Miss Kitty's back legs in their enthusiasm. The mare didn't seem likely to do anything more than enjoy the attention they lavished on her, but I kept watch just in case.

Marnie raised her hand as though we were in a classroom.

She looked a lot like Marilyn, with thick, dark hair that tumbled over her shoulders. "Is Mr. Ty your husband?"

The question brought out a round of giggles from the rest of the girls. I resisted the urge to turn around to catch Ty's reaction. Would he scowl, groan, roll his eyes? Look horrified at the very thought? I didn't want to know.

"Mr. Ty is not my husband." I put a prim edge to my voice, as though that could stop me from thinking about what having him for a husband would entail. Not the time or the place to get carried away with those thoughts. I wasn't sure he was even the marrying type. The rest of it, though—he was definitely *that* type.

"Does Mr. Ty have a wife?" Marnie asked, scrutinizing him over my shoulder without shame. She didn't look like she approved of the idea. At only six years old, she couldn't see much appeal in a big, slightly scruffy, brooding man. At twenty-nine, those qualities did more than a little for me. Add in his persistent care for me, his honesty, and his hard work ethic, and he was just about irresistible.

I can respect a man like that.

"Mr. Ty doesn't have a wife." I knew the direction of little kids' questions well enough to guess where this was headed. Right about now, Ty was probably wishing he'd opted for that cup of tea and purse bourbon.

"You should marry him," another girl said, nodding until the braided ends of her cornrows bounced.

Marnie gasped. "Then all the horses would be yours!"

So would a grouchy, stubborn man. It didn't put me off the idea.

I shushed the squealing that followed before Miss Kitty could get agitated. I wasn't entirely sure Miss Kitty could get agitated anymore, but if she could, the squealing of fifteen little girls would do it.

"That's probably not the best reason to get married." I looked over to Crystal, who flashed an apologetic smile.

"Girls, let's pay attention, please," Crystal said. "Who hasn't had a turn brushing the horse?"

I waited a few minutes before risking a glance over my shoulder at Ty. He stared at me from beneath his Stetson, his eyes hard and unreadable. Yep, he definitely looked like he wished back the whole afternoon.

After grooming practice came time for the big show. I put a saddle on Miss Kitty, another task I had mostly learned from YouTube. Ty had helped me figure out all the saddle parts the day before, so I knew I had it secured right. Then I fastened Miss Kitty's bridle and snapped a lead rope on before taking her out of the barn. Little hands reached out to gently touch the horse's soft, short hair as I led her into the round pen. The girls fanned out along the pen fence, bumping together as they sought first place in line for their ride.

"The quietest, most respectful girl will get to go first." The line straightened out, silenced in a flash.

Crystal had brought an adjustable riding helmet for the girls to wear as they each took their turn. She winked as she handed it over. "Let's hope it isn't lice season."

I selected the first girl and helped her into the helmet before boosting her onto the saddle. Ty followed us out to the pen to watch the girls take their rides. I stared at him a moment, our positions reversed from the first day I'd come out here. His heavy gaze shivered through me, all heat and intensity, until I finally had to turn away.

Two passes around the pen per girl seemed about right, even though they would have happily ridden all evening. Miss Kitty didn't mind either the walking or the stopping to have her rider exchanged. My back strained from boosting up all the little bodies, but it was worth it to see the girls' happy faces once on top of the old horse.

By the time I'd led the last girl on her walk around the pen, the afternoon sun had just started its descent to the tree line in the distance. The first parents pulled into Ty's drive to collect their children as I gave the tail-end of my closing speech.

"Congratulations, Daisies. You earned your Horse Fun badge!"

The girls squealed and whooped as Crystal handed out their iron-on badges embroidered with tiny ponies, showing them off to each other like they were Olympic gold medals. Parents came forward to collect their daughters, last longing glances were cast at Miss Kitty, and the group split apart.

One little girl moved away from the others to approach Ty. He stooped down to her level, wincing as he moved his body forward. I couldn't hear her over the goodbyes shouted all around us, but whatever she said seemed to startle him. His sternness melted away, and he smiled down at her.

"You're welcome," was all he said.

Their conversation over, she trotted off to her mother, who waited by the barn. I didn't have time to ponder the sweet little interaction long before Crystal and Marnie walked over to where Ty and I stood.

"Thank you both for today," Crystal said. "This means so much to the girls, you have no idea." She held a check out to Ty. "Our program fees. June said you didn't want to take payment, but it's only fair."

"She did all the work." He didn't make a move to take the check. "The money should be hers."

Crystal cut an apprehensive look at me. "I wrote the check out to Ty. Can you two maybe...?"

"We'll work something out." I took the check.

"Thank you!" Marnie called as she and Crystal walked across the yard to their car. Soon, they disappeared down the dusty drive, and the ranch quieted again. Man, fifteen kids could be noisy.

I gave Ty the smuggest look I knew how. "Pretty good, right?"

"Not bad."

The trace of a smile on his face was praise enough for me.

I folded the check and moved closer to him until we stood toe to toe. Being in his space proved a delightful, dangerous indulgence. I didn't give myself long to savor it, since I didn't know just what I might do in that closeness. Careful not to touch his injured chest, I slipped the check into his shirt pocket. Stepping away again, I worked against the powerful pull that tempted me to move right back to him.

"I'll cash it and have the money for you tomorrow."

"Ty," I said softly. "Don't be an ass."

His mouth twisted into a crooked smile, and he nodded as though I'd offered him sage words of advice instead of a fond insult. "I'm working on it."

"What did that little girl say to you?"

"Maybe it was a secret," he said, his voice low and teasing.

I smiled up at him until he relented.

"She just said 'thank you'. She said she'd never been up close to a horse before, and..." He cleared his throat, looking away. "She said she loves horses more than anything. No big deal."

"No big deal," I repeated. "For someone who says he doesn't have the personality to be around kids, you sure won her over quick."

He gave a disinterested tilt of his chin. "It's the horses that do it."

"That must be it."

Miss Kitty waited in the round pen, stepping lazily along

the edges, looking for stray grass that hadn't already been chewed to the dirt. The rest of the horses had been turned out before the Girl Scout lesson started, and they roamed the pastures. Still plenty warm out, but the worst of the day's heat had just about burned off.

"You know what I feel like doing?" I said, fresh inspiration dancing in my thoughts.

Ty looked like whatever I wanted to do was sure to be a bad idea. "You want to try shoeing them next?"

"I want to go for a ride."

One of his eyebrows quirked. "When was the last time you were on a horse?"

"Not that long ago."

He blinked slowly. "It was at that Girl Scouts trip, wasn't it?"

"Yes, but I did very well. Your Gram named me Least Likely to Get Kicked in the Chest."

"That's low."

I grinned up at him. "I could handle Miss Kitty. She was so patient and good all evening, she deserves a reward. She's a real sweetheart."

"That she is, but I can't ride out with you." His mouth pulled at one corner like he wished he hadn't admitted it. At least he'd come to accept that he wasn't doing his recuperation any favors by pushing himself so hard day in and day out.

"I wouldn't be gone long. I just want to ride out in the back forty for a little while."

"Oh, the back forty?" he said with a short laugh.

"You know what I mean."

I didn't know what to call the part of his land not used for his training business. The large, fenced pastures closest to the barn were covered in thick grass for the horses to graze on, with a few trees and shade shelters, but past that, the land was still in its natural state. Ashes and oaks towered over sages and laurels, and the creek that supplied the horses' watering pond shone gold in the sun. I had only caught glimpses of that wilderness since I'd been out here, but exploring it on horseback sounded perfect.

He gazed down at me as though assessing every inch of my horse-riding abilities. "You haven't been on a horse in eighteen years, and you're asking me to let you go for a ride all alone."

I stood straighter. "Seventeen years."

"That's not as reassuring as you think."

"I have earned it, you know." I laid on an entirely fake air of casualness. "The bet, and all."

"I figured we'd hold off on paying up until I was better."

"Then I'll just have to ride twice."

He laughed at that, even if the effort caused him noticeable pain. "All right. You win."

"Really?"

His pride seemed to want to disagree, but he nodded. "The bet, the ride. You won fair and square. You've done nearly two weeks of work and didn't run for the hills."

I must have grinned like a maniac. This many compliments from Ty Hardy taken all at once would go straight to my head.

"Let's get you saddled up before I change my mind."

I went back into the round pen with Miss Kitty to adjust the saddle's stirrups. Ty gave instructions over my shoulder as he helped me get everything ready for my ride.

When I first started working on his ranch, I took his color commentary on my efforts as not-so constructive criticism, but the thought hit home that he liked showing me around his horses. As much as he had fought with me at the beginning, I think he enjoyed sharing this side of his life with someone. I liked being that someone more than was sensible.

I reminded myself my time out here had always been on

strictly a temporary basis, and he'd just conceded our little bet. Technically, I didn't have to come out here anymore. Fine, technically, I'd never needed to. But winning the challenge I'd foolishly thrown down lost some of its thrill when it meant I wouldn't come back to his ranch tomorrow. I wasn't prepared to give up my place out here so quickly. Maybe not for a long time.

And how would that be, side by side with Ty for the long-term? Sharing just a small part of the work out here, sharing ourselves, sharing *life*? What if, instead of going back to Austin, I came home to Ty? Want blazed through me like a forest fire, scorching and all-consuming.

I finished securing the stirrup, my fingers trembling as I adjusted the leather straps.

See? Not at all sensible.

From the round pen, he led me to the lane that divided the pastures, one hand gripped tight on Miss Kitty's bridle. "Keep going this way, and you'll find a walking trail. She'll know what to do and isn't likely to pick her own path. Whole property is fenced if you try to wander off."

"I'm not stealing your horse, you know."

"I wouldn't put anything past you." The mischievous light in his eyes turned serious. "I want you back in thirty minutes."

"Half an hour? I might as well stay in the round pen for that." I'd pictured a leisurely walk among the shade trees, not an in-and-out sort of thing.

"It's enough for a greenhorn like you."

I would have bristled at his description if not for the note of affection in his gruff voice.

"Anyway, if you have her out much longer, she's likely to eat her weight in all that uncut grass. Keep her walking, or she'll stand around and graze until she's sick."

"Can do."

I put my hands up on the saddle, but paused. It *had* been nearly twenty years since I'd last been on a horse. What if it wasn't like riding a bike, and I sat up there like a nitwit not knowing what to do? Watching a video about grooming a horse was all well and good, but no amount of videos could make up for my lack of experience as a rider.

"I'm not really in a fit state to give you a boost into the saddle." A current of amusement ruffled Ty's voice. "Do you want a box?"

"I can do it."

I grabbed the pommel, put one foot into the stirrup, and swung my other leg over. Seated in the saddle, I let out a quick prayer of thanks I hadn't failed the first test. The rest should be even easier.

Should be.

Ty's eyes were sharp on me beneath his Stetson as though he could read my thoughts. "You good?"

"I've got it." I put a touch more confidence in it than I felt.

He handed up the reins. "Hold them loosely, remember, but don't be afraid to remind her you're in charge." He took a step back and nodded, giving me the okay to set off.

I made a clicking sound in the back of my throat as I nudged Miss Kitty with my heels. Obedient girl that she was, she started down the pasture lane. We weren't moving any faster than I might walk, but my heart thrilled anyway. I probably looked as ecstatic as any of the Girl Scouts had, finally getting my long-awaited ride. I petted Miss Kitty's neck, thankful Ty had at least one well-behaved horse in his barn full of troublemakers.

"Thirty minutes!"

Ty's voice rang out behind me, but I knew already thirty minutes would never be enough.

I PACED the length of the empty barn, stopping at each turn to stare out the doors, up the lane between the back pastures. Thirty minutes, I'd said, and I knew she'd heard me because she'd argued the point. I should have just said no to the whole idea and waited until I'd healed enough to ride out with her. Who let a green rider out on his acreage all alone?

I checked my watch, my anger egged on by the pain drumming in my chest with each step. She had already been out fifty minutes, and no sign of her. She was probably just lost in thought, but the idea she might actually be *lost* gnawed at me.

My property wasn't big enough to get truly lost in, but that wouldn't stop someone as determined to rile me as June. The back acreage rambled, and although I knew every rock and tree as well as I knew my own house, June had never been out there before. At least not as an adult, and anything she might have done as a Girl Scout didn't count.

I stopped in the open barn doors and squinted up the lane, searching for a sign of her. Every time I thought I saw movement coming my way, it turned out to be a trick of the light. And that was another problem. Twilight was falling, and while it wouldn't be full dark for at least another hour yet, the change wouldn't help June find her way back any faster.

All kinds of things could happen to her out there in the fading light, falls worst of all. Miss Kitty's gentle nature made her easy to lead, but she could still put a foot in the wrong spot or get spooked by a snake just as easily as any other horse. I'd never had a horse fall, with me or on me, but I'd never let anyone else ride my horses alone before, either. I wasn't running a hobby farm, dammit.

What had I been thinking? I'd let her round up the colts, let her bring a whole gaggle of girls onto my ranch, and now, I'd let her ride out all alone. These kinds of foolish decisions weren't like me. It didn't make sense. I'd never lacked for backbone before, so why was it so hard to tell June no?

As though I didn't know the answer.

She'd been gone a full hour now. That decided it. I would saddle up Bonanza and go after her. It would hurt from start to finish, but at least I would know where she was, and wouldn't be stuck standing around unable to do anything. This useless waiting burned me up as much as the way she'd ignored my advice.

I'd headed to the tack wall to grab a lead rope when June finally appeared at the far end of the lane. Eager to get home, Miss Kitty cantered the last stretch, making June bounce in the saddle. I might have laughed at her obvious discomfort if my blood weren't so hot.

I stormed over to meet them before they reached the barn. Miss Kitty came to a slow halt just feet from me, June pulling on the reins. She beamed down at me, but even that show of pure joy couldn't break through my frustration.

"What kept you so long?"

The delight in her eyes faded. "What time is it?"

"You've been gone an hour." I took hold of Miss Kitty's bridle to stop her wandering steps.

"Oh. I'm sorry. I didn't realize it had been that long."

She swung her right leg over to dismount, but unused to riding, her legs had turned to jelly. She tumbled against me, and I wrapped my free arm around her, my chest lighting up from the contact. Even as my whole body flared with sudden fire, the soft scent of her curled its way into my senses like an aphrodisiac.

She stepped away, holding onto the saddle to keep herself steady.

"I'm sorry," she said again, glancing at my chest as though she expected to see a broken rib sticking out of my shirt. "I didn't mean to land on you."

"Anything could have happened to you out there," I said, ignoring the urge to pull her to me again. "You could have been injured, or worse."

She looked at me as if I were talking nonsense. "I was just on a little ride."

"Alone."

"You're acting like I took her without permission. You said I could go."

"And I never should have, it's too dangerous."

The little smile she tried to hide only fired me up more.

"Miss Kitty is perfectly well behaved."

The horse snorted as if in agreement, ready to be brushed down and turned out again. June was already leading her to her stall as though our conversation were over. I trotted along beside her, feeling like the one on the lead rope.

"Her foot could have found a gopher hole, and then where would you be? I don't think this is funny, June."

Her smile threatened to turn into a laugh, as if my worry was the silliest thing in the world. "It is a little funny, getting a lecture on safety from the professional who got kicked by his own horse."

"Dammit, June, this is serious."

"I'm sorry, I'm just a little surprised by your reaction."

Frankly, I surprised myself. I knew I was being an absolute ass. The whole thing had been my own fault, and yet, I couldn't stop lecturing her as though it were hers. No harm had come to her, but all the things that might have gone wrong still tormented me. I couldn't explain it if I tried. Here I was all twisted up in knots over her, and she laughed at my concern. I'd never been so sick with worry; it wasn't like me. More than anything, I wanted that dark, greasy feeling to go away and stay gone.

Once Miss Kitty was in her stall, she occupied herself with her leftover hay and water while waiting to be brushed.

June turned to me, all smiles and sunshine once more. "Thank you for your concern. It's sweet."

"It isn't sweet." I took the two steps to her, pulled her into my arms, and kissed her.

All my worry finally seeped away, overpowered by this raw, urgent need. My chest hurt to hold her so tight against me, but not holding her hurt worse. I needed this. I needed *her*.

She responded with delicious intensity, as if she'd been waiting for this, too. She drew her hands along my shoulders to the back of my neck, and a soft sigh escaped her as I kissed her harder. Her mouth was the sweetest thing I'd ever tasted, I wanted to drink her in. My blood pounded in my veins as she explored me in return.

Somewhere in the part of my brain that could still think straight, I knew this was a mistake. Once again, I was crossing a line I'd sworn to myself I'd stay clear of, and worse still, I didn't regret it. She fit perfectly in my arms, like she'd been there a thousand times before. I just wanted a few minutes of this wonderful woman all to myself.

I traced my fingers from her chin to her jaw, cupping her face in my hands. She sighed against my mouth, and I swallowed the sound, hungry for more. Untold sounds of delight waited inside her, and I wanted to unlock them all.

My chest seemed to rip apart with each breath, halting me from satisfying the hunger that drove my thoughts and pulsed through my veins. Just kissing her could never be enough, but my lungs already burned with white fire.

Stopping seemed a worse torment, but the pain finally became a wall I couldn't climb. I broke the kiss, June's face still in my hands. A long moment passed before she opened her eyes, as if she didn't want this moment to end, either. She gazed up at me with eyes so full of desire, my blood churned harder for more.

"I didn't know you were that worried," she breathed.

"I was. Anything could have happened."

Anything could happen now. I could toss her in the hay rick and reassure myself she was safe and sound by exploring every inch of her with my hands and mouth. With my chest aching from one powerful kiss, anything more would probably send me to the hospital as she feared. With that kind of a trade-off, I would go willingly.

Slowly, I came back to my senses. I released her, letting my touch linger on her as long as possible. "I'm sorry. I acted like an idiot."

Her mouth curled into a smile. "True."

"I couldn't stop thinking about you lying hurt out there somewhere."

She still looked amused, but tempered with soft understanding. "I never pictured you for the worrying type."

"I'm not. Or, I wasn't. I don't know what I am now. You keep taking me by surprise until I don't know if I'm coming or going."

"I didn't think I was doing all that."

"You don't know the half of it." I took a step back, as though that could rid me of the temptation to kiss her again and never stop. "We can't keep doing this."

She closed her eyes and inhaled slowly, as if gathering all her strength to her.

"Give me one good reason why not," she said when she opened her eyes again. "And it can't be your brother."

I ground my teeth together. "He's part of it."

I wouldn't be like him, indifferent to everyone's wants but my own.

"Haven't you ever been with someone you knew you shouldn't have?"

"Yes." The image of Delia driving away with a casual wave flashed through my mind. "I don't want to be that for you."

"*You* wouldn't be. Dating Bret was just about the stupidest thing I've ever done."

Her words seemed to cut through the air between us as I turned over what she'd said.

"When my mom died, my whole world fell apart." She spoke softly, but her voice carried an urgency, too, like she needed to get the words out, make me understand. "I stayed out here a few weeks, but Dad thought I should return to Austin, back to the life I had there. So I went back to my apartment, lost and alone and shattered."

I twined my fingers with hers, offering some small measure of comfort.

"I was adrift and numb, barely noticing the weeks that passed. I lost my job. I don't know if you knew that." She looked like she feared I might judge her for it. I squeezed her hand to let her know I never could. "I was too much of a mess to meet with clients, I couldn't keep myself together. That's when I started the online work. Nobody had to know how broken I was inside."

It killed me to think of this sweet, loving woman trying to work through her grief and sorrow all on her own.

"Then one day, I ran into Bret at this random coffee house I'd been to a hundred times before. We hadn't talked in years, and we stopped to catch up. Handsome and charming, everything about him was polished to a shine. He didn't look at me with pity in his eyes, or talk about my mom, and he never, never asked how I was feeling." She gave a small shrug. "I didn't recognize it as indifference at the time."

I had accepted that's just how Bret was with women—in it for a good time, not for a long time. He'd had a parade of women go by, some he brought to town, others I heard about only in passing. Some part of me had hoped he'd grown past all that and was ready to do right by June. I should have known better from Day One.

"Our time together was a distraction. Being with Bret let me forget my grief for a little while, but that wasn't really what I needed. If I hadn't been so shattered by my mom's death, I wouldn't have dated him at all. I would have realized we just didn't connect, that there wasn't anything real between us, we didn't really know each other. Not like you and me."

This last came out a whisper, but I felt every word. Her gaze dropped to somewhere in the vicinity of my broken ribs, right close to that part of me that ached like a demon when she spoke this way.

"This," she said, tugging on my hand, "doesn't have anything to do with Bret. This is about you and me."

She leaned closer, inching toward my face. A replay of that night in my truck, but now that I'd kissed her, the anticipation thrummed so much worse for knowing just how glorious a kiss from June could be. Her lips finally brushed against mine, soft and sweet, before she lowered back down to her heels.

"Bret's a fool," I said. She smiled up at me until my chest seemed to explode all over again.

If my brother was a fool for letting June go, what would that make me in a few days when I would have to do the same thing?

june

FROM THE FIRST minute I'd walked through Fine & Dandy's doors, I'd wanted to move in. The shop was filled top to bottom with the sorts of homey accents I loved to snap up for my clients: rustic wall art, plush decorative pillows, cozy throws just perfect to cuddle up in by a fire. All the little finishing touches that made a house feel like a home.

A few customers browsed the store, but Marilyn buzzed straight over to greet me.

"I hoped I'd see you here." She moved right in for a hug as though we did this every day.

After half a second's pause, I returned her brief embrace. "Thought I'd stop in and see what you've got today. I've always loved the things you find."

"Thank you," Marilyn said with a little wave of her hand. "But you're the interior designer. I just round up things I would want in my own house."

"Well, you've got great taste."

She glanced around the store. "Sometimes, it takes all my willpower not to buy one of everything just for myself. I have to be satisfied to enjoy them in here, and resist the urge to bring them all home."

Two women appeared at the counter, and Marilyn excused herself to ring up their purchases. I made a slow circuit of the store, taking in the wide assortment of home decor. Marilyn had reasonable prices, too, nothing like the markup some Austin stores charged for similar items of lesser quality. Yet another little benefit of small-town life.

Once the women had left the store with their bags, Marilyn made her way back to me. "Would you like to sit down with me for a little while? I have some sweet tea in the back fridge."

I had meant to say hello as I'd promised and wander the aisles a few minutes, but I hadn't expected to turn this into a social call. A stray memory of my mother flitted through my mind, leaving guilt in its wake, but I shushed it out again. "I'd like that."

We took over a back corner of the store in two overstuffed chairs with a table covered in floral teacups between us. Marilyn set out a tray with glasses of tea and a few chocolate cookies. It reminded me of my Grandma Evans's sitting room, if Grandma Evans had been a hoarder with terrific taste.

We eased back into the plush chairs, and I took a long sip from the iced tea. Not quite how my mom had made it, but it tasted good.

"Thank you for hosting Marnie's Girl Scout troop," she said. "Those girls were just over the moon afterwards. I've had two excited calls already. Marnie's told me so much about it, I feel like I earned my own horse badge."

"I loved doing it." Once my bout of nerves wore off, anyway. "I'm glad the girls had a good time."

"You'll pass my thanks along to Ty, won't you?"

"I'll do that."

"Ty seemed less sure of the whole plan. He didn't mind too much, did he?"

"I don't think so. He got used to the idea."

He didn't get used to the idea until the whole thing was over, but he didn't lecture me about it afterwards, either. He'd had other lectures for me, about safety on solo horse rides. My cheeks warmed as I thought about his worry for me, and the delectable kisses that worry had brought out.

"He seems like a man set in his ways."

I snorted into my tea. "You could say that."

"He comes by it naturally. Victor Hardy was just about the most immovable man the town's ever seen." Marilyn laughed lightly. "But of course, he had Abigail to soften him. Sometimes, a man needs a woman to soften out his rough edges."

Ty certainly had some rough edges, but he seemed pretty content to stay that way. "What do you do when they don't realize they need it?"

"You help him figure it out."

If only it were that easy.

I had told Ty my regrets about dating Bret, and how different my feelings for him were. And Ty had...well, he'd said nothing I didn't know. *"Bret's a fool."* He had seemed pleased with my confession, but he hadn't said anything in return. Even a simple, *"I feel it, too,"* would have been something, but he hadn't offered a similar confidence. Eventually, I'd gone home, feeling at once closer to and just as distant from Ty as I ever had been.

As much as our conversation pressed on my thoughts, opening up the can of crazy that was my situation with Ty didn't really fall in the *social call with Marilyn* category.

"So do you have one supplier, or do you pick and choose?" I asked.

The abrupt change of topic didn't seem to bother her. "I

have several. Some catalogs, some individual vendors, some local craftsmen. I've collected a little bit of everything over the years. I don't like seeing the same thing when I go into every store in the area. I like to offer my customers a little something different."

"It shows. The eclectic mix in here could keep even my pickiest clients happy."

"I've been all over your website. Is that a strange thing to admit? I feel a bit like an internet stalker." She laughed again, but she seemed nervous about something other than light internet stalking. Her fingers toyed with the puffball edging on a tea towel hung over the arm of her chair. "I like the style of the work in your gallery—home, but better."

"That's my goal. I don't want to change people's houses so much that they can't see themselves in them anymore. I want to create the best versions of their homes, not some magazine spread of a celebrity's house that nobody feels comfortable in."

"Exactly. That's what I've always tried to help my customers achieve, too. Some of these houses are so overdone, it's a wonder people can call it *home*." Marilyn took a drink of tea, watching me with avid eyes. "Are you happy where you're at, work-wise?"

I searched for a nice, pat answer, but couldn't find one. "It's all right. This online job was supposed to be a short pit stop. Just until I got back on my feet after—after my mom died."

She nodded, sympathy shining in her eyes. If I expected to find awkwardness, it didn't come from her. She listened without judgment or jealousy.

"I was planning to start a firm with a friend, but that fell through a while back. I guess I haven't decided what I want to do next."

"I don't suppose there's any chance you'd consider coming back to Magnolia Ridge, would you?"

I fumbled for an appropriate response. I'd been thinking about coming home for more than just a visit, but for all the wrong, rancher-related reasons.

"I've always liked the idea of having an interior decorator set up shop back here." Marilyn glanced around as though envisioning something more than the furnishings around us. "An in-house designer would be a wonderful addition, don't you think?"

I looked around, too, my eyes following hers through the store. I could almost see a work table set up in the far corner, stacked high with specialty fabric books and furniture catalogs. Working out of a shop like this could be ideal for a decorator just taking off on her own. She'd have independence, but she wouldn't be completely alone. I tried to contain the zing of excitement fluttering through me in case I'd read too much into the conversation.

"My girls both went into teaching," she went on. "And I'm out of my depth when it comes to customers asking anything more than 'How many throw pillows is too many?' I've had a steady increase in sales the last five years, and we get a lot of foot traffic. If you were interested in working with me, I'd like to keep it in the family."

That brought me out of my fevered imaginings of bolts of damask and rolls of wallpaper.

Marilyn looked back at me with a mix of trepidation and boldness. "Your father and I haven't been together very long, but I know what I feel. I had thirty-one wonderful years with my husband, Darren, before I lost him six years ago to a heart attack. I didn't think I could ever love another man like that, but here I am. And I do love your father."

She smiled softly, her eyes glistening. Whatever innocent infatuation I'd imagined between her and my pop disappeared in the light of the real love glowing plain as day in her face.

My eyes stung with tears over my own selfishness. I had been so caught up in how I felt about my father dating again, I hadn't given much thought to what it meant to him. Seeing how much Marilyn truly loved my father made me want to wrap my arms around this woman and beg her to never let him go. He had loved my mother dearly, and had grieved her since she'd gone. If Pop could have that kind of happiness again, I wanted it for him with all my heart.

I reached across the display table and took Marilyn's hand in mine, tears finally spilling from my eyes. "I'm glad he has you."

TWENTY-EIGHT

"THANKS FOR TURNING your schedule around again," I said as Aaron let the last horse into the pastures for the evening. They'd spent the day cooped up in their stalls beneath circulating fans and were ready to run free in the fresh air all night. "I know you've got a lot on your plate."

"No problem." Aaron secured the pasture gate behind Opie, who galloped the length of the enclosure twice before he settled down. "I wouldn't have my job at Belton Grove if it weren't for your recommendation. I owe you my start, man."

"Remember that one day when you're training world famous racehorses."

He laughed, but a spark of determination fired up in his eyes. "One day."

We walked to the barn, where he hung the halter he'd been using on its peg on the tack wall. I paused, breathing in short, sharp gasps until the stitch under my arm eased away.

"You okay?" he asked.

"I might have overdone it yesterday."

"Just yesterday?" He grinned over his subtle dig.

"Hard to pinpoint it."

All I knew for sure was that the ache in my chest had worsened. Probably just all the excitement of the last few days, what with bringing the horses in from the storm, and then holding June to me like she could patch together all my broken pieces and make me whole again. One or the other.

"You want me to clean out the stalls, or is your friend coming by?"

I hesitated. After her ride and our incredible kiss, we hadn't gotten around to logistics. "I think you'd better do it. She doesn't need to keep doing this."

"Why on earth not?" came a voice from behind me.

The woman lived for catching me by surprise. I turned around to see June smiling innocently at me.

"How long were you standing there waiting for your cue to pipe up?"

"Long enough to hear you admit you've been overdoing it. I needed to savor the moment." She strolled up to me, her eyes on my chest like she had her X-ray vision turned up high. "Are you in worse pain?"

"It's fine."

She pursed her lips at me.

"You need to get that tattooed across your chest." She left me to pull on a pair of my rubber work boots, grab her gloves, the tools, and the wheelbarrow, and moved down to the first stall. "Hi, Aaron."

"Good evening, Miss June." He tipped his hat to her like a genuine cowboy.

"What do you think you're doing?" I asked her.

"I'm cleaning the stalls," she said without breaking her rhythm.

Lord help me with this stubborn woman. "The bet's over. You won, and you already got your reward."

"Part of my reward," she corrected. "There's still the little

242

matter of the public declaration of my competence with a pitchfork."

"Is that a euphemism?" Aaron asked under his breath.

I shot the kid a look of fire that sent him back to the tack wall.

"Anyway," June continued, thankfully ignorant of Aaron's comment, "the work needs to be done, doesn't it?"

"I do pay Aaron."

She stopped to level a curious look at him. "How many stalls have you cleaned today?"

His hands paused in doing their nothing over the tack. He glanced from her to me like he didn't want to answer. "About thirty."

"You've earned a break, then."

"You can't just dismiss my hand, June," I said.

She gasped in mock surprise. "Look at me. I just did."

Aaron ran a hand over his mouth to cover a laugh. I cut him a sharp look, but it didn't sober him much.

"I don't really want to be in the middle of this," he said. "I think I'd better get going. See you tomorrow." He bobbed his eyebrows at me as he sidled past and out the barn door.

After laying out new straw in the stall she'd just cleaned, June moved on to the next.

"You're never allowed to call me stubborn again. Are you like this with everybody, or is it just me?"

She stopped and glanced over at me as she considered. A smile tugged at her lips, her contentiousness gone. "I think it's just you."

That answer cozied up inside me like a kitten getting comfortable by a fire. What was it about her that made me want to contradict her and then pull her in close for a kiss? She'd busted her butt working at my ranch for weeks, and here she was back for more. She wasn't doing it to antagonize me—

although it did do that—but because her heart was too big for her own good.

My heart tugged and ached as I watched her muck out my horse stalls, unasked, with nothing to gain but the satisfaction of helping me. For years, I'd been sure I had to do everything on my own, ignoring just how much I wanted someone out here with me. I wanted someone else to be as invested in my ranch as I was. Someone to work beside me. Someone to share my life.

All the tender feelings for June I'd tried to hide away from the first day I met her had only grown stronger. I was in a real bad way to lose myself entirely to this woman who had swept in and made a home in my heart. Even if every last owner came to haul their horse away tomorrow, with her beside me, I would be the happiest man in Texas.

June glanced up as she moved on to the next stall and stopped short. "Are you sure you're feeling okay? You're doing that thing again."

"What thing?"

"Smiling." She smirked and disappeared in the stall.

I ran a hand over my face. Well, look at that. I *was* smiling.

That smile disappeared when my phone rang. My guts sank into my boots, but it wasn't any client on the line to let me know they were about to come collect their horse. Checking the screen, I saw it was my mother calling.

I left the barn and headed out toward the round pens before answering.

"Tyler Edwin Hardy!" my mother squawked. "How dare you?"

I sighed and braced one hand against the pen fence. This would be a long one.

"You get knocked senseless by a horse and don't even have the decency to call your mother to let her know? I had to hear it from Sandra Stevens, that gossip, fishing for details. She sent me a message about it, asking if you needed anything." Mom finally took a breath. "She said it happened weeks ago. What's the matter with you?"

"How's your vacation?"

"Don't you start with that," she said, some of the fire easing from her voice. "Don't try to distract me. Tell me everything."

"I got kicked. I have a couple of cracked ribs. The world continues to spin."

She *tsked*. "Why didn't you call us?"

"There wasn't anything to do about it."

"We still might like to know. Honestly, son."

"Ask him if he needs any money," my father called.

"Do you need any—"

"I've got it all under control." I would rather cut off any talk of money before Dad could get started. "How's the cruise?"

"The cruise is a sight, honey. The windmills are magnificent, and the gardens...*oh*. Wasn't the National Museum glorious?" Dad grumbled agreement in the background. "Has Bret been by to help you out?"

"He hasn't been by, no."

I hadn't called him, but that was just a technicality. No way Bret would have dropped anything to come help me out around the ranch. Bret didn't know a thing about horses and had no interest to learn. Like in everything else, June had been right about us—my brother and I weren't much alike.

"I'll call him. I'm sure he'll move some things around for you."

"Don't do that. I'm doing just fine."

"Hmm. What does the doctor say?"

"That bones take time to heal."

"We could cut our trip short," she offered.

But I heard the hesitation in her voice. And why not? Who

wants to run home early from their European vacation? I wouldn't have them change their plans, anyway.

"No, Mom, I don't need you to do that. You finish your trip. I'll still be right here when you get back next week."

"I still think you should have called us."

"I didn't want you to worry." Worry, flip out, scold me for carelessness. All of the above.

"I'm your mother, that's what I do."

This was true, to a dizzying extreme. Hence, the lack of a phone call.

"Ask him if he has health insurance," Dad said.

"Do you—"

"Yes, I do," I grumbled.

"What about savings?" Dad said.

"It's covered."

"Ask him—"

"I'm not asking him another thing. You talk to him yourself."

There was a muffled sound of the phone changing hands before my father's voice boomed into my ear. "How are you holding up?"

"I'm doing fine." I kept saying it, but no one took me at my word.

"A horse finally got you good, huh?"

Where my mother had sounded frantic with worry, my father's voice held amusement. Another reason I wouldn't call Bret. He shared our father's scorn for the ranch, and thought the whole thing some experiment in living out a childish dream of being a cowboy. Bret would find my injury funny, and that would just piss me off.

"That's about the size of it."

"I keep trying to tell you it's not a safe career, son. Physically or financially. There's too many risks in what you do." He paused, and I could have predicted his next question word for word. "Have you thought any more about putting the business side of your degree to use?"

I ground my teeth together until my jaw hurt. "I run a business already."

Dad's laugh came out almost a sigh, as if he found my ignorance tiring. "I mean a *real* business."

That qualifier turned my stomach to lead. My father wanted me to start a *real* business, just like Delia had gone back to her *real* life. Like nothing I had was legitimate or worthwhile. Just a temporary pit stop before moving on to something better.

"You could do well for yourself if you'd just apply yourself a bit more. Sell that land, split the profits with Bret, and go into the management side of things."

I gripped the pen railing so hard my knuckles turned white. "My answer's the same as it always is."

"I thought this would have shaken a little sense into you, son."

"Give me that back," Mom said, followed by more muffled sounds. "Don't pay him any mind. We won't keep you any longer, honey. We'll see you next week. Tell Beverly we're sorry we can't make the wedding. Call your brother!"

We said our goodbyes and hung up. For all of Mom's attempts to keep Dad's contempt for the ranch in check, I was plenty familiar with it. His warnings about the realities of ranch life had never made a bit of difference to me.

I stared out at the pastures I loved more than anything, the horses I tended and trained wandering aimlessly as the sky turned orange in the west. Dad's solution to any problem on the ranch was always to sell the land. That's why Gram had left the ranch to me, and not my father. I would never sell it. Just like Gram, this ranch was in my blood. It was my whole life.

I wasn't an Austin lawyer, or even a Magnolia Ridge ranch

manager. I started young colts; I worked every day in the dust and muck. My life was smelly and dirty, with hard days and short nights.

I had to let go of these dreams about June I'd been spinning. As soon as Booker and Eden's wedding was over, June would go back to Austin. To her *real* life.

I didn't want to be the one to hold her back. And what could I possibly say to change her mind? She had a good job and her own hopes and dreams out there. Sooner or later, she would realize exactly what I was—a simple rancher with modest prospects—and these glorious days of her looking at me like I was everything to her would come to an end.

TWENTY-NINE
june

I FINISHED WASHING up for the evening and found Ty sitting in the twilight on the bench in front of the barn. He watched as the horses wandered around in the pastures, tearing at the short grass with each lumbering step. I sat down next to him, leaving the barest sliver of space between us.

The sun sank low, casting red and purple streaks through the deepening sky. It led to a peaceful kind of quiet, with crickets chirping in hidden corners, and the occasional neigh rolling in to us from the grounds.

"You're right," I said. "It is pretty romantic out here. You need a porch swing, though."

Ty sighed, looking out at the horses. His gloomy mood had returned, and I had a feeling I wouldn't like whatever he was getting ready to say.

"I appreciate all you've done out here, June."

"You could have fooled me, with all of your growling and complaining the last few weeks." I hadn't minded most of it, but if he knew that, he would probably just take it as encouragement to complain more.

His mouth twitched, but he didn't smile. "You have no idea how hard it is to be around you all the time."

"And here I thought you'd gotten used to me."

"That's just it. I am used to you." He turned to me, and the tenderness in his eyes made my breath catch for all the hope it ushered in. "Every day, you show up in your tiny little car, and you work harder than anybody else I know. Every day, you do a thankless job for no good reason. Every day, you sass me like your life depends on it."

I lit up at his teasing. "I do know how to get to you, don't I?"

Softer, he said, "Every day, I have to fight the urge to pull you to me and hold on tight."

That admission curled through me, growing and expanding until I became nothing but pleasure. I wanted to both savor the moment and rush right into the next.

"Why do you have to fight it?" I breathed.

He gave an almost imperceptible shake of his head, as if maybe he didn't know the reason himself. I leaned forward, careful not to press hard against him, until my face hovered just a breath away from his.

He stayed as still as stone while I drew nearer. I hesitated, knowing if I kissed him, he might tell me it was a mistake all over again. But not kissing him seemed the kind of thing only a superwoman could have done, and I didn't have that kind of strength.

Our kiss was so slow and gentle, we hardly moved. He groaned a little against my mouth, but he didn't stop kissing me. Ty put so much sweet emotion in the kiss, my senses over-loaded on it—all I knew was his taste, his touch, his scent. He was everything I wanted.

Love spun through me like leaves on the wind. I was falling in love with Ty, and I couldn't stop it now if I tried. And I wouldn't try. That much I knew. I would jump in with both feet if it meant the chance of being with him.

He groaned again, but with a note of pain in it this time. I broke the kiss and drew away. Lines etched the corners of his eyes and the set of his mouth, his breathing ragged from the combination of the kiss and his aching lungs.

"June," he breathed.

Just my name, but I heard the reprimand in his tone, a prelude to another attempt to talk me out of everything I wanted. Everything I needed.

"For the love of God, if you mention your brother again, I will punch you in the chest."

That provoked a smile, but it faded again almost as quickly as it had come. "This isn't your life. You're leaving in three days."

The reminder shot ice water through my veins, and not just because of these newfound feelings for Ty. This visit had showed me everything I loved about Magnolia Ridge, everything I missed when I was gone. My family, my friends, a community that had each other's backs. My snug little apartment in Austin seemed a sad replacement for the true home I had here.

"What if I didn't leave?"

The idea of Marilyn's offer had barely taken hold, but new *what ifs* followed the first, a series of possibilities I hadn't let myself truly consider before. What if I stayed? What if I set up shop in Fine & Dandy? What if I reclaimed the home I left so long ago?

Hope and surprise flashed through his eyes, but he shut them down again. "You would regret it. The career and life you want are in Austin. You don't want to be stuck in Magnolia Ridge with a bunch of ranchers."

"I like ranchers. One in particular very, very much."

Tenderness and disbelief seemed to battle in his eyes, and I willed his tenderness to reign victorious, but at last, disbelief won out.

"You'd get tired of him, believe me."

His voice was final, like he'd already resigned himself to the fact that the man I wanted could never be him, even as I was beginning to realize he was the only man I needed. He'd underestimated me once before, and I'd proved him wrong. I would just have to prove him wrong again.

"You sound awfully sure."

"I've seen it before."

"What does that mean?"

Before he could explain, my phone rang in my back pocket.

"Oh no, I completely forgot. I'm supposed to go out with Eden and the girls tonight." I'd planned to go straight to Pop's after my chores around the ranch, but it had slipped my mind. Being around Ty made a lot of things slip my mind.

He lifted his hand, encouraging me to leave. "Go. Party it up."

I needed to stay here and convince Ty he was wrong about us, that I couldn't imagine ever being tired of him, but my phone still rang in my hand, Eden's face on the display. I had promised my cousins one last girls' night before the wedding and didn't want to let them down.

"I should take this," I said as I stood to go. "But we're not done here."

I did my best Ty Hardy impression, echoing the assertive voice he used with the horses. That at least brought a whisper of a smile to his face.

"Call me if you get into the sangria and need a ride home."

I leaned down and kissed him on the cheek. I could see him warring with himself again, battling back all the desire that flashed in his eyes, until at last, I couldn't be sure it had been there at all.

"I'll see you later."

"Goodbye, June."

The ominous tone to that simple phrase sent a shiver up my spine as I walked away.

june

"I KNOW WE SAID CASUAL, but dang, girl."

Eliza gave me a pointed once-over, taking in my dirty jeans and grungy old T-shirt. I hadn't had enough time to go to my pop's to change, so I'd met my cousins at The Broken Hammer in my mucking clothes. In retrospect, that might have been a bad call.

The others dressed casual in the sense none of them wore a skirt or pearls, but they still looked ready for a night on the town. I looked like the only thing I was ready for was a shower, my hair mostly still in a bun, my makeup nonexistent. I had at least slipped into The Hammer's restroom to freshen up a bit, but judging by Eliza's upturned nose, it hadn't done much good.

"I had to come straight from Ty's." I pulled up a chair between Harper and Eliza. Eden already had a beer poured for me and passed it over.

"You were at Ty's?" Eliza's scorn disappeared as she leaned on the table between us, eager for gossip. "What are you not telling us?"

Only Eden knew about what had been going on with Ty and

all the time we'd spent together these last weeks. Even then, I'd glossed over just how closed I'd become with him in favor of detailing how closed I'd become with manure. The manure required a lot less explanation.

"We had a bet," I said simply, taking a sip of beer. "He thought I couldn't handle his chores around his ranch, so I said I could do them for two weeks."

Eliza leaned closer, a devilish look in her eyes. "And what did you get if you won?"

"A ride on one of his horses."

Her eyebrows darted even farther up her forehead. "And what did he get if he won?"

"Me out of his hair."

Her expression fell. "Snore. I thought you'd at least ask for a ride on *him*. Save a horse, ride a cowboy, that's my motto."

"That's not your motto," Eden said.

"He has broken ribs," Harper put in. "Sexual favors are pretty unlikely right now."

"The man's not dead, though, right?" Eliza flashed a comical wink. She loved to get in a good cheeky remark, but lately, I'd begun to suspect it was all for show. Her sauciness protected her tender heart, not all that different from how my grump protected his with his dismissive attitude.

"It hurts for him to even breathe hard, I think he'll be out of commission for a while."

Our kisses had seemed to bring him almost as much pain as pleasure. In the barn after my ride, he'd been passionate, sure, but controlled and careful. What would really be wild? Ty Hardy *not* being completely in control of himself—but I wasn't sure he would ever let me see that side of him.

"I know that look," Eliza said. "You're wishing you'd chosen a ride on the rancher for that bet."

I couldn't stop my smile. "Maybe."

"Maybe?" Harper repeated. "Are you doing more than ranch work over there?"

"Not much more."

That prompted a round of whoops from my cousins.

"Fill us in," Eliza said. "I want all the details. I didn't realize you were actually getting down with the hottie rancher, not after everything with Bret."

"That has been a bit of an issue," I admitted. "I don't know if he's trying to protect me from himself, or if he just feels bad about kissing his brother's ex. Maybe both."

Eliza slapped my hand. "I need to know about the kissing. Is he good? He's good, right?"

Toe-curling, knee-weakening, mind-numbingly good. "He's basically the best, yeah."

"I thought there was something going on with you two after the bachelorette party."

I tried not to groan at how obviously I'd mooned over him even then. "Nothing was going on at the bachelorette party."

"I still shipped it."

"But it's more than just that, isn't it?" Eden asked. Pragmatic to the core, Eden would know there was far more going on with me than just the rush of kissing a man, no matter how rancher-hot. "You skipped unemotional and went straight to France, didn't you?"

I laughed at our terrible nationality metaphors. I'd been a downright lousy unemotional robot.

"I care about him a lot. I think I love him."

Saying it out loud in front of my cousins touched on all those sweet, growing emotions like plucking a guitar string. A comfortable warmth seeped through me as though Ty were right here with me in the room. I had only just left him, but I missed him like he held a piece of my heart inside him.

"But?" Eden prompted.

I sighed, and that warmth dissolved. "But I'm not sure where I stand with him."

She made a face. "Strong, silent types can be hard to read."

"Look at it this way," Eliza said. "Either he's madly in love with you and doesn't know how to say it, or he's not and doesn't want to hurt your feelings."

"Was that supposed to make me feel better?" I tried to play the tremor in my voice as laughter, but worry coiled in my chest.

She shrugged. "It's a fifty-fifty chance, right?"

I took a long pull from my beer, hoping against hope I had better odds than that. I thought I did, but until Ty actually said something, I couldn't know for certain. In that light, fifty-fifty didn't sound so bad.

"You need to just have it out with him," Eden said. "Tell him how you feel. Directly ask him how he feels about you. Then you'll have your answer."

The worry in my chest hardened into a spike of fear. "Is that what you did with Booker?"

"Are you kidding? He said *I love you* first."

"Must be nice," Harper said with a wistful little sigh. "You're really lucky, you know that?"

Eden nodded. "I do know."

The smile she wore was full of such pure love, I couldn't help the twinge of jealousy rippling around inside me.

"This is your last chance." Eliza's teasing tone butted into the moment. "I could call a stripper. I bet I could get one to come right here to our table."

Our collective groans made heads turn around to look at us.

"You're stupid, but I love you." Eden spread her arms as though she could hug all three of us at once. "I love all of you."

I love you echoed around the table, filling me up with something I hadn't had enough of in far too long. I loved these

257

women who had been my best friends since childhood, and my closest confidantes in adulthood. And not just them, but my father and brothers, Annie and the boys, my whole hometown. I had left Magnolia Ridge trying to find what I needed, but maybe that same impulse would bring me back home again to the people I loved.

Before I could think better of it, I blurted out, "I'm going to move back home."

A slight pause as the three women parsed what I said, then another round of whoops erupted from our table. Harper and Eliza squeezed me from either side, and Eden reached forward to clasp my hand.

"Nothing's decided for certain, but I miss everyone so much, and I want more than just weekend visits now and then."

"This doesn't have anything to do with a certain rancher, does it?" Eden asked.

"Only a tiny bit," I admitted.

Maybe I was falling for Ty, and maybe I was gearing up to have my heart broken, but that could happen no matter where I lived. What I couldn't have in Austin was the feeling of being home I so desperately missed.

I was ready to be back home in Magnolia Ridge, Ty or no Ty.

THIRTY-ONE

"WE SHOULD HAVE PUT money on this," Booker said as he laid out a royal flush on my kitchen table. "I could have paid for my honeymoon."

I tossed down my hand, a pair of twos and trash. About par for how I'd been playing all night. "Thanks for not taking advantage."

I took a pull on my beer and leaned back in my chair as best I could before the ache in my ribs stopped me short.

Booker had turned up not long after June left, a six-pack in one hand and two pizzas in the other. I would never refuse that kind of hospitality, and we'd settled in. If I'd known he was going to win at poker all night, I might have turned him away at the door.

"You want to try Go Fish?" he asked.

"Shut up and deal."

His smug smile just begged to be wiped off with a full house, but I'd lost all night. A string of bad cards, and bad choices. Kind of summed up my life right now.

I looked at my hand. A king, a seven, and a three. Any other night, I might have made it into something, but tonight, I just couldn't break my losing streak. I finished out the hand with a pair of sevens that couldn't touch Booker's straight.

"Let me deal." I pulled the cards to me across the table. The movement hurt, but I needed that edge of pain. It kept me from thinking too much. Or worse, feeling too much.

"Want to talk about it?"

I glanced at him, but he wasn't giving anything away. "What's there to talk about? I'm having a run of bad luck, that's all."

"That's all, huh?" Booker shrugged. For a P.E. teacher, he sure knew how to lay on the theatrics. "Whatever you say."

"My head's not in it." I looked at my cards and swore.

He laughed. "Maybe your mind's on something else."

He motioned for me to deal him two more cards, and he smiled when he looked at them, not bothering now for a straight face. I might as well fold.

"Maybe I'm just cursed by the Poker Gods tonight."

"You never lose this much. Does a certain pretty brunette we know have anything to do with that?"

I threw down my cards. If we'd been betting tonight, I'd have run out of cash an hour ago.

"Why would June throw off my game?" I growled.

"Don't play with me, man. We've been best friends for almost thirty years. You really think I don't know how you feel about her?"

I took another pull from my beer, not sure I wanted to do this, even with Booker. I'd tried so hard to keep my feelings for June out of reach, talking about them couldn't possibly make anything better after these last weeks with her.

"How long have you known?"

"From the first time you told me about her." He tipped his beer bottle toward me. "You flew into a rage about your no good, show-off brother bringing home a sweet girl like that, how he was sure to break her heart, she deserved better. Etcetera. You always knew Bret was a dog, but it never seemed to bother you that much until her."

Guys who wanted to keep things casual didn't normally bring women home to meet their parents, but Bret wasn't like other guys. He'd figured out in college that no matter how light he kept things with a girl, if he brought her home to Magnolia Ridge, she thought he was all in. I mostly ignored the girls he brought to family dinners, figuring they would be gone again soon enough.

I'd never been able to ignore June.

"She's been coming out here every day, working in the barn and tending the horses. Cleaned my house, did my laundry. Stubborn like you wouldn't believe."

His mega-watt smile lit up. "Sounds familiar."

"She talked me into letting her take Miss Kitty on a solo ride. She strong-armed me into letting her have a Girl Scouts troop out here."

"She strong-armed you?" He feigned amazement. "Tough woman."

I had to smile over how easily she got me to do whatever she wanted. I was wrapped around her little finger, and the only word on my lips was *more*.

"But this is just a side trip for her," I said, shutting down those thoughts as fast as they came up. "She's heading back to Austin after the wedding."

He splayed a hand. "I don't see the problem. Austin isn't that far."

"It's worlds away from the life I have here and you know it. Even if my wildest dreams for my training business came true, it wouldn't be much compared to the sort of life she has in front of her."

"You realize cars exist? She could come out here on weekends—"

"I'd never be satisfied with just seeing her on weekends. I'd want it all with June." And that was the heart of it. I wanted things with June I'd never even thought of for myself before. I wanted a life, a home, a family. But not when June would be the only one paying the cost. "I can't make her choose between me and her career. She's just getting her future off the ground. The right thing to do is to let her go."

Booker rolled his eyes. "You're too noble for your own good, you know that?"

"What can I offer her? I work this ranch twenty-four-seven. I haven't left Magnolia Ridge in years, I can't. This is my life, I chose it. She doesn't have to make that choice."

He grew more somber. "Have you told her how you feel?"

I cocked my head to the side. "Last time I told a woman how I felt about her, it didn't go so well."

"I love you, man, and I say this to you with all due respect, but you have got to get over yourself."

His fake-polite advice slapped me across the face. "Excuse me?"

"You've got to get past this Delia thing. I'd been dumped a dozen times before I met Eden—you were probably there for half of the dust-ups—but I wasn't going to let that stop me from grabbing that woman and making her mine. You think I don't know every day I'm the luckiest guy around? She figured out a long time ago I'm nothing but a washed-up college basketball player who couldn't go pro." He shrugged. "She loves me anyway. Doesn't make sense, but I'm not going to question it. You need to get over this."

I was over Delia in all the usual ways. I didn't miss her or want her back, but I couldn't just forget that kind of humiliation, either. When she came to the end of her training at the winery in Magnolia Ridge, I had opened up my heart like a fool. Or I'd started to. I had barely gotten more than a few words about my feelings out when she stopped me. Told me this thing between us had been a good time, but she would ruin her life if she stayed here with me. Said I knew her real life was in Dallas, not playing around with cowboys out in the sticks.

The idea of June tossing out a casual 'this was fun' over her shoulder the way Delia had tore me up until I ached from it. I had more at stake this time around. This time, I had my whole heart on the line.

Booker gathered the cards together and shuffled them. "I know you don't want to wind up dumped again, but you've got to climb back on that horse. Get back in the game. Rock that woman's world. When you're not completely incapacitated, that is."

"See, this is why we don't talk about our feelings."

He pointed the deck of cards at me like a threat, his eyes narrowing. "You got kicked by a horse."

"I recall."

"So are you going to quit your job? Leave training horses behind forever? Or are you going to heal up, put it behind you, and get back out on that court?"

Was it really as simple as that? Just try again? Lord, I wished it could be so easy.

"You mixed your metaphors there."

He shrugged. "I'm a high school basketball coach. Sue me."

When he dealt our cards, I held an ace and a king.

Maybe things were looking up.

THIRTY-TWO

june

I GOT to the Myler Manor earlier than I'd planned. After a rough night's sleep, tossing and turning while my mind drifted restlessly from Ty to my excitement over the wedding prep, I'd been up since dawn. Now that the decorating day had finally arrived, I couldn't get started fast enough.

The Manor's dining hall would have been gorgeous enough without any additional decoration. The rich hickory floors were set off by rows of tables laid out with plain white linen. Giant casement windows stretched from wall to wall, providing stunning views of the maples and wisteria in the gardens beyond. The wedding itself would be in the Methodist church a few miles away, but to my mind, a ceremony under the canopy of trees would have been perfect.

The reception would be an indulgence in book-themed decor. In addition to the copies of *Pride and Prejudice* for the bouquets, I'd salvaged dozens of classic books from thrift stores and garage sales, arranged them by color, and tied small stacks with gauzy ribbons. Each one would get a few of the paper flowers on top, perfect centerpieces for a bookworm's wedding.

"This is the last one," Jed said, toting in another carton of books.

I'd brought him along to do the heavy lifting, and he had been happy enough to do it until around the fifth trip out to his truck. After that, he set boxes on the growing stack with increasingly dramatic sighs and once, pressed the back of his hand to his forehead like an overtaxed chambermaid.

"Now you get to help me stack books."

In the reception hall, I pulled one table off to the side and stacked it high with my thrift store finds. The end result was a precarious but artistically pleasing backdrop for the photo booth Eden wanted set up there, complete with instant cameras and an assortment of fake mustaches on little sticks. The book display looked marvelous—I just hoped nobody bumped into the table during the reception, or they risked the whole thing falling down.

"Couldn't you have just printed out a poster with books on it?" Jed asked.

"And half-ass the theme? No, thank you."

He stretched to place a book at the top of one of the stacks. "What are you doing with all of these after the reception?"

"Donating them to Eden for the next library book sale."

"I was thinking kindling for a fire pit." He paged through a tattered copy of *Great Expectations,* its green hardcover splotchy with watermarks.

"Don't let Eden hear you talk that way. She had a hard enough time cutting up a few books for all these flowers. If you threaten books with fire, she just might set *you* on fire."

"I'll keep it to myself, then." He snapped the book shut and placed it on top of the stack.

I watched him, debating saying anything about my plans yet but too excited to keep my good news quiet. "Can you keep something else to yourself?"

His eyebrows twitched with mischief. "I love secrets."

"I'm serious."

"So am I. You have no idea how easy civilian secrets are to keep."

I hadn't considered that. Anything I had to tell him would seem like nothing compared to everything he never spoke about from his time in the military. "Do you have a lot of Top Secret secrets?"

He smiled serenely.

Right. Secret-keeping.

"Okay. So." I started to lean against the table stacked with books but thought better of it and jerked away. "I'm going to move back to Magnolia Ridge."

"Cool."

I scowled at him. "I thought you'd be more excited than that."

"Am I not jumping up and down?" He mimed squealing like Dylan and Beau. "Better?"

"I guess."

"What prompted this change? Or should I ask?"

"It's not that," I said quickly, knowing his hint meant Ty. "Marilyn offered me space to work out of her store."

That news took a little of the laughter out of Jed's expression. "She did?"

"We haven't talked about all the details yet, but I've been wanting to start my own business, and this is the perfect opportunity. I can still do the online stuff while I build up a clientele at Marilyn's."

"That's awfully generous of her."

I nodded, running a finger along the spine of a worn book. "I guess she and Pop are pretty serious."

"Are you okay with that?" His hazel eyes weren't teasing now.

"I'm not okay that y'all kept it from me for so long, but yeah, I think I'm okay with it. I just want Pop to be happy."

"I think he is." He paused and seemed to evaluate me. "What about you? Is this move going to make you happy?"

"I miss you guys. Dad, Wade, Annie, the boys. Eden and the girls. I miss being *home*."

"You're really done with Austin?"

The question sounded so stark, so all or nothing, but my answer didn't feel any less true. "I think I've been done for a long time. After we lost Mom, I thought coming back here would mean giving everything up, you know? It would prove I couldn't deal, prove I couldn't really make it in design. I think I wanted to come home even before that—I just didn't know that was what I wanted."

"I know what you mean. Come here."

He wrapped me in a hug and held on tight. I sank into his embrace, grateful he'd been kept safe all those years in Afghanistan and wherever else he'd gone that he never mentioned and wouldn't talk about. When he let me go, his eyes were sly again.

"First thing on your agenda has to be making friends with women we're not related to."

"You're not using me to get dates, Jed."

"Then what's the point of you coming home?"

THIRTY-THREE

AFTER WALKING down the aisle at the Methodist church three times, I wasn't sure I would be able to do it again for the wedding tomorrow morning. The wedding party had to stand on a dais at the front of the sanctuary, and it was those four little steps up to it that killed me. Up and down, up and down I'd gone, gritting my teeth that something so simple could cause so much pain. Today would have been a good contender for those pain meds I'd set aside weeks ago, if it weren't for all the lightheadedness that came with it. Didn't seem wise to risk fainting dead away in the middle of the church.

June watched me too closely for me to think she'd missed my discomfort—she picked up on everything. But between listening to the preacher's sneak peek at his mini-sermon about love being patient, kind, and understanding, and the wedding coordinator's determination to keep us all moving with military precision, June hadn't found a chance to say anything much to me at the church.

That was likely to change. I pulled up in front of the Robin-sons' massive old Queen Anne home where cars were already parked three deep in the curved driveway. Booker's parents liked throwing parties even more than mine did, and they'd invited most of the guest list to the rehearsal dinner. From the looks of their trampled lawn, they had a full house.

Laughter drifted from the open front door that led into the heart of the house. I walked through, nodding to guests I knew here and there, but not in much of a mood to talk. My chest hurt like blazes, and with all the excitement of getting to the church on time this afternoon, I'd forgotten to take my double dose of ibuprofen. I'd figured I would make a quick appearance and high-tail it back out again, until the smell hit me.

Walking into the Robinsons' kitchen was like stepping into a tidal wave of every delicious food smell I could think of. Fried chicken, biscuits, some kind of pie, and I didn't know what else. Platters were ferried out to the back yard as fast as Beverly Robinson could spoon them up. Chloe winked as she scooted by me, cradling a heaping bowl of homemade macaroni and cheese that had my mouth watering from a single glance.

I supposed I could stick around a little while.

Beverly turned and spotted me. "Ty! What are you doing hanging back there, come on in."

I moved closer to kiss her on the cheek.

She patted me lightly on the shoulder with a meaningful look at my chest. "Booker told us you got hurt. How are you doing, honey?"

"Better." Even though I'd known Beverly most of my life and thought of her as a second mother, I still didn't feel much like opening up about my pains like an old man.

She hummed as she peered up at me, her deep brown eyes shining like she could read my every hidden ache. "Does your mama know about your accident?"

"She does." I wasn't about to admit that my mother had only just found out yesterday. Beverly wouldn't approve, and I was in no state to receive one of her spirited lectures or her follow-up ferocious hugs.

"They're in Holland, is that right?"

"Admiring the windmills, that's right. They asked me to pass on their apologies again for missing the wedding."

She waved her hand in the air, tossing the apology away. "That's nothing. If Douglas had booked me a non-refundable European cruise, we would have missed the wedding, too."

Her laughter eased a little of the tension that wound through me. There was no way to be unhappy or uptight in the Robinson house. It had always been one of my favorite places as a kid, second only to Gram's ranch.

"I'm sure your mama's disappointed she's not here to nurse you back to health."

I grimaced, thinking how that would have gone. "I'll be through the worst of it by the time they get back."

"Well, let me tell you something, you don't look like you're through the worst of it yet. You look like you should be sitting down. What do you need? Want me to kick Grandma out of the easy chair?"

"Nah, I think some of this food you're making will cure me. Your fried chicken smells like heaven."

"Get on out there and grab some, but find a seat once you do."

The worried once-over she gave me warmed my soul. My mother's concern was all sharp edges and to-do lists, but Beverly's care was of a softer sort.

"Will do." I wrapped an arm across her shoulders so I could kiss her on the cheek again before sidling past her out the back door.

As I suspected, the Robinsons' yard teemed with people. Booker and Eden's family and friends mingled beneath huge blue awnings that provided a little shade but did nothing to combat the oppressive heat. I recognized some of the guests from around town, but a lot of the faces were strangers to me. Judging by the all the men over six-foot-six, Booker's entire college basketball team had shown up for the festivities.

A long line snaked away from the tables laid out with all the delicious food Beverly and Douglas had prepared, and it wove its way between folding chairs where people sat elbow to elbow as they savored the meal. Children played cornhole and horse-shoes in the yard beyond the feast, and enthusiastic kids had already put a massive bucket of bubble solution to good use, the results glittering as they floated through the air.

I scanned the crowd of well-wishers until my eyes lit on June. It had only been an hour or so since I'd last seen her, but I ached at the sight of her like we'd been apart for days. Unlike the physical pain I had to grit my teeth through, this ache had a sweetness to it, affection mixed with longing that sent my heart galloping in my chest. A loose sundress billowed around her as she laughed over something one of her brothers had said. She glanced over and met my eyes, pausing mid-laugh before breaking into a wider grin. I wanted to make her smile like that every day.

She left her family and came straight to me through the crowd. Her smile was tempered by the little line that sat between her eyebrows, and I could guess what she had in store for me.

"I'm surprised to see you here after the pastor put us through the paces at church. Don't you think you should take a rest?"

"You couldn't pay me enough to miss Beverly's fried chicken."

"But you look a little—"

"June." I put the slightest edge in my voice, both amused and exhausted by her constant fussing.

She raised her hands in surrender. "Okay, you win. I was just about to get some dinner. Want to join me?"

"Lead the way."

We took our place at the end of the line, and I wondered just how long it would take to reach the food, get a plate, and sit down. I didn't like to admit it, but June and Beverly were right, I could use a rest. What I needed was some ibuprofen, an ice pack, and my easy chair, but I wouldn't get any of them anytime soon.

"June," Isaiah said up ahead of us. "That is some dress." He took the excuse to let his eyes drift over her, flashing a charming grin.

I took a half step forward until my arm jostled against hers. The line needed to move faster.

"Thanks." June didn't move away from my touch, but leaned into me, her body warm against mine as we crowded together in line.

Maybe the line could move a *bit* slower.

"Are you coming out with us tonight after dinner? We're driving into Austin for one last pre-game. It's bound to get a little wild." He looked at me as if I'd appeared out of thin air. "And you, too, Ty. Gotta have the Best Man."

"I don't think I'd be much fun tonight."

"That's too bad, man." He managed a believable look of regret, but I knew he didn't care if I went out with them tonight, and would probably prefer it if I didn't. "June, you'll join us, though, right? Maid of Honor, and all."

"I'd better not. I've got plenty left to do tomorrow morning, and I don't think a hangover would do me any favors."

"We'd take real good care of you."

He grinned until I wanted to shove him face-first into the sweet potato pie.

"Thanks just the same."

"Let me know if you change your mind." Isaiah affected an easy come, easy go attitude but cut a last glance my way.

I nudged a little closer to June like a Neanderthal staking my territory, and he finally turned back to his own business.

We finished filling our plates and were shunted away from the buffet. A smarter man would have taken his food over to Booker's table and not looked back. As if reading my mind, June cocked her head to the side.

"Come on."

I followed.

She led me over to where her dad and brothers sat beneath a sprawling old ash. As soon as Clint saw us, he started waving us on like a coach calling his runner home from third. Jed moved out of the way to clear space for us, and with some careful maneuvering, I sat down between him and June.

Marilyn Wells sat next to Clint at one end of the table, the two of them sharing secret little looks. I would have bet money they held hands beneath the table. I stole a glance at June, but she seemed more comfortable with the idea of them together than she had been. Or at least, she was trying to get used to it, which was more what I suspected.

"You're looking a little worse for wear tonight," Clint said.

"It's not so bad as it was." I liked to believe I was improving little by little, but today, walking up and down a few stairs wore me out— that was still pretty bad.

I dug into my food, hoping the conversation would turn a new direction. One bite of Beverly's fried chicken sent my eyes rolling in the back of my head. The woman could cook circles around every restaurant in this town. No surprise I'd spent half my childhood trying to finagle an invite to stay over for dinner. Every dish was the most delicious thing I'd ever eaten.

Wade gestured between June and me with his fork. "Are you two doing speeches tonight?"

June shook her head. "At the reception. Tonight, it's just going to be Uncle Joel and Mr. Robinson."

"I hope somebody sets a timer," Clint said. "Joel will talk all night if you give him the chance."

"Douglas will just wrestle the microphone out of his hands," I said. Booker's father loved a good opportunity to tell embarrassing stories, as he had thoroughly proven at his kids' high school and college graduation parties. "He's probably got ten pages of speech notes tucked away somewhere."

"What about you, Junebug?" Jed grinned at her from behind a chicken drumstick. "Are you ready for your speech tomorrow?"

She gave him a sassy little look. "I hope everyone has a hanky ready, you're all going to be in tears."

"It's going to be that bad?"

She glared at Jed but turned to me. "Yours is ready, right?"

I feigned surprise. "I have to give a speech?"

Her eyes went wide, just as I'd hoped.

"Relax. I'm not that incapacitated."

She swatted me on the shoulder, but then let her hand fall to the crook of my arm. She rested it there, her thumb running little circles along my elbow, as if touching me like this was perfectly natural. Nobody else seemed to notice the gesture, but all my attention focused on it like a laser beam. The warmth of her fingers, the hypnotic circling of her thumb—my mind blanked out, I was so gone over the smallest touch from her.

An older woman came up to our table, a smirk set on her face. "Wade Evans, are those your boys stripping down to their altogether out under the magnolia?"

Wade spun his head around so fast, he probably gave himself whiplash. He choked on a bite of food and sprang up out of his chair, beelining to his two little boys who romped half-naked not far away.

Annie looked over her shoulder until she spotted them. She grumbled and turned back to the last of her food.

"I'm seeing a lot more of your boys this trip than I was expecting to," June said.

Annie made a face. "Try living with them. They think it's clothing-optional at our house."

"And the Robinsons' back yard," Jed said.

The woman gave Annie a once-over. "Honey, you look like you're about to pop. You aren't fixing to give birth during the wedding, are you?" She laughed, missing the look of death Annie shot her way.

"I've got two and a half months to go." Annie stood from the table, one hand cradled beneath her belly. "I think I need some cobbler."

"Oh, honey, you want to be careful with that, the baby weight gets harder and harder to lose. It's one of the worst things about pregnancy, you know."

Annie took a deep breath like she was gearing up to let Miss Opinionated have it, but Marilyn spoke first.

"I'm not sure about that, Peggy." Marilyn's voice came out sugary sweet. "I always thought receiving unsolicited advice was the worst thing about pregnancy."

Peggy pursed her lips as if she'd had a taste of something sour, then gave a pert little nod. "Good seeing y'all."

She sauntered away, and the minute she was gone, Jed burst into laughter. "Nice one, Marilyn."

Annie grinned at her rescuer. "Thanks."

"Some people need to learn to keep their thoughts to themselves." She stood and put an arm around Annie. "Now let's go get that cobbler."

The two women walked off toward the dessert table arm in arm. June smiled at Clint as though he had been the one to swoop in and save the day, and he just smiled back, apparently as pleased as could be.

"I don't think it's going so well for Wade." Jed nodded in that direction.

We all turned to see Wade chasing after one naked kid, with a second tucked under his arm like a football. Every time he got close to the loose one, the one he'd caught laughed and kicked until the kid nearly slipped from his arms.

"That's really not my wheelhouse. Is one of you going to help him, or are we just going to take videos?" Jed pulled his phone out of his pocket and tried to get a bead on them.

"I'll help him," Clint said as he left the table. "I've been down this road a time or two."

He wandered off while Jed captured the moment for posterity.

June laughed, and it was all I could do to contain my own laughter for fear of the spasms of pain it would cause. Her arm brushed against mine, and she still held my elbow with her other hand, sending a tingling warmth cascading through me.

I gazed down at her, and the whole world seemed to pause so I could take her in. Her eyes were full of joy, her smile all for me. Being with her was the only place I ever wanted to be. My thoughts were foolish, but if I had to be a fool, at least I was a fool over a woman like June.

As though the world knew just how to ruin a moment, I looked over her shoulder to see Bret in the crowd.

june

SITTING under that old tree with my family and Ty, another pang of what I'd been missing back in Austin tugged at me. I needed this sense of belonging and togetherness, being surrounded by the people I loved. And it *was* love tying me, not just to my family, but to this quiet man at my side. The way Ty gazed down at me, I would have sworn he felt it, too.

He glanced away, and his expression darkened like a storm cloud rolling in. I turned to see what had caused his happiness to so totally disappear, knowing what I would see before my eyes reached him. Bret stood not far away, overdressed for the warm day in a dark blue suit jacket and slacks, reminding everyone he was a big shot lawyer.

All the cozy, comfortable feelings that had been swirling inside me turned sour. Bret watched me with an odd look on his face.

I turned to face Ty. "Did you know he was coming tonight?"

His scowl deepened. "He didn't tell me a thing."

Jed seemed to realize something was up, and he, too, turned to see what it was. Bret walked toward us through the crowd, pausing a couple of times to shake someone's hand, but moving ever closer.

Jed stood up at the same time Ty did, ready for trouble. I couldn't say whether they were going to put a stop to it or looking to get some started. I took a deep breath, already thrown off my guard even with such support on my side. I stood to face Bret, flanked by my brother and Ty.

Bret stepped in front of us but hesitated. He glanced from Ty, whose rancher's muscles stood out beneath his pale blue button-down, to Jed, who hadn't lost any of the lean hardness he'd gained from twelve years in the Army. Finally, he looked at me. I didn't cut the same imposing figure as either of the men beside me, but I could still glare daggers at my ex.

"June." Bret said my name with the same shade of affection he'd used when we dated. Even he must have realized how fake that sounded now. He shifted his weight on his feet with another quick glance at my companions. "Ty. Jed."

"Dickface," Jed said. "How's it going?"

Bret's façade slipped. Half a second later, his confidence kicked back on, as bright as ever. "How have you been, June?"

"I've been great." I kept my words flat so he wouldn't think I was happy at all to see him.

"That's good to hear." He swallowed hard, casting brief glances at the men beside me. "Work going well?"

"The best. I'm starting my own design business."

Ty shifted at my side. Maybe it made me petty to throw that out there, but I didn't have a lot to toss in Bret's face right now. *I've been kissing your brother* was one, but I wasn't feeling *that* petty.

"That sounds great." Bret glanced around the crowded yard. When his eyes landed on me again, I caught a glimpse of nerves behind his composed veneer. "Would you talk to me alone for a few minutes? Please?"

Ty moved as though he might put himself between me and his brother, but he didn't quite do it. Neither he nor Jed said anything—they just made their presence undeniable as they stared Bret down in the middle of the party.

"Sure." My fake friendliness needed work, but I tried.

He gestured for me to go first, so I walked toward the little grove of peach trees that stood on one side of the Robinsons' house.

"I'll watch for your signal," Jed called after us, reminding me of his willingness to throw a punch if needed.

I clenched my hands together as I reached the stand of trees. We stood far enough away from the wedding guests to be out of earshot, but still somewhat in sight of them. I wasn't sure I wanted to be completely alone with Bret. I had no fear of falling for his garbage again, but I didn't want to give him the perfect opportunity to peddle it, either.

In classic Bret style, he smiled at me as if nothing at all could be strange about seeing each other again after so many months. "It's been a while."

Seeing him brought back memories, but probably not the ones he hoped. All I could think about was our last day together, and how long it had taken him to get around to telling me he'd started seeing someone else. We'd had dinner, walked through my favorite park and up to my apartment door before he finally started in on the real conversation. Even in the moment of telling me our relationship was over, it took him way too long to do it.

When he didn't come right out and speak up, I considered going straight back to my table. This was so like him, to have something to say and not actually say it. "Well?"

"You look gorgeous."

"You could have told me that in front of Jed and Ty."

"I'm not sure about that." He flashed a cheeky smile, but it faded when I didn't budge.

Still the Bret I'd known last year, more comfortable with the shine of a confident exterior than exposing anything real. He looked so much like Ty, with the same broad forehead and strong jawline, and hints of similarity around the mouth. But where Ty's eyes reflected his heart, however conflicted it might be, Bret's eyes didn't let me in at all. He was all flirt and charm, with nothing underneath. I kicked myself for never recognizing his lack of sincerity when we were together.

"June, I owe you an apology."

He looked so contrite all of a sudden, I almost laughed at the change. This, too, seemed more like a show than a glimpse of true regret. He was sorry now?

"You already apologized."

"No, I didn't. Not really." He took a deep breath that felt like another stalling tactic. He ate up plenty of time just making a show out of everything. "June, I didn't treat you right. I never should have—" He raked his fingers through his hair. "I thought you knew we were just casual."

He had no idea how close he was to getting slapped. Only the sight of the wedding guests over his shoulder stopped me from giving that remark the answer it deserved. "Was that seriously your apology?"

He winced, but what could he have expected? Gratitude?

"I'm sorry. I screwed up. I was a complete and total jackass, I know that now."

I didn't have anything to say. Hurt and anger swam through me all over again, and I tucked my hands beneath my elbows so he couldn't see them tremble. When he broke things off with me I'd been so surprised, everything had seemed to happen all at once. Now, time slowed so I could memorize every word of this pointless conversation.

"I don't expect you to forgive me. I wouldn't forgive me. But

I still wanted to apologize."

"Why?"

He smiled, but there was no joy in it. "Samantha left me for someone else."

It would have been a good moment to get a dig in about karma, but I didn't have the heart. Even if it served him right, I couldn't pour salt in that wound, not when I knew exactly how deep it cut.

"One of the partners in my law firm, to be precise," he went on. "It's been a little..."

He didn't clarify, but I could fill in the blanks. *Shocking. Painful. Humiliating.*

"I found out a few months ago. I thought about getting in touch with you then, but I didn't think you'd want to talk to me."

Leave it to Bret to make it my fault he didn't do the right thing. What had I ever seen in him? He was charming and confident, always up for anything. His desire for nonstop action had been just what I'd needed when we reconnected, but it couldn't suit me now, even if he had never thought about cheating.

Now, I wanted someone who didn't need to put on a show, who was down to earth and kept true to his values even when it hurt him financially. I wanted someone who put me ahead of his own selfish interests. Now, all I wanted was Ty.

"I'm sorry I didn't break things off with you before I—" Bret grimaced, apparently unable to admit his mistakes even when he apologized for them. "I thought I'd find the right time, but—"

Most of his apology went unsaid. That fit. As a lawyer, he probably had some credo against self-incrimination.

"Ty kept telling me to man up and be honest with you, but I guess I was too much of a coward."

The warm cocoon around my heart shattered. "Ty knew?"

Bret made a helpless gesture. Why wouldn't he have told his brother? I'd always assumed Ty found out after the fact just like I had. But no, Bret had told Ty, and Ty had kept the secret. I went cold, untouched now by the afternoon's stifling heat.

"I'm sorry, June. I learned my lesson too late, but I wanted you to know."

I doubted the lesson would stick. A long pause followed where he seemed to expect me to say something, probably offer forgiveness. I stayed silent. He took a step toward me, arms out as if coming in for a hug. I jabbed a finger over his shoulder for him to leave.

"Right, right." He turned and walked away.

I moved deeper into the peach trees that blocked the Robinsons' yard from view of the street, tempted to run all the way to my pop's. Maybe that would get rid of the sick feeling that coiled around me, pressing in and suffocating. Blood pounded through my veins, pulsing at my temples until the sound filled my ears.

Ty hadn't told me. Not then, not now. He'd kept Bret's secrets.

I wasn't sure how long I'd been in the trees when a new voice came from behind me.

"June?"

Ty.

I turned around to face him, my heart cut to shreds by the sweet worry lining his face. I'd wanted that kind of openness from him for weeks, longed for it—but now, how could I trust it?

"Are you okay?"

I shook my head, willing away the shock that clouded my thoughts. "No."

"Oh, sweetheart." He moved closer, but I held up a warning hand.

"You knew?" My voice was low, but he stopped as though I'd shouted. A part of me had hoped I'd misunderstood or Bret had misspoken, but Ty's hesitation confirmed all my fears. The churning in my gut had me reeling. "You knew he was seeing other girls, and you didn't say anything?"

The tenderness in his eyes seemed to harden up and close down, like he was packing it all away. Shutting it up in a box labeled *Feelings* he'd stuff away in an attic.

"I didn't know what to say."

"How about the truth?" My voice came out too loud, but music thrummed through the night, and the rehearsal dinner went on undisturbed. I clenched my fists, my nails digging little half-moons in my palms.

He looked unsure of himself, at a loss for what to say. His stricken expression reminded me of when he'd been lying in the dirt, injured and broken.

"I didn't want to hurt you."

"Well, you did." I found some satisfaction in his flinch. Did he think he'd *spared* me? "How long did you know?"

"June—"

"Tell me."

He tried to draw in a deep breath but stopped with a wince. "A few months."

The wind seemed knocked out of me all over again. After Bret's evasive admission he was seeing someone new, the question of just how long I'd been deluded had tormented me. How long had I thought our relationship was good enough, when in reality, it had been broken beyond repair and I just didn't know it yet? And now, I knew. Months. At least.

Did *everyone* think I was too fragile to hear the truth?

"You should have told me."

"I was afraid."

"Afraid of what? What could the Unbreakable Ty Hardy

possibly have been afraid of?"

He held his hands out as if grasping for the right thing to say but found nothing. This man who kept powerful animals in check, who worked in the harshest elements without a second thought, whose glare could make any rational man take a step back—what was he afraid of? It sure as heck wasn't me—he'd proven that time and again. He could only have feared angering his brother if he told me the truth.

"Were you afraid you might lose your ranch if you crossed Bret?"

He jerked his head back as though I'd shoved him. "I'm not afraid of Bret."

"Then what?"

He shook his head like he couldn't find the answer. I wanted to believe he *had* an answer, but now, I wasn't sure. A scummy ooze crept through my stomach as doubt swelled. I had stormed over to his house again and again these last weeks, involving myself in his ranch, in his home, in his life. He had never once asked me to do any of it, never asked me to come back, never asked me to stay. He'd told me to keep away, and I hadn't listened. I'd kept barging in, thinking he needed my help —thinking he needed *me*.

"Is *all* of this just because you didn't want to hurt my feelings? Was any of it real?"

What I wouldn't give for a tender declaration of his growing feelings, a confirmation that yes, there was something between us, it wasn't all on my side. But Ty clenched his jaw, biting back whatever he felt.

If he felt anything at all.

That was what decided me, the silence. I couldn't fall for someone who had no intention of loving me back. Hadn't he been trying to tell me this whole time? I'd been too caught up in my own crazy hopes to listen.

"I'm such an idiot." Humiliation filled my stomach like a dead weight, creeping outward until I thought I might be sick. I'd done it again, projecting everything I wanted onto a guy instead of seeing the truth right in front of me.

"June, no."

The tenderness in his voice skated too close to an apology, too close to pity for me to stay out there with him any longer.

"I'm not doing this again." I moved to slip past him, but he reached out to me.

"Wait."

"Forget it." I pulled my arm away, shivering from the soft touch of his hands. "After the wedding is over, I'll leave you alone, and we can go back to our real lives."

I managed to say the words without a trace of tears. Maybe I had some unemotional robot in me, after all. Ty's expression froze as if something in that statement cut him, but whatever it was, he didn't say.

Of course he didn't say. He was the Unbreakable Ty Hardy. I was the one who had broken.

"Right." His eyes grew shuttered, distant. Just like he used to be, before I barged in and got us tangled up in this mess. "We can go back to our real lives."

Well. That sounded final enough. My heart crumpled in on itself until it became a tiny speck. I turned, walking as fast as I could toward the ash tree where my family waited, trying to clear my expression before anyone caught sight of me. This was no place to cry. After the rehearsal dinner, I would shut myself up in my childhood bedroom and let my heart shatter in private.

Maybe I could try to forget I had fallen hook, line, and sinker for another Hardy, and this time, I'd been stupid enough to think he actually loved me back.

THIRTY-FIVE

I STOOD IN THE ROBINSONS' yard, June's words echoing their misery in my head.

"We can go back to our real lives."

She would go back to Austin. It was what I'd expected all along, what I thought I wanted, so it shouldn't hurt this much to hear her say it. She would start her own business and make a name for herself, just like she wanted, and I would go back to my ranch.

I closed my eyes, a cold throb settling in behind my broken ribs. The thought of going back to my ranch all alone left my heart aching for everything I'd lost. Everything I had just let slip away. I opened my eyes again, and the sight of Bret walking across the lawn turned that cold ache into an angry fire. I glared as my brother came close enough I could smell his awful cologne.

"I heard you got kicked by one of your horses."

Bret's smirk did it. After everything he had put June through and made me endure by proxy, he'd decided to lead with a smartass remark? I snapped. I socked him square in the mouth. Pain ripped through my chest like a Mack truck thundering over my ribs and tore a shout from my lungs, but I'd do it again to give Bret a small taste of what he deserved.

He stumbled back, putting a hand to his bleeding lip. Should have at least knocked him down, but I didn't have the energy to get in a better punch. The one I'd landed left my head swimming and sparks flashing in my vision as it was.

"What was that for?"

"You had it coming." I put one hand over my blazing chest, sure I'd felt my bones pop out of place with that punch. Worth it, but it cost me. "What did you say to her?"

"I apologized, you ass." Bret dabbed at his mouth and inspected the blood on his fingertips. Probably afraid it would drip on his fancy jacket, the pretentious jerk. I should have known better than to think he might throw a punch in return. Couldn't sully his image. Leaving women left and right didn't faze him, but he wouldn't stoop so low as to fight for one.

"It's a little late for that, isn't it?"

"Better late than never." He fished around in his pockets but must not have had anything to wipe his hands on. "What's gotten into you?"

"Nothing." I stormed around him, trying to decide if I wanted to punch him again. The first one hadn't been very satisfying, but maybe another would do the trick. I might pass out from the pain straight after, but that didn't stop me from wanting to land a second blow.

Even with a bloody lip, he managed a smirk. "I guess a better question is, what's going on with you and June?"

I shook my head, still prowling around him. I wasn't about to have a heart to heart with my baby brother, especially not over her.

"Come on, man, I might be a jackass, but I'm not an idiot. I know you like her."

"You don't know anything." Like wasn't nearly the word.

287

This was more than *like* burning through me, eating me up whole from the inside out.

"I saw the way you used to watch her when we were together. I know that look. You wanted her from the first day I brought her home."

I couldn't deny it. I'd been taken with her from the first moment I saw her. I'd tried to accept I could never be with her, but that hadn't made me want her any less. These last weeks, all that wanting had stretched and grown until I couldn't contain it any more. I put my hand on my chest, somewhere over my busted up heart. This wasn't a passing interest I could put out of my mind, or an inconvenient attraction I would forget as soon as she was gone. For the first time in my life, I was in love.

In two days, the woman I loved would go back to her real life in Austin, her future laid out in front of her, all shiny and new. I wanted to break something.

"You know, I used to wish you'd make a move on her so I could bow out and it wouldn't be my fault." Bret flashed his *I'm a jerk but what can I do?* grin.

I took a step closer, and he flinched. "The minute you thought that, you should have done the right thing and ended it with her."

"I know. I'm a coward. I admit it."

"You're a coward and a cheating snake."

"That, too." He kept his tone light, but something in his eyes said he felt the truth of it. He could be a selfish jerk, but I had never really thought him heartless. He just couldn't stop himself from screwing things up with women.

"Did you ever care about her?"

He hesitated, and that was answer enough.

"I wanted to."

I exhaled an imitation of a laugh. He'd *wanted* to. I couldn't stop thinking about the woman, and the idea of not being with her made me feel like I was drowning, but oh, my little brother *wanted* to care about her.

"You are a piece of work."

"Yeah." His smile seemed a little more genuine. "I've got to admit, I'm not real thrilled about my brother dating my ex-girlfriend."

"You don't get a say," I said, my lungs burning in my chest. "And we're not dating. We're not anything." My voice broke. It was the truth, but Lord, it felt like a lie. June was everything to me.

His smile disappeared again. "You really care about her."

I shot him a glare. "I'm not talking about this with you."

"Fine. You look awful. You want me to get you a glass of water or something?"

My vision swam. I put my hands on my knees, waiting for the dizziness to pass. I'd been on my feet more than half the day. Too long. The punch hadn't done me any favors, either, but I couldn't regret it.

He placed a hand on my shoulder. "What do you need?"

A bottle of Tennessee whisky and about a hundred years to forget.

I brushed his hand away. "Get off me."

Booker suddenly appeared beside us, a wide, fake smile on his face, and fire in his eyes.

"Gentlemen," he said, as if breaking up a fight at the high school. "I am here on behalf of my future wife to let you know if you go on making a scene like this, she will murder you both with her bare hands."

Over his shoulder, a few people in the dinner crowd cast cautious glances our way. Even if our shouting had been muffled by the music, the punch I'd thrown hadn't gone unnoticed.

Dammit. The one thing June had asked of me was to make nice, for Eden and Booker's sake. This wasn't what she'd meant, but it clearly fell into the *don't wreck the wedding* category.

I straightened. He clapped me lightly on the shoulder, and I had to stifle a groan.

"Are you two done here?"

I looked at Bret, who had the sense to lose his default smirk. "We're done."

With another dab at his bloody lip, he nodded at Booker and walked away.

Concern pulled at Booker's eyes and mouth as he glanced me over. "Are you okay?"

Was I okay? I might have just undone the last few weeks' worth of my bones healing, but that wasn't what had my chest feeling flayed and laid bare like it would never be whole again.

"I'm wrecked."

He nodded. "Come on. Let's get you a drink."

june

I SAT in Jed's truck, my arms tucked tight around my chest. I'd plastered on a fake smile through two long speeches, silently ticking down the minutes until the rehearsal dinner finally broke up for the night. I hadn't looked for Ty, and he hadn't come looking for me. I'd stared straight ahead and done my best not to have an emotional breakdown in front of all of Eden's guests.

I should have been proud of myself for walking away from Ty—I'd wished more than once over the last year that I'd had the good sense to walk away from Bret. This time, I'd nipped it in the bud. No humiliation, no getting blindsided by a break-up, just a quick goodbye.

Instead of feeling like a badass, confident woman, every step I'd taken away from Ty had cracked a new fissure in my heart.

This was all my fault. If I'd been a little more logical and hadn't chased after my feelings the way I always did, I might have avoided this crushing heartache. Ty had tried to tell me I was risking my heart, and what had I done? Ignored his practical advice and instead run headlong toward him.

"Does your Irish goodbye have anything to do with the bloody lip I saw Bret sporting at the end of dinner?" Jed asked.

All my woe-is-me thoughts crashed together in an epic wreck. "What?"

I'd been so intent on not looking for Ty, carefully not missing him sitting beside me, absolutely not thinking about his infuriating strong, silent act, I'd barely paid attention to the rest of the rehearsal dinner.

Jed looked even more satisfied than he had the night of our embarrassing family dinner. "I'm guessing he and Ty had words."

I was still trying to make sense of the image. "You think Ty hit Bret?"

"Can you name anyone else who would want first pick? It wasn't you or me."

He had a point. "Ty isn't supposed to exert himself like that. That can't be good for his healing."

Jed's laughter finally broke free. "I guess someone had better tell him."

I'd been fussing over Ty against his will for the better part of three weeks. I guessed he could take care of himself. But *why* had he hit Bret? And why hadn't he done it so I could see it play out in all its glory?

"I'm the last guy who should be giving anyone advice on love," Jed said. "But are you sure hiding out at Pop's is really what you want to do right now?"

No, I wasn't, but I couldn't trust myself to be sure of what I did want right now. My head wanted to go to my pop's, drink a fifth of Jack Daniels, and forget Ty Hardy entirely. My heart wanted to run right back to him at the Robinsons', confess all my feelings for him in a stupid, messy speech, and hope somewhere deep down, he felt the same.

My heart was an idiot.

Rather than tell Jed all that, I stuck with the facts.

"Ty knew Bret was cheating. He *knew*, and he never told me."

Jed didn't take this news as hard as I had. He made a *so what* gesture with his hands on the steering wheel. "What was he supposed to say?"

"I don't know, maybe *My brother is cheating on you, thought you should know*."

"You were close with Ty when you were dating Bret?"

He didn't say it like an accusation, but surprise wove through the question.

"Not exactly close. Not at the end, anyway."

"Uh-huh. So you're mad he didn't rat out his brother to someone he wasn't exactly close with?"

My mouth dropped open, but I shut it again. Maybe Ty and I had been a little too comfortable together at the beginning, but by the last couple of months of my relationship with Bret, he'd stopped coming to the family dinners. He hadn't been around to tell me anything. Did I really think he should have run to my apartment in Austin to tattle on his brother?

"Well, we're close now." I refused to let go of my righteous anger so easily. "He's just as bad as you and Pop and Wade, keeping secrets and thinking you can't tell me anything."

"Interesting how you just tossed Ty onto a list with the three men who love you most in the world."

I swiveled my head around to look out the window, even though I saw nothing but darkness. I wanted him on that list, but that didn't mean he qualified.

"He doesn't feel that way about me. I thought maybe..." Heartache nipped at me, threatening to pull me under. "I guess I was wrong."

"Hey." Jed reached over to squeeze my hand. "I know your heart, June. And your heart's never wrong."

"It was wrong about Bret."

"Yeah, but did you love Bret?"

I sagged against the seat. That had never come into play. Sure, I'd had feelings for him and blinded myself to his lack of them for me, but actual, gut-wrenching, heart-leaping out of your chest *love*? "No."

"What about Ty?"

I loved him more than was sensible or safe.

"Just drive."

THIRTY-SEVEN

MY HEAD POUNDED, and my eyes ached, but I managed to lay out the last of the decorations in the Methodist church. I'd turned the whole sanctuary into a romantic librarian's dream come true, down to the last artfully arranged book.

I scurried around the building in my regular clothes and my hair pulled into a loose ponytail, using up precious preparation minutes. Eden and the other bridesmaids were already tucked away upstairs in the bridal ready-room, doing each other's hair and makeup. I wanted to make sure everything was perfect for the ceremony before I got myself ready, but that was only part of what kept me nudging paper roses and adjusting banners.

My thoughts were stuck on repeat, memories from last night burned on my mind without mercy. Ty's tender *Oh, sweetheart* when he sought me out, followed by the image of him packing all his feelings away right when I'd needed to hear them most. A glimpse of all I'd hoped for, and then the brutal reality of what was.

This wedding was going to be so much worse than it would have been if I had just left well enough alone. I'd gone out to Ty's ranch hoping for a semblance of friendship, however strained. Now I knew without a doubt I loved him, and he didn't feel the same. Yeah, that wouldn't be awkward at all.

He felt *something* for me, I was sure of it. But whatever he felt, it wasn't enough for him to break his silence. That reminder made me stand a little taller as I did my final walk-through of the church. I deserved someone who was all in. If Ty couldn't be that, then I would just have to move on. How, exactly, I couldn't imagine, but I would figure it out eventually.

Upstairs, the bridesmaids jockeyed around dueling vanities that stood at either end of the bridal room, putting final touches on their makeup and hairdos. At least three floral perfumes wafted around in the air, threatening an immediate headache. But when Eden turned from the full-length mirror, I forgot all my selfish troubles.

In full Greek goddess mode, she looked even more radiant than she had in Brides Galore. Her blond hair was swept up into a complicated bun, with delicate ringlets falling on either side of her face, her grin bigger than I had ever seen it. The woman positively sparkled with joy.

"You look gorgeous." I wrapped her in a quick embrace, careful not to crease her dress. "I'm so happy for you."

"Don't cry or you'll make me cry, and I already have my makeup on."

"You're going to cry through the whole ceremony anyway," Harper said, dabbing a tissue under one eye.

"Shush." Eden jabbed a finger in her sister's direction. "Just let me get through the pictures. My face can fall apart after."

"Any bets on how hard Booker blubbers through his vows?" Chloe asked.

Eden seemed delighted by the thought. "He's going to cry so hard."

"That man loves you more than he loves himself."

I hurried into my blush rose bridesmaid dress and sat still

while Eliza did my makeup and curled my hair into soft waves that fell loose over my shoulders. I tried to close off my mind and focus on the wedding, but Ty just couldn't stay out of my thoughts. Soon enough, I would see him again, and I wasn't sure yet what I should say when I did.

I needed to stop letting my heart lead me around by the nose. I needed to be logical for a change. The most logical thing would be to do as I had always planned: Play nice through the wedding and reception, smile in an approximation of happiness, and get out of there. Robots didn't cry over broken hearts. Lucky jerks.

The wedding coordinator summoned us to the hallway, and we lined up in order as we waited for our cues to go downstairs and walk down the aisle. I had never been particularly anxious during the other weddings I'd participated in, just giddy for my friends and grateful for the excuse to wear a fancy dress. Today, nerves ate up my insides like they were looking for some of Beverly Robinson's fried chicken.

One by one, my cousins and Chloe filed down and away until only Eden and I stood on the stairs. I turned to her and flashed a huge grin. She grinned back, her eyes already full of tears. So much for her grand plans of not crying until after the photos.

"I love you," I whispered.

"I love you, too."

My cue came, and I walked downstairs and into the sanctuary on auto-pilot, focusing on taking slow, reasonable steps. My nerves eased as I passed friends and family, and my fears of having to fake smiles disappeared entirely when I saw my pop, Jed, and Wade. Their faces propped up my heart, keeping me afloat, and I had to stifle a laugh at Jed's cheeky wink.

Marilyn sat at Pop's side, beaming at me. Seeing them together was still jarring, but the smile on his face eased away whatever bitterness I'd harbored about their relationship. My pop's happiness meant more than anything else.

Just before I climbed the steps at the front of the church, I made the mistake of looking up at the waiting line of men. Booker's huge smile showed his unquenchable joy on his wedding day, as if he'd been granted three wishes and every one of them was *marry Eden*. As predicted, tears already streaked his cheeks, and he hadn't even caught a glimpse of her yet. I was dimly aware of the other groomsmen in line, but Ty's expression made my breath catch. Standing at the front of the church in his perfectly tailored gray suit, he watched me with such intensity, I could almost believe he was trying to talk to me without words.

Well, that would make sense, since he had used as few words as possible with me for weeks now.

I took my place next to Chloe, the wedding march started, and everyone stood. My nephew, Dylan, and one of Booker's little cousins trotted up to the front of the church, Dylan going at a fast clip to get his job over and done with, the little girl relishing her time in the spotlight. She spread petals one by one until the whole church rumbled in laughter at how seriously she took her role.

When the dedicated flower girl finally reached her mother and was herded off to the side, Eden appeared on Uncle Joel's arm. Everyone craned their necks and whipped out handkerchiefs, but Eden and Booker might as well have been alone. Watching them watch each other like no one else existed pinched at my heart as much as it warmed it. Crazy to want this moment for Ty and me, absolutely crazy—but that didn't stop the wanting.

I kept my composure all through the pastor's sermon, the two Bible readings, and the musical interlude. I was careful to hold my gaze someplace safe and neutral, like Eden's back or the reader's lectern, *not* on the Best Man.

Everything went fine until the vows. When Booker said he would take on Eden's burdens as his own, my gaze darted to Ty. His eyes were already on me, telegraphing a message I couldn't interpret. My stomach bottomed out and my heartbeat skipped at the look in his eyes. I clutched my bouquet tighter as I glanced away again, willing my heart and mind to quiet down.

Any tears that fell down my cheeks afterwards were solely because of Eden and Booker's happiness, nothing more.

The happy couple were declared husband and wife, and leaned in for an extravagant kiss. I smiled over them even though my stomach twisted into a pretzel. They finally came up for air and darted down the aisle to cheers and wolf-whistles. Lumbering forward like a wall of gray linen and muscle, Ty offered me his arm. *Showtime*. I flashed a fake smile just like I'd practiced. Maybe weaker than I wanted, but the best I could do. His eyebrows drew together, but he didn't return the favor.

Ty escorted me through the sanctuary and outside to where the photographer waited to take photos. I tried not to listen, but Booker's repeated declarations of how stunning Eden was and how much he adored her were hard to miss. They sank into my heart, searing a little for all the foolish wishes they conjured. Foolish wishes had gotten me into this mess in the first place.

While Eden and Booker posed wrapped in each other's arms, I stood with the rest of the bridal party off to one side of the churchyard.

Ty spoke nearly in my ear, he was so close. "You're the most beautiful woman I've ever seen."

I gave him another thin smile. Beautiful. Ordinarily, it was a heck of a compliment, especially from a man of few words like Ty, but it paled compared to what I really wanted to hear.

I have feelings for you, too.

You're not in this alone.

I'm all in.

Any one would have done just fine.

I shook off those regrets and stuffed them far away. I had to get through this entire wedding day, and getting weepy over Ty would make that ten times harder.

"How are you feeling?" I'd asked him so many times, it was second nature now. Even his tailored suit and freshly shaven face couldn't hide the tension that lined his mouth and eyes. I guessed he'd had a bad night. Well, he wasn't the only one.

"I'm fine."

His answer was just as reflexive as my question. I could see he wasn't fine, knew his chest must hurt from all of this standing and walking around, and the day had only just begun. But if he didn't want to give an honest answer, I wouldn't push it. That hadn't gotten us anywhere.

"How are you?" he asked.

I glanced away. "I'm fine."

See? We could both lie.

THIRTY-EIGHT

I COULDN'T HAVE BEEN HAPPIER for Booker, that was the truth. I just wished the man's reception would go by a little quicker. I'd smiled through all the photos, which wasn't too hard, since I'd been looking at June. I'd cheered right along with everyone else when Booker and Eden were ushered into the Myler Manor as Mr. and Mrs. Robinson, ignoring the blaze that flared up in my chest with every clap and shout. Now, I had to endure dinner as a spectacle, sitting at the head table next to Eden while everyone watched me eat.

Not that anyone really watched me. Any glances my way were aimed at Eden and Booker, wrapped up in each other's happiness like twists of taffy. I'd never had so many cameras and phones turned toward me in my life. I did my best to keep a light smile on, hoping any wide-angle shots focused more on June than me.

I tried not to stare at her down the table, I really did. With her hair all done and the slinky bridesmaid dress on, she was almost too beautiful to look at. Though if I had to choose, I preferred her in jeans and a T-shirt, stomping around in rubber boots on my ranch.

The thought of never seeing her there again left me sick inside. I'd barely slept last night for misery. I'd managed not to drown myself in the bottle of Johnnie Walker Bullet's owner had sent me, though it'd been tempting. Anything to kill this ache in my heart and the growing sense that in trying to do the right thing, I'd gone and done the opposite. I wouldn't hold June back, tie her down to me and my ranch when she deserved so much more, but I couldn't shake the feeling I had crushed my own happiness under my boot.

"How are you doing, Ty?" Eden broke through those depressing thoughts, shining the full force of her joy on me.

"I'd think you would be more concerned with how your husband's doing."

Her grin widened on the word *husband*, like it was her new favorite word. "I'm just checking in."

I noticed the photographer moving around in the audience, her huge camera lens trained on us. Ah. Candids. I smiled and played along.

"I'm fine. How does it feel to be Mrs. Robinson?"

"Like I'm the luckiest woman in the world."

Her happiness amplified the ache in my own heart, a bright spotlight on the longing I'd been holding onto for two years. And I was going to just let June drive away in a few hours? *Not the time.* I could at least get through my best friend's wedding. Then, I could retreat to regret and Johnnie Walker.

"Booker's going to spend the rest of his life trying to make you as happy as you are today, you know that, right?"

She nodded, blinking back tears. I hadn't meant to make her any more emotional, but it probably wouldn't take much to get the waterworks going today. Booker had cried all through the ceremony, the sentimental sap. All told, they were pretty perfect for each other.

Our fake-casual conversation came to an end when the

wedding coordinator slipped up to the table, clipboard in hand, and passed me a microphone. The worst part of my Best Man duties had arrived.

I stood, and the coordinator clinked a spoon against her wine glass, drawing attention to the head table. One hundred faces turned toward me as I stood up. She slunk away, disappearing into the edges of the audience, leaving me to my task. I pulled out notes for the speech I'd written months ago from an inner pocket.

"I'm Ty Hardy," I said into the microphone, lifting a hand in greeting. "I've known Booker since we were kids. You'll never meet a guy with more enthusiasm or more heart. He's got a big personality—that means he's sometimes an obnoxious ass."

Laughter rumbled around the audience, to my relief.

"But his big personality gets things done. He's the kid who started Magnolia Ridge's annual downtown pet parade through sheer force of will. He's the guy who petitioned for—and got—extended lunch periods our senior year of high school. And as an adult, he's the guy who encourages his students to be the best they can be every day."

Booker had fresh tears in his eyes, and I'd just gotten started. I'd wanted to avoid mooning and getting too sentimental, but I loved the guy.

"That's what Booker does—he lives life with no regrets and takes every opportunity that comes his way. So when he started dating Eden, our sweet, kind, smart librarian, he didn't waste any time. They'd been together about a month when he said to me, 'Ty, Eden's it for me'. If you've seen them together, you know he's right. They fit. Eden, you might have to deal with his occasional obnoxiousness, but you'll never have to question that this man would do anything for you.

"If there's one thing we can learn from Booker, it's how to—"

I froze, the words I'd written all those months ago blurring across the page like I viewed them through fog. Then they sharpened, so bold and clear, they squeezed my heart in a vise grip. For a second, I couldn't breathe—I just let the words rattle around in my brain, shaking me out of my stupid fears, pushing out all my doubts, all my insecurities. My world lurched, shifted, and righted again.

The success I'd worked so hard to build wouldn't comfort me if I sacrificed a life with June to keep it. I didn't know how it would all fall into place, but I knew what I wanted without question. I loved my life, my ranch, my work—but I loved June more.

Was I really going to let the woman I loved slip away from me without putting up a fight? Not today.

I cleared my throat and tried again. "It's how to take hold of happiness when it comes our way without fear, and live in the moment. To Booker and Eden. May your years be long, your joy great, and may you never want for more."

The crowd toasted and cheered, but I hardly heard the noise. My whole focus centered on June. She stood to give her toast, our fingers brushing as I handed over the microphone. My heart slammed against my ribcage, pounding out its eager tattoo. I finally fulfilled her wish to avoid some public scene, since it took every last ounce of self-control I had not to take her in my arms right in front of everyone and tell her how much she meant to me.

If Booker could move past his disappointments to claim the love of his life, I could, too. No more hesitation, no more fear, no more garbage excuses. June was it for me, and I wouldn't go another day without telling her.

I just hoped she would still give me a chance to say the words.

june

I STOOD FROZEN in front of the whole wedding reception, my skin buzzing from Ty's microphone hand-off. His sweet speech had filled me with fireflies, but when our eyes met, every one exploded in a shower of sparks. His eyes held so much yearning, so much tenderness and vulnerability, that for a moment, I couldn't speak. I just stood there soaking it in.

A cough in the crowd snapped me out of what I hoped had been a very short Ty-induced daze. I dragged my gaze away from him and tried to focus on Eden and Booker. My hands shook so I could hardly hold the small cards I'd written my speech cues on, but I had to plunge ahead. I took a deep breath and dove in.

"For those of you who don't know me, I'm Eden's cousin, June. I grew up with these women, and I always considered myself the fourth Webb sister. It was either that, or accept I already had two older brothers, and that was unthinkable."

The audience's laughter eased some of my nerves. Giving an emotional speech should have been a slam dunk, but with my senses on high alert and Ty watching from feet away, tension pulled taut inside me.

"Eden and I were always close, and as a kid, I idolized her as if she were my own big sister. I remember watching her ride her bike, this huge pink Huffy, when I still had training wheels on, and I thought, 'I want to be like that'.

"Later on, I watched her graduate valedictorian of her high school class, and I thought, 'I want to be like that'. In college, she figured out exactly what she wanted from her career and went after it. And I thought, 'I want to be like that.'"

I took in a shaky breath. "One night last winter, Eden invited me to come to town so I could have dinner with her and Booker. They were disgustingly happy, as most newly-dating couples are, and it was pretty hard to take, to be honest. Even then, I could see how perfectly they matched each other, how their strengths brought out the best in each other, how they encouraged and supported each other.

"There was this one moment where Eden's shawl slipped off her shoulder. In the middle of telling me a story, Booker reached over and moved the shawl back without thinking, like taking care of Eden came as naturally to him as taking care of himself. And I thought, 'I want to be like that'."

My voice broke, but I was determined to hold it together. "Booker and Eden see each other for who they really are. They love with their whole selves, no selfishness, no holding back. I have no doubts about their future happiness, because they put each other first." I turned to face Eden and raised my glass. "Of their love story, may we all say, 'I want to be like that'."

While the audience toasted and cheered, Eden stood and wrapped me in a huge hug.

"I told you not to make me cry," she said in my ear.

"You knew I would if I could."

We sat down again for another quick speech from Uncle Joel, thanking everyone for coming. I still buzzed with nerves from being center stage while my brain malfunctioned over Ty. Worse, he hadn't taken his eyes off me since before my speech. No matter how he stared, I couldn't look at him. If I did, I would start to cry, and absolutely all of this mess had happened because I didn't want to cause a scene at my cousin's dang wedding.

With the speeches wrapped up, it was time for dancing. I wasn't sure I had the heart to dance all night, but it was Eden's special day—I would do whatever I could to make it perfect. The crowd slowly made their way into the next room, where the dance floor spread out beneath strings of fairy lights. Ty followed close behind me, and though we didn't touch, the weight of his eyes on me had my heart in my throat. We had one last official duty as Maid of Honor and Best Man. A fake smile was one thing, but fake happy-dancing? I should have brought the purse bourbon.

Booker and Eden were introduced again as husband and wife, to room-shaking applause. They swayed together in the middle of the dance floor while "Love is Here to Stay" by Ella Fitzgerald played. Eden grinned up at Booker as if she were etching the moment on her heart, and he gazed down at her like he'd been handed the whole world.

My heart squeezed as if giant hands had wrung it out. *I want to be like that.*

Ty stood next to me at the edge of the crowd, close enough his body heat warmed me from the outside in. I stared straight ahead, looking through Booker and Eden, pulling all my pride and self-respect together. I could do this. One last dance. And then...what?

I didn't have a clue, but the only way out was through.

Louis Armstrong's "The Sunshine of Love" started, and I recognized my cue. The bridesmaids and groomsmen were

GENNY CARRICK

supposed to join Booker and Eden out on the dance floor for the second song, but the party would really start when the third song played.

"Are you ready for this?" I asked Ty.

"I think I've been waiting my whole life for this."

He held his hand out to me, a silent invitation. Fighting the gravitational pull threatening to crash me straight back into my foolish hopes, I slipped my hand into his. He walked us onto the dance floor beneath the twinkling lights, then drew me to him. Held close in the comfort of his arms, his hand warming the small of my back, all my plans to be detached and distant evaporated. I wanted to sink into his closeness forever. My heart seemed to swell up with that want, even though I knew I should flatten it back out.

"June." My name sounded like longing on his lips, a secret confession in that one word. "I should have told you as soon as I knew Bret wasn't being true to you. I'm sorry I let you go through that."

The desperation in his voice squeezed my chest, slowing my breath. The song played on, the bridal party swayed in time, and all around us, other guests watched us dance. But for me, nothing else mattered but Ty.

"I wanted to tell you, but how could I? Your heart would be hurt either way. I was the only one who stood to gain anything. I was crazy for you from the day we met."

My heart thundered in my ears until I had to strain to hear his words.

"I looked forward to every conversation I had with you, every glance, every stray touch of your hand. I thought it was okay, because I was the only one who would get hurt. But what did that make me, falling for my brother's girl? I couldn't stand seeing you with Bret, who didn't understand you, and didn't deserve you."

308

His hand holding mine tightened, his thumb stroking my knuckles as his words soothed my bruised heart.

"When he stupidly told me what he was doing, I didn't know what to do. I couldn't be the one to end your relationship that I'd come to hate. I knew I was being selfish either way. How could I pretend I was only doing right by you when I wanted you for myself?"

His soft words of confession were a balm on my soul, sweeping away all my doubts and worries. Hope spread its wings and soared, filling me with a giddy lightness. I might have been floating for all I knew, held to earth only by Ty's hands as we danced circles with the bridal party.

"And I do want you, June," he said, his voice hoarse, as if every word cost him. "Maybe I'm still being selfish, but I love you, and I don't want to lose you."

I stopped swaying as though I'd come up against a wall, and we stumbled together, Ty wincing at the contact. Those three marvelous words flooded my senses, obliterating all coherent thought.

"You love me?"

Raw emotion etched his face. "Hell yes, I do."

My heart was fit to burst, a star exploding from joy. "That's good, because I love you, too."

Relief and victory lit his eyes before he leaned down to press his mouth to mine. Sweet and tender, the kiss conveyed everything he felt for me in those soft touches. When he finally drew away, he rested his forehead on mine.

"I don't know what I could do in Austin, but if that's where you need to be for your new business, then that's where I'll be."

I pulled away, my mind shifting gears to try to follow that left-turn. "What? No."

Doubt crept back into his face, lining his forehead and tugging at his mouth. "No to which part?"

"No to Austin." My selfless, ridiculous man. I would never ask him to quit ranching for me, but his offer made me love him that much more. "I'm moving back to Magnolia Ridge."

He let go of my hand and drew both arms around my back, tugging me close until I pressed against him from knee to waist. "Since when?"

"Not that long ago." I loved the way he held me as if I was the most important woman in the world. As if I was the only thing he could ever want. "I'm going to partner with Marilyn. Do some work out of her store, strike out on my own a little."

His dazed look melted into a grin. The warmth of his smile only rivaled the heat from his hands on my back.

"You're really staying? You're not going back to Austin?"

"I didn't become a pro at mucking stalls for you to give up your ranch now."

He kissed me again, pressing his lips to my mouth, my forehead, my temple. "You only love me for my horses."

"I love *you*." I pressed close against him as "Hey Ya" by Outkast started up. "The horses are just an added bonus."

* * *

Long after Booker and Eden were ushered off into the night as Mr. and Mrs. Robinson and the reception had broken up, I snuggled against Ty in his recliner. Most of the lights in the house were out, but moonlight streamed in through the front window. We were both exhausted from the day's celebrations, yet not quite ready to say goodnight.

"Are you sure this is okay?"

I gave his injured chest as much room as possible, even as I tucked myself up against him. I didn't try to hide how I breathed him in now, letting his scent swirl through my senses.

He ran one hand along the leg I had casually draped over his lap. I still wore my bridesmaid's dress, but I'd kicked off my shoes long ago. His suit jacket hung over the arm of the sofa, and he looked more like himself with his messy hair and rumpled shirt.

"It's more than okay. I only wish I were a little more recuperated."

His voice rumbling in my ear sent shockwaves of anticipation up my spine. "We've got time."

He made a sound in the back of his throat, but he pulled me closer. "I'm not patient."

"So you keep saying." I glided one hand along his arm, exploring the firm bicep there now I was free to touch and caress him as I liked. "You still owe me, you know."

He kissed the crown of my head, his hands wandering over my body. "You'll have to be more specific. I owe you plenty."

"The public declaration."

"Oh, that. I'm willing to make public declarations every day, if you want." He shifted, and I tilted my head up to look at him. "I, Ty Hardy, do solemnly swear I'm crazy in love with you, June Evans."

I grinned until I could have lit up his whole house. "I am never going to get tired of hearing that."

We kissed, long and luxurious in the peaceful quiet. His hand moved over my hip, up my arm to stroke my neck, sending sparks cascading over my skin, and I sighed against him.

Eventually, he broke the kiss, resting his forehead against mine. "You should probably go soon. I don't want to get on Clint's bad side right out of the gate."

"I'm a grown woman."

"Doesn't mean your dad wouldn't bust my head."

"I'll go in a few more minutes." I snuggled back under his

311

arm. "Anyway, Pop thinks the world of you. I'm pretty sure he's been rooting for you all along."

Ty made a sound low in his chest. "You mean the dinner thing?"

"That, too. He's been dropping hints."

"Hints." He pulled me in as close as he could without crushing me to him. "Clint's never struck me as devious. You, on the other hand..."

I laughed against his chest. "I am not devious, Ty Hardy. I'm just—"

"Stubborn."

I made an indignant sound, but before I could argue, he cut me off. "It's one of the things I love about you."

I settled back against him. Nope. I would never get tired of hearing that.

From my vantage point in his lap, I could see into the kitchen where the white cabinets stood out in the dim light. Moonlight glinted on the warm hardwoods, impressing me all over again that he had remodeled the house by himself.

"Can I ask you a question?"

He hummed his assent as his hands roved along my back and legs.

"Why didn't you just ask me to help you come up with ideas for your remodel? Other than the obvious problem with asking for help, I mean. We could have figured out something that suits you."

"This does suit me. This house is exactly how I want it. The only thing that's missing is you in it." He ran one hand down my arm again until he played with my hand, lightly rubbing my bare ring finger with his thumb. "I thought you'd already figured it out. I did all this for you. I didn't know if you would ever even see it, but all the time I was working, deep down inside, I was doing it to make a home for you."

I closed my eyes, breathing in the warm smell of him as I turned my face to his chest. Held close in his arms, I couldn't imagine anywhere else I would rather be.

"*You* are my home, Ty."

epilogue

TY

ONE YEAR *later*

I let June pull ahead of me so I could watch her ride, a thrill I indulged in every chance I got. Her comfort and skill on the horse did something visceral to me. A swell of pride, sure, but something deeper, too—a rock-solid certainty she was meant to be out here. The same certainty that said she was meant to be *mine*. And very soon, if I didn't blow everything I'd planned this afternoon, I would make sure she was mine for good.

Corazon cantered along, excited as always when we explored the back acreage. I'd searched several breeders before I finally lit on the right horse for June, and Corazon had proved a perfect match for her—good-natured, but spirited, too, with just enough sass in her to keep June happy. The two had become near inseparable these last months, and I often caught

June in the barn, whispering sweet nothings to her chestnut quarter horse.

Jealousy over a horse—a new one for me. Not that I'd begrudge June anything. Seeing her take so well to life out here brought satisfaction like nothing else.

Well. Almost nothing else.

She slowed, coming up on our favorite spot. I kept my eyes on her, waiting for the moment she noticed the change. When she swiveled her head toward me, the look of wonder on her face was worth all the sweat and curses I'd endured out here yesterday.

"When did you do this?"

A wood-slat glider sat beneath the shade of a live oak, looking out toward the stream that ran through the property. It made a pretty picture, if I didn't say so myself. Though it would look best with her sitting in it.

I basked in the sunbeams she shone my way. That smile was the best part of every one of my days, the sparkling center to every morning, noon, and night. "I might not have had as much fence-mending to do out here yesterday as I claimed."

Her grin warmed me, even as nerves roped through my stomach, pulling tighter the closer we got to the glider. I didn't have much fear over how she'd answer me, but my heart rate ratcheted up anyhow. I wanted to get this right. Couldn't very well do that shaking like a jittery colt.

We dismounted, and I tied Bonanza and Corazon to low branches on opposite sides of the big old tree. They'd got on well so far, but nothing would wreck this moment like two horses having a dust-up. I patted my shirt pocket, as if the soft weight there hadn't reassured me of its presence the whole ride out.

June stood in front of the glider, her grin all pleasure and satisfaction. Maybe a touch of smugness in there, too. After the ones I'd put up at the barn and the house, this made her third swing on the property.

"All I said was, it would be nice to have a place to sit out here."

She'd said it two weeks ago, lying in the shade on the picnic blanket we usually brought with us. Like with everything else, she'd been right.

Now and then, she gloried over just how right she was, but I didn't mind. She'd earned it. Her experiment with hosting Girl Scout troops had proved a boon for my business, bringing in referrals for both boarding and training to the ranch I now owned outright. She'd held a couple more weekends for the girls in the year since that first one, and I couldn't get enough of watching my woman show off her love of my horses.

The Girl Scouts hadn't been the only thing to bring in more business. Owning up to my injury and subsequent training delays had done more for my reputation than I'd ever have guessed. Apparently, what clients liked even better than an unbreakable trainer was an honest one. I'd feared a long-term setback to my training work, and instead, I'd seen an uptick. The last year had been the busiest one I'd had yet. If I owed it all to June, well—I didn't mind being in her debt.

Bringing myself back to the significance at hand, I gestured at the oak glider. Spots of sunshine glittered on it through the tree's branches, just waiting for her to try it out. "Go on and sit, then."

She sat down, easing the glider back and forth in a smooth slide. "It's perfect."

I cleared my throat, nerves fastening down tight inside me. "You know I'd give you anything you asked for."

She cocked her eyebrows up, suddenly saucy. "Anything?"

The heat of her teasing unwound a little of my nervousness.

"No question. After giving you my whole heart and soul, everything else is easy."

I stepped closer, and she stopped rocking. The smile slipped off her face as I lowered down to one knee in front of her.

"June, I love you more than I have words to say. I want to give you everything I have, every part of who I am, for the rest of our lives." Reaching inside my shirt pocket, I slipped out the little black box, swallowed down the lump in my throat as I opened it. "Will you marry me?"

I just caught how her eyes widened and her mouth dropped open before she launched herself at me. I held her close, reveling in how perfectly she fit against me.

"Yes! Yes, I will marry you!"

Elation and a pure sense of rightness filled me to overflowing as we kissed. She pulled back enough for me to slip the ring on her finger, admiring the pretty thing. It sparkled at me a second before she pressed her hand to my chest. I let her push me back into the grass, circling her in my arms as we kissed our silent promises to each other.

This woman was mine, now and forever, and I was every bit as much hers.

She pushed up to hover over me, sunlight dancing along her grin. "I heard somewhere this means the horses are all mine now."

I chuckled, running my hands over the scoop of her waist. "You and your schemes."

She slid her fingers through my hair, her gaze full of more love than a man deserved. "You're a romantic after all, aren't you?"

I hugged her closer, my heart content. "Only for you, June."

also by genny carrick

acknowledgments

First, I want to thank YOU for reading my book! It's truly a dream come true to finally see my words in print, and know someone else out there is experiencing this story, too. Thanks for taking a chance on June & Ty.

Thank you Laura, for shopping this book to publishers. It didn't get picked up, but it meant a lot that you believed enough to try. Thank you to Gwen, Amanda, Allison, Claire, & Becca for giving helpful feedback along the way. Shout-out to my first readers who saw the potential, but saw the flaws, too. In the very first draft, Ty wound up sick with pneumonia, and his love declaration came during the ride to the hospital. You can thank Kelly & Lindsay for nixing that!

Thank you Jeri for lending your expertise on horses—any mistakes or implausibilities regarding Ty & his horses are solely on me.

Big thank you to Zee, for bringing out this manuscript's heart!

Special thanks to Melody for creating such a beautiful cover!

And finally, I couldn't have done any of this without Pete, Ruby, & Oliver. You keep me going with goofy business name suggestions, supportive notes, and reminders that romance is gross, respectively. I love you 3000.

about the author

Genny Carrick is a sucker for an HEA, especially if there's a whole lot of laughter along the way. She writes romances and rom-coms about stubborn women and the men who fall for them.

When she's not lost in swoony reads, she's probably up to something crafty or trying to get her dog and two cats to love her.

Genny recently moved to Texas after a lifetime in the Pacific Northwest. She brought her brilliant husband and two hilarious kids with her.

Stay up to date with book news at gennycarrick.com

Made in the USA
Las Vegas, NV
11 April 2024